KERRIE O'CONNOR has been making up stories since she was eight years old. She became a journalist at the age of eighteen and learnt how to 'stick to the facts', but was always tempted to sneak stories about talking animals into the newspaper. While working for ABC Radio, she made a series of documentaries about war in Eritrea. 'It is the children who remain with me: brave, optimistic, damaged, hungry . . . and still ready to party.' *Through the Tiger's Eye*, her first novel, draws on this experience, although it is set in a magical country where the jungle is thick and tigers still prowl.

Kerrie was born in the Year of the Tiger, and once (when she was a little girl) owned 21 cats. 'I thought I was so lucky! It took me years to work out that we just couldn't afford to get them desexed.' These days she doesn't live with any cats, much to the relief of the water dragons in her creek . . . but she still says 'Hi' if she meets one.

THROUGH THE
TIGER'S
EYE

KERRIE
O'CONNOR

ALLEN&UNWIN

First published in 2003

Allen & Unwin
83 Alexander Street
Crows Nest NSW 2065
Australia
Phone: (61 2) 8425 0100
Fax: (61 2) 9906 2218
Email: info@allenandunwin.com
Web: www.allenandunwin.com

National Library of Australia
Cataloguing-in-Publication entry:

O'Connor, Kerrie, 1962– .
Through the tiger's eye.

For children.
ISBN 1 86508 538 3.

1. Rescues - Juvenile fiction. I. Title.

A823.4

Designed by Jo Hunt
Set in 11.5 on 15 pt Berkeley by Midland Typesetters
Printed by McPherson's Printing Group

10 9 8 7 6 5 4 3 2 1

Contents

This book is dedicated to my parents,
my partner and my son; and to Joan Yule and
Jim McCall, who, confronted with a tiger cub
in the classroom, opened the cage . . .

Thanks to all those who read early and (very) late drafts: Michael, John, Fay and Helen Panckhurst; Mary, Alice, the two Karls and Carmel; Susanne, Vuli and Bheki; Felix and Ruth (who jumped up and down when the phone call came); Hilary, Lila and Natalie; Jenny, Mark, Timiny and Bearyn; Alison, Peter, Heather, Duncan, Angus and Erica; Fiona, Dave, Tom, Xanthe and Jelly Bean; Anne and Jessie; Matilda, Sara and Kevin; Anita; Andrew Stevenson; Di Fitton; Sarah and Henry. For their patience, I thank Oscar, Sam and Gabriel, and for their sharp eyes, Claire Gerson, Ros Walker and Judy Gill, who always said it would be done.

Special thanks to skilled fellow travellers Erica Wagner and Sarah Brenan, who trimmed without torment.

Prologue

In the still of a summer night, no one noticed a handsome ginger cat wriggle through the kitchen window of an ordinary house in Kurrawong. The cat showed no interest in the remains of a peperoni pizza on the table, but padded purposefully across the hall, through a doorway, into the bedroom of a sleeping twelve-year-old girl with long dark hair. The cat leapt lightly onto the bed and gazed intently at the girl. She didn't stir, nor did the puppy on the end of her bed.

But Lucy's dream changed.

One minute she was playing dream soccer on a flashing dance floor; then the driving bass and techno beat became . . .

Gunfire!

A smiling soldier in a brown uniform raises his rifle triumphantly to the sky. On his shirt is the image of a black bull, with red eyes and yellow horns.

Seconds stretch silently . . . and explode. Children scream, run for their lives, run from brown uniforms and guns.

In this sea of panic a little girl sails toward Lucy, calm in the eye of the storm. She has black curls, a glorious pink-and-gold dress hemmed in snowy white lace, shiny black shoes. She is staring right into Lucy's eyes. Her eyes are black. Her little hand reaches for Lucy's. Her skin feels like paper.

A woman glides across the grass towards them.

The smiling soldier shouts at her, but she is already squeezing a scrap of paper into the little girl's free hand. The tiny fist clenches shut.

The woman's black eyes are burning into Lucy's.

'My little girl is yours now. You must look after her until you find —'

Rough hands pull mother and daughter apart. Over the shoulder of the brown-shirted soldier who carries her, the little girl's black eyes hold Lucy's. In the midst of screams and chaos, she hasn't made a sound.

1

Retardo Ricardo

'Is that it?' Dread wriggled out of Ricardo's mouth like a worm. 'We can't live *there* . . .' he said.

He wanted to say 'because it's a dump,' but Mum would get upset. Again.

Lucy didn't care, though.

'It's a dump, Mum! Retardo's right for once. It's not even worth getting out of the car.' Before Mum could say, 'Don't call your little brother names!' Lucy wound up the window.

Why did Mum want to look at the worst house in Kurrawong?

You couldn't *get* any further away from the beach. It was way up in the bush, at the end of a lonely dirt track that snaked up the escarpment. The escarpment looked like one of those giant slippery water slides at a fun park, except that it was a couple of kilometres long and you'd slide right into the Pacific Ocean. It was covered in rainforest and stretched as far as you could see in either direction. Ten thousand kids could hold hands and slide down, if they didn't mind getting wedgied on giant gum trees.

At the very top, stretching forever, was a jagged wall of rock.

That was the end of Kurrawong. The only things that escaped over those cliffs had wings. And Lucy was no angel.

Below the cliffs, hidden in a dense jungle of towering green, was the last house in town.

The last place Lucy wanted to live.

A real dump.

The sign nailed to the fence had said 'To Let' until someone scribbled an 'i' between the words. Probably the last loser who drove all the way up here for nothing. The verandah sagged in the middle as though a giant bum had sat on it. Faded paint hung off the walls in strips, and the roof was rusty brown. Whoever had nailed up the 'Toilet' sign had found the only bit of fence still standing. No way would it keep in a hyperactive puppy called T-Tongue.

The grass was long and the roses had gone psycho, twisting all over a wonky archway above the front gate. They were probably holding it up. A gang of red and green parrots landed on the crooked verandah rail. Great, parrot poop, something else for Ricardo to step in. There was a shriek overhead and a gang of white cockatoos dive-bombed a gum tree, yellow crests flaring. Just what a family needed, cockatoo crap.

Mum nervously opened the driver's door.

'Lucy . . .' she began, but Lucy jumped in furiously.

'Don't call me Lucky. I'm not lucky. If I was lucky we'd still be living at the beach and we wouldn't have to rent a house at all. If I was lucky we'd still be living —'

Lucy was *about* to say 'with Dad in *our own* house', but

suddenly Mum looked as if she was about to cry, so for once in her life Lucy shut up.

Too late. Her unspoken words hung in the air. She might as well have hired an aeroplane to write them in the sky in humungous letters.

Lucy felt a wet nose on her ankle and picked up the squirming black puppy with the white chest and white-tipped tail. She buried her face in puppy fur so she wouldn't have to look at Mum's face.

'I'm *not* lucky,' she whispered to T-Tongue.

He was. He got in three licks on Lucy's face before she remembered how he got his name: Tyrannosaurus-Tongue.

'Come on, kids, just take a look at it,' Mum pleaded. 'I know it doesn't look terrific, but sometimes houses are really good on the inside, even if they look terrible, and the agent says it's great inside.'

Even Mum didn't believe that. Her voice went wobbly again.

'And we're allowed to have T-Tongue . . . *and* it's really cheap. It will give us more money to spend on other stuff. If we have to pay too much rent, there'll be no lunch orders when you go back to school.'

That got Ricardo out of the car.

'You can't do that! I'll starve to death!'

'Good!' Lucy shot back. 'Can you start starving Retardo today, Mum?'

Uh oh. She'd gone too far. Here came the '*Be nice to your little brother or else*' speech . . . or maybe worse. Lucy took diversionary action.

'All right, I'll look, but we're not living there! Because it's a *dump*!' She jumped out of the car, marched across the

5

road with T-Tongue scampering along beside her, and ripped opened the rickety old gate.

It tumbled off its hinges and Lucy fell over.

T-Tongue was delighted. So was Ricardo.

2

The Mermaid House

The first thing Lucy saw when she scrambled up the rickety stairs was a naked woman. Well, a naked mermaid; a heavy, cast-iron mermaid. You picked her up by the tail and rapped her scaly bum on the huge, old-fashioned door. The door *had* been dark green but the paint had blistered and peeled, revealing veins of undercoat, like dried blood. Lucy shivered. It was a corpse of a house and it probably had a corpse in it.

'And I bet the toilet's outside,' she said accusingly as Mum stepped up brandishing a mega bunch of keys.

'Find the right one!' Mum said to Ricardo, ignoring Lucy's outstretched hand.

Ricardo examined the keys. Big ones and little ones, shiny silver and greasy gold ones. He picked out a small silver key. It worked, turning with a clunk and a creak.

A wave of musty air hit Lucy as she peered down the hallway. It seemed to go forever. An old rug with a faded blue-and-yellow pattern stretched all the way to a blue-and-gold glass door at the far end.

Lucy took a deep breath and stepped onto the rug. She was standing on a faded mermaid with gold scales and long dark hair. It coiled into the next mermaid and the next, all the way up the hall. She stepped onto the next mermaid's tail, cautiously, and after that it was easy – she just kept walking from scaly tail to scaly tail. Mum made Ricardo take off his shoes, and they followed.

Whoever had lived here had been a mermaid freak. There were mermaids painted all over the hallway walls. Lucy opened the first door she came to. Every centimetre of the huge floor was painted with mermaids, shells, dolphins, angelfish, seaweed, giant clams, turtles. Even though it was covered in dust, everything looked alive.

'Awesome! It's like Sea World,' said Lucy, stepping gingerly away from a shark.

A chandelier above her head dripped with glass sea creatures, dust and spiderwebs. The sun streaked through filthy windows, chequered blue, green and gold.

'It's a ballroom!' exclaimed Mum.

She pointed at the grand piano, grey with dust, in the corner – but Lucy was already next door in the bathroom, where the water spouted out of dolphin-shaped taps. Glass starfish glittered in the windows.

Every room was decorated like an underwater cave. And there was something else strange: the house was bigger on the inside than it seemed. Little rooms came off big rooms, opening into other larger rooms, which opened into alcoves that were really just cupboards, big enough to walk into. It was as if the house never really ended. Lucy wanted a map. It was like one those wooden puzzles you got on Christmas morning that looked easy-peasy until you tried to work them out, and you still hadn't finished by the time Grandma called you for Christmas dinner.

'See,' said Mum, 'I told you things can be nice on the inside even when they look awful outside'.

Silently, Lucy admitted she was right. The house was weird, but cool. Of course, it was nothing compared to their own renovated house, with its shiny floors and brand-new kitchen. But still . . . weirdly cool. And think of the parties she could have in that ballroom!

At the end of the hallway, near the blue-and-gold back door, were two other doors, one on either side. The door on the left opened into a big kitchen with an ancient fridge, almost as big as a small car, and a long wooden table with high-backed chairs. It was set with dusty plates, cutlery and candelabra as if ready for a banquet. But it was the other door that caught Lucy's eye. It glowed wine-red, the dust settling in the deeply carved scales of a dragon. Two Chinese vases stood guard on either side. They were taller than Ricardo and painted with red-and-gold dragons that glared at Lucy.

T-Tongue was sniffing feverishly at the gap under the door. Lucy tried the handle. Locked. She grabbed the keys from Ricardo and went straight for one with a funny, loopy decoration. It worked. She swung the door open and T-tongue let out a strangled bark as something small, lithe and supremely fast jumped off an old black bed in the corner, streaked across the floor and out an open window, leaving lace curtains swinging in the breeze. Lucy looked out into a wild back yard, just in time to see a ginger cat race up a steep path and disappear into the rainforest. T-Tongue tried to jump out the window, pulling on his

9

lead so hard he almost strangled himself. He tried to bark but it turned into a coughing fit.

Holding fast to his lead, Lucy checked out the room. Two iron beds on either side. A big, rug faded to dusty brown. The only room with no mermaids or sea creatures. In fact, it was the most boring room in the house. So why was it locked?

She kept exploring. The house was full of odds and ends, as though whoever lived here before hadn't had time to pack up properly. Ricardo found a really old-fashioned piggy bank, actually shaped like a pig! When he shook it, he could hear coins rattling.

'Put that down,' said Mum.

Even Mum got excited when Ricardo found a big wooden chest, carved with dragons and strange faces and shapes, but none of the keys worked on its heavy lock.

They didn't find one dead body.

The toilet was definitely inside.

Back at the real-estate agency, Mum kept telling the agent, Nigel Adams, how much she loved it and she didn't mind how old and dusty it was and it didn't matter that it was way too big for three people. He had a funny look on his face but stretched his mouth open in a big smile and said he'd talk to the owner and let Mum know that night.

Weird, thought Lucy, they'd all stopped hating the worst house in Kurrawong at the same time. One minute even Mum couldn't pretend to like it, then the next they were all exploring like excited kids. Maybe the house had cast a spell on them? Maybe old houses got lonely, just like old people, and wanted humans to move in? Maybe the house didn't want to die with all its paint falling off and the verandah caving in.

She couldn't wait to get back there.

That night they told Grandma all about it. Mum muttered something about not getting everyone's hopes up, but she was the smiliest she'd been in weeks. Since the night she'd had the really big fight with Dad – the night both of them cried, first Dad, then Mum. When Mum had stopped crying she'd packed up clothes and soccer balls and books and moved them all into Grandma's. That was right at the beginning of the school holidays, just before Christmas. Ricardo was worried Santa wouldn't know where Grandma lived. Grandma said Santa definitely *did* know, but what if Santa didn't know Ricardo had moved? Ricardo rang Dad, who said he would email Santa. And the Tooth Fairy. And the Easter Bunny.

Over dinner, Mum and Grandma chatted happily about the mermaid house. Everyone was in a good mood. Ricardo even had a bath without anyone having to yell at him.

So Lucy rang Dad to tell him the good news, about Ricardo getting in the bath. She told him about the house, too, and he said that was good, but he didn't sound all that happy. Then he said he was flying to China in the morning for a conference and would be back in a few days, and he'd see her after that.

Then Mum got on the phone to Dad and spoke in that frozen voice she used when they weren't going to fight but they weren't going to make up either.

Then Nigel Adams rang. They could move into the mermaid house straight away.

And that was that. Sort of.

First they had to help Mum clean it.

'Aawwww!'

'Or no TV for the rest of childhood.'

That was a lot of TV.

3
Minty Puppy

The kids were up to their armpits in hot water in the back yard of their new house. Poor T-Tongue was in it up to his nose. He didn't like baths, Lucy could tell, because of the way he was shivering, even though the water was warm and they'd made it smell nice. Lucy had convinced herself that puppies liked roses, so she'd filled T-Tongue's bath with red rose petals. Ricardo had convinced himself dogs liked minty things, and Lucy had to stop him squeezing toothpaste into the water.

Lucy let go of T-tongue's collar to grab the toothpaste, and he seized the chance to run inside, leaving a trail of wet pawprints, looking over his shoulder as if they were traitors. Now he was hiding somewhere in the big old maze that was their new house.

Maybe it was his doggy DNA. Lucy had read about DNA in one of Dad's magazines. He kept his science mags in the toilet, and they built up and built up until Mum went psycho every few months and threw them out. In between psycho attacks, Lucy had read a few stories. As far as she could work out, you were born with the right DNA for having brown eyes or curly hair. Or, in Ricardo's case, the DNA for treading in gross things. Maybe all puppies were born with the DNA for hating baths. Come to think of it, Ricardo had that sort of DNA too.

Lucy finally tracked T-Tongue down to the room near the back door, where she and Ricardo would have to sleep tomorrow night, until the furniture van came with their beds. It was the one with the dragon vases standing guard outside, the ratty old brown rug on the floor and the two old iron beds, which is why they had to sleep there. Ricardo didn't mind because it was closest to the kitchen and therefore closest to food, but Lucy hated it. The rug was too grungy.

T-Tongue, cowering under one of the beds, didn't look as if he liked it much either but he also didn't look as though he was planning to leave in a hurry. He had squashed himself almost flat against the wall, and when Lucy got under the bed and grabbed his collar and dragged him gently out, his body was completely stiff and he made a funny kind of whimpering sound – a 'No, no! Not the bath! Please not the bath!' sort of whimper.

As she began to wriggle out, Lucy noticed a face under the bed. Or at least two big round eyes and the vague outline of a shape, woven into the old rug. How weird was that? The rest of the rug was just a gross, faded brown with no patterns at all. Mum reckoned it would be full of fleas, dust and life-threatening germs that scientists hadn't discovered yet. She said if they didn't rip it up and cremate it, Lucy and Ricardo wouldn't live long enough to graduate from school.

Just then T-Tongue made a wild bid for freedom, twisting and almost slipping out of Lucy's grip. She hauled him back, scrambled out and ran outside in time to see Ricardo squeezing toothpaste into the bath, a whole tube of it, like a fat white worm. For the minty freshness, he said. They washed T-Tongue in it anyway.

Then Mum realised what they were doing and got mad and made them get back to the housework.

'Come on, you two. That disgusting old rug in your room's got to go. I hate to think what kind of life forms are hiding in it.'

Lucy and Ricardo started at either end of the rug and rolled as fast as they could until they hit the rickety old bed. Then Lucy said, 'There *is* an animal sleeping in here already. Look'.

'I'm not looking at fleas!'

Lucy half-dragged, half-pushed the bed out of the way. The light from the window fell directly on the faded face staring up at them. Lucy went shivery. Deep golden eyes. Cat's eyes, no, tiger's eyes. There were the stripes to prove it.

'Cool!' said Ricardo.

It was definitely a tiger, not a spotty leopard or a cheetah, but it looked as if it could disintegrate into dust and flea-poo at any moment.

'Let's wash him!' said Ricardo unexpectedly.

'OK,' said Lucy. Washing a tiger, even a mangy rug tiger, would be a lot more fun than washing walls.

'Do you think tigers like minty things?' asked Ricardo.

Lucy ignored him and began dragging the bed over the roll of rug onto the newly exposed floorboards.

'We better not roll him up,' Ricardo said. 'He might not be able to breathe.'

'She's not a he, she's a she,' growled Lucy. 'And anyway, she can't breathe with your feet so close. Come on!'

They dragged the first iron bed into the corner and then went back for the second. As they lifted it away from the wall, Ricardo dropped his end.

'Loser!' said Lucy. 'What did you do that —'

Then she saw what Ricardo was looking at. Another face, peering intently at them in faded carpet colours. A golden monkey.

'My monkey!' screeched Ricardo.

'What do you mean, your monkey?'

But Ricardo was grinning insanely at the carpet monkey and wouldn't answer.

4

Corpse on the Rug

The next night Lucy and Ricardo had their first real dinner in the house: baked chicken with lots of spuds and gravy, pancakes, icecream and chocolate sauce. Lucy made the pancakes and Ricardo made the chocolate sauce. It had a slightly minty flavour.

They slept in the tiger room, even though the light switch didn't work and they had to use candles.

That day they'd washed every surface in sight – windows, walls, floor – and carefully put the sun-dried rug back down. The tiger and monkey were a little brighter. Mum hadn't said anything else about throwing it out. She'd even helped them drag it up the hall.

They hopped into their sleeping bags and lay looking wearily at the rug until Mum came in to make sure they were zipped up.

'Now, Lucy, keep that torch where you can grab it if you need it. Ricardo, if you have another nightmare, just call out.' She kissed them both and blew out the candles.

'Wimp!'

'Lucy!'

'OoooKaaay.'

It was fun, just like camping. The house felt big and empty. That's because it was. They had only a few of their things in it – clothes, kitchen stuff, enough food to shut Ricardo up, and boxes and boxes of books. Mum had had a big fight with Ricardo because he wanted to take the TV instead of all the books. She won. But he had won the argument about the Lego, stuffed animals and gaming magazines. Lucy had won the one about the soccer balls, all six of them. Mum said the removal truck would come soon with their furniture. In her imagination, Lucy began to pack up her old bedroom but she was asleep even before she'd found her soccer boots at the bottom of the cupboard.

If anyone had looked through the window just then, they would have seen buttery moonlight melting on the three sleeping faces of Lucy, Ricardo and T-Tongue. And on two other faces that never slept, not now, and not through all those long years when the iron beds blocked out the light of sun and moon. And that's when Lucy started to dream.

She is on a rainforest track, stumbling on heavy stone legs. A light burns ahead. She is almost there. Gunfire! She falls but is dragged relentlessly forward, slithering on her belly, like a stone python, closer to the fire.

A smiling soldier points his gun at the night sky. He's firing at the moon.

She is crawling on her belly, trying to see. There are kids in front of her, lots of them, lining up for school or something. But it's night and they're skinny, really skinny, and they look scared. They're wearing rags. A little boy limps slowly into line and the smiling soldier yells at him, raising his gun threateningly. In the firelight, Lucy can clearly see a bull with red eyes and yellow horns on his brown shirt. A girl with dark hair twisted on top of her head darts out of line and puts her arm around the little boy, and helps him get in line.

At a shouted command, another soldier empties the contents of a big pot onto the dirt near the fire. It looks like rice. The kids fall on it like hungry animals. In seconds it is gone. The little boy was too slow but the girl with the twisted hair shares hers. Another shout and the kids line up, then march through tall barbed-wire gates into a rickety old house. The limping kid trots to keep up. The girl holds his hand.

Just as they reach the gate she looks up, but not at the soldiers. She looks longingly at the trees where Lucy lies like stone.

She's looking for help.

Something is going to happen . . . Thunder builds in Lucy's stone mind, and rumbles into life – a roar from the darkness that makes kids and soldiers freeze.

In the heartbeat between fear and flight, a creature springs from the shadows, knocking the nearest guard to the ground, vicious claws raking flesh. Before the others can raise their weapons, the tiger is gone, and a soldier's screams fill the night

No one notices two skinny children at the end of the line melt away into the shadows – no one but Lucy, who is wondering if that terrible roar came from the jungle or from her own stone heart.

Thump! Lucy sat up in bed, gasping, accidentally kicking T-Tongue. He yelped and she cuddled him, which calmed her too.

Moonlight shone on the tiger rug and Lucy's eyes followed its path. Suddenly her heart was thumping again: there was something human and very dead on the floor. She wanted to scream but couldn't, which was lucky really, because it gave her time to notice that the corpse had blond hair, was wearing her brother's pyjamas and was in a sleeping bag. Ricardo. She had never been so pleased to see him.

The feeling didn't last long.

'Retardo,' Lucy whispered. 'Wake up!'

She grabbed the torch and beamed it at him, but he just lay there, right on the golden monkey's head. The thump that woke her must have been him falling out of bed.

Lucy struggled out of her sleeping bag and shook him. He muttered something. It sounded like 'ids'. She shook him again. Just then T-Tongue got involved. One sloppy lick and Ricardo opened his eyes wide in the moonlight, looked deep into the puppy's eyes and said very clearly, 'They're mean to the kids'.

'What kids?'

His eyes closed again.

Lucy shone the torch in his face.

'What kids!'

He opened his eyes and, dazzled, promptly shut them again.

'Ricardo, what kids?'

But all he said, eyes shut tight, was 'They're mean to the kids'.

She couldn't get any more out of him, no matter how hard she shook him, so she went back to bed.

5

Video Brainwaves

Next morning, when Lucy woke up, she was still clutching the torch and the smell of mint was right in her face. T-Tongue was licking her. The bedroom was still quite dark but Lucy could just make out Ricardo standing in the middle of the floor, staring down at the tiger. Lucy shone the torch at him. He kept staring at the tiger with a funny expression.

'Hey, Retardo! Do you think it's going to talk to you?'

Instead of glaring at her as usual, he said seriously, 'It does talk. I heard it'.

Lucy did her best fake laugh. Ricardo didn't respond. She did it again. Still no response. He just turned and ran out of the room, through the back door into the garden. T-Tongue chased him, with Lucy right behind.

When Lucy burst out onto the concrete, she was glad she still had the torch. It was *really* early. She turned east towards the ocean and saw the first golden arc of the rising sun just breaching the horizon. The sky was streaked a sleepy purple-pink but the back yard was deep grey and mysterious. Suddenly scared, she turned on the torch and stood in the wet grass examining the shadowy garden.

The rainforest rolled back up the hill to the cliffs. If the mermaid house had had a back fence once, it was long gone. The trees and creepers had eaten it. There was only dense forest between the garden and the wild, steep slopes higher up, where the last trees clung for their lives. The cliffs above were just catching the light of the rising sun, sheer rock glowing pink, splintered by black shadows and secret places. It was so quiet Lucy could hear the faint roar of the waterfalls that spilled over the cliffs on their way to the sea. The smell of the bush was overwhelming: gum trees and something lemony.

Ahead, the shadow that was Ricardo plunged into the trees, with T-Tongue's smaller shadow in pursuit. Lucy gave chase. She reached the trees and heard Ricardo calling cajolingly, 'Here, puss, puss, puss,' but she couldn't see him. She kept walking and the trees seemed to open in front of her. Then she found Ricardo on a path she had never been on in her life, *yet she remembered it clearly*.

'Look,' Ricardo said triumphantly, pointing up the path. In the dim light, Lucy could just make out a set of stone stairs. She shone the torch. Maybe they used to go somewhere, but the somewhere – an old house? – had vanished. There was just a curtain of vines and creepers and the dark trunks of trees. Lucy couldn't even tell if the track continued into the dense shadow above the stairs.

Sitting on the top stair, as though waiting for them, was a cat: a distinctive ginger cat. And it was looking at them with the golden eyes and serious expression of the tiger in their bedroom.

For once Lucy had nothing to say. She felt the hairs on her arms stand up.

T-Tongue was standing at the bottom of the stairs, growling low in his throat, all the hackles along the ridge of his back bristling like a doggy mohawk. The cat turned its golden gaze towards him and T-Tongue's growl became a disappointed whimper. He flopped down on the ground with his nose between his paws, but didn't take his eyes off the cat.

Meanwhile, Ricardo was acting weirder than ever, grinning insanely at the cat.

'I know who you are,' he babbled, 'you're the tiger from our bedroom. But you didn't eat your vegies and you shrank. Or maybe you jumped out of the rug like T-Tongue's fleas because we were going to wash you, and you ran away and hid in the bush and a tiger would have looked too con-con . . . con-see-you-us . . . you know that word? So you had to be a ginger cat. How come you can talk? Have you seen my monkey?'

Lucy stared at the cat, perched on the muddy old stairs as though on an ancient Egyptian throne. She thought the cat *was* going to talk for a minute because it sat looking at them so intently. Then it yawned, licked a stripy paw, washed behind a stripy ear, jumped lightly off the steps and began rubbing and twisting around her legs. Its fur brushed thick and luxurious on Lucy's bare skin and she felt shivery again. She reached down to stroke it, but it stalked a few steps away before turning to fix her with a compelling look.

'Why don't you talk?' pleaded Ricardo, but the cat leapt off into the bush.

Lucy finally broke her silence.

'Because it can't, you idiot! It's a cat. You know, miaow and all that!'

Lucy's brain was working harder and faster than ever before. In the growing light her eyes felt super-sensitive, as if she was seeing for the first time . . . and she had certainly never seen *anything* like that cat.

It *did* look like a tiger. It was stripy all over. Its fur was deep, burnt orange and its stripes were proper stripes: charcoal along the length of its back and face, with chalky white marks on its face and chest. Tigerish. A Tiger-cat!

It didn't seem too strange to Lucy when the Tiger-cat appeared again, dragging something out of the bushes with its teeth – not a mouse but a piece of tin, about the size of a car numberplate. The Tiger-cat was tugging at it, trying to dislodge a corner caught on a vine. Lucy stepped forward to help, and the Tiger-cat dropped the metal and began to purr.

The surface was muddy but not rusty. Each corner had a small hole drilled in it and when Lucy looked closer she could see writing. It must be a plaque, like the one outside their doctor's surgery.

She rubbed at the metal and tried to read the words, but just managed to smear mud all over it. Somehow she knew she had to read it. The Tiger-cat purred and twisted against her legs. Lucy reached down to rub its head and it let her, staring at her fiercely even as it purred with pleasure.

It jumped lightly back onto the top step and stared commandingly at Lucy, right into her eyes. Holding that golden gaze, all of a sudden Lucy began to shake. She wasn't scared, quite the opposite. Lucy didn't know why her body was doing what it was doing, but for some reason she didn't want it to stop. She felt an ache in her chest and in the middle of her forehead and then . . . her skin just dissolved into the air around her! The air rushed in where her skin used to hold it back, and her body rushed out. Or the air and her body got all swirled up together and there wasn't any difference any more.

All the time she was staring at the Tiger-cat and the Tiger-cat was staring at her. Their line of sight was a golden rope holding her fast, and Lucy didn't need her body any more.

The odd thing was that even though Lucy couldn't feel her skin, she knew she was smiling. She was one big smile. Then she felt a tug, as if the Tiger-cat had yanked the rope that joined them, and a picture began to form in her mind. The Tiger-cat's golden eyes changed subtly and Lucy knew something even weirder was happening. She was still in that same suspended smiling state, her mind holding fast to the Tiger-cat's mind at the other end of the rope. *Only the Tiger-cat was changing.*

The Tiger-cat's stripes blurred into the distance. Lucy felt as though she had been blown gently backwards down a long tunnel and could barely see the other end. Then the tunnel suddenly shrank and Lucy floated forward again, like a dandelion seed-head on the wind, and saw *the tiger-striped face melt into a person's face, one lined with old age.*

Like a camera shifting focus, one minute the Tiger-cat's image was sharp and clear, the next it blurred and shifted, and when it sharpened again Lucy was staring at . . . *an old lady, with a wrinkled face and eyes the same gingery-gold as the Tiger-cat's. The old lady's tawny eyes filled with tears and Lucy's smiling feeling vanished. She was flooded with sorrow.*

Lucy blinked and the Tiger-cat's face was back. A second later it shifted and changed again, this time into a face Lucy recognised. *The girl from her dream! The one with the twisted hair, the one who had looked into the jungle and asked for help with her eyes and then escaped with the little boy.*

Lucy blinked again and found the Tiger-cat gazing at her fiercely from the top of the stairs.

Shivering, Lucy felt herself slowly come back inside her skin, aware of her body again, tingling all over. It was as if her skin was an envelope she had stepped out of for just a moment. Then she grew back inside it, filling it up again.

Her mind was spinning. Who was that kid, and what about the old lady with the ginger eyes? Maybe she'd been right about the house the first day she saw it, when she thought they might find a corpse inside. *The old lady in the Tiger-cat's mind was scared about dying all alone.* Lucy was as certain about that as if the Tiger-cat had said it out loud.

She had a sudden vision of Grandma getting sick without anyone in her family knowing. What if she died and had no time to say goodbye to the things she loved? – like her favourite red rosebush and her chickens and her grandkids.

'An old lady lived here and we have to find her,' she said suddenly to all the trees and the moist morning air and the sunlight – and the Tiger-cat.

The Tiger-cat must have thought she had said the right thing because it relaxed and began washing itself, still sitting on the top stair. T-Tongue gave a relieved whimper and stretched, before inspecting the first stair from every angle, sniffing the stone warily, keeping a prudent distance from the Tiger-cat. It looked perfectly innocent, licking

26

a stripy paw and washing behind a rounded ear; but weren't cats supposed to have pointy ears?

Ricardo's voice broke into her thoughts. 'I know we have to find the old lady, stupid! The Tiger-cat just told us that. Do you think I'm deaf or something? I *told* you it could talk.'

Lucy wasn't about to get into a fight with Ricardo over whether the Tiger-cat could talk or not. Even if she hadn't heard it talk, *it had beamed video clips right into her brain.* And it had made T-Tongue behave.

Ricardo began chattering away to the Tiger-cat, 'Don't worry. Grandma will know where the old lady is. She knows everyone. And those kids – you tell us where to find them and we'll help them too. That's a slack school they go to – teachers shouldn't have guns in the play-ground. They should tell their mums and dads and they should complain about the food too – it looks gross and they shouldn't chuck it on the ground. They shouldn't have wild animals from the zoo there either. We've only got chickens at our school. We've got a rooster called Ugg Boot and . . .'

The Tiger-cat must have worked out that Ricardo would have kept talking all morning because it twisted lightly, leapt off the top stair into the shadowy jungle above . . . and disappeared.

T-Tongue gave a strangled bark and bounded up the stairs after the Tiger-cat . . . and disappeared too! Lucy dropped the plaque and ran, with Ricardo right beside her, clambering up the slippery stairs. One, two, three, four, five . . . as Lucy hit the top stair, one foot slid into space. For a nanosecond she was suspended, one leg and arm dangling into nothingness, one hand clutching Ricardo. Then, like a slow-motion replay, she watched first herself then her little brother tumble off, with Ricardo desperately clutching at thin air. They were catapulted, cartwheeling, into blackness.

6

Into the Pit

Thump! Lucy did a somersault and landed in what felt like a nest of snakes, half-buried in mud and wet sand. There were slimy coils all around her, under her hands, under her back. She lay stunned, unable to breathe or speak. But T-Tongue licking her face, Ricardo whimpering beside her and the thought of snakes were enough to get Lucy on her feet.

Miraculously, she was still holding the torch. In torch-light the snaky things resolved themselves into the roots of an enormous tree, some thicker than her arms and legs, fanning out everywhere over the floor of a muddy hole. It was a pit, but not a snakepit. Phew. Shining the torch up, Lucy could see where they were. The offending step was still there, and she could see the early-morning sky, but so far above her head that it was hopeless to think about climbing. There must have been a landslide or something, sweeping away the track above the stairs. Only the roots of the gigantic tree held the rest of it in place above their heads.

Ricardo was clutching his arm, crying. Forget about the holidays, Mum was going to ground Lucy for the rest of childhood.

'Give me a look.'

She shone the torch on Ricardo's arm. He was holding his elbow. He must have whacked his funnybone on the way down.

'Can you bend it?'

Ricardo gingerly flexed his arm once, twice. He started to breathe again.

'Can you clench your fist?' Lucy asked, remembering first aid.

He could, both of them in fact

Just then T-Tongue decided to take matters into his own paws. He sniffed the air, stiffened, barked and shot across the floor of the pit towards what looked like a dark wall – and disappeared!

'T-Tongue!'

Amazingly she heard a faint bark, as though he had already gone quite a long way. She shone the torch on the wall, revealing a gaping hole behind a pile of broken wood. Huge beams poked up out of the mud and sand like dinosaur bones. Lucy scrambled past, and the hole became a tunnel with smooth earth sides – a hungry mouth disappearing into the blackness of the hillside.

T-Tongue had decided to go adventuring under a mountain that might collapse on his head any minute. Great. Lucy heard his barks grow faint, then stop.

'We have to get him!'

The thought of her puppy lost at the end of that tunnel was too much. She took off into the blackness, calling and whistling desperately. Ricardo stumbled after her, determined not to be left behind.

The tunnel seemed to go forever. The further they went, the smellier it got. A dark, dank, watery smell. And the air got colder. Lucy felt as though they were tramping into the very centre of the earth. She tried not to think about cave-ins.

And then a crisis: the tunnel forked. In the weak torchlight Lucy could see that the left-hand fork sloped downwards, further into the mountain. The right-hand fork sloped upwards, towards where the sky should be. Ricardo thought T-Tongue would have gone up, not down. Lucy thought T-Tongue wouldn't even notice a second tunnel if he were chasing something. If the something had gone down, so had T-Tongue. Lucy looked at her torch and saw how pale and yellow the light was. The batteries were running out.

'T-Tongue!' she screamed down the left tunnel.

No answer.

'Let's try this one,' she said, moving into the right, up-sloping fork. She couldn't face heading down that other dark wormhole with a dodgy torch.

'If he's not up here, we'll go back home and get more batteries,' she said, trying not to think about how they would get out of that hole. Ricardo was only too happy to agree.

The tunnel went steadily upwards and in a little while Lucy felt a change in the air.

'I think we're getting close to the top,' she said.

As she said the words, she felt the panic she had been squashing down rise in her throat. She almost choked with fear. That was weird. She had been scared back there but hadn't had time to really notice. Now they were almost back up at the surface, she felt weak with relief.

They rounded a bend and saw sunlight spearing through a mass of creepers and vines. Lucy and Ricardo smashed through, emerging scratched and hot into a different kind of tunnel, one the jungle had grown itself. The canopy above their heads was so thick that little sunlight filtered through, but the colour! The trees and shrubs glowed fluoro green. Lucy had never seen anything like it.

There was a faint path, but in some places the creepers and bushes were so thick that Lucy and Ricardo had to crawl on hands and knees. After a few metres, Lucy looked back and couldn't see the tunnel. She glanced up, and between the towering trees caught a glimpse of the cliffs looming behind.

'Look,' she said. 'That's the escarpment, so that way's west. All we have to do is head downhill away from that and we'll hit our back yard again. Or one of the neighbour's. Or at least we'll hit the road.'

But there was a warning voice in Lucy's head. She knew stories of bushwalkers lost for days without food on the escarpment. She looped her red hair-scrunchie on a bush to mark the path to the tunnel.

'It's hot as,' said Ricardo, panting.

His face was streaked with dirt and sweat. It *was* really hot – hot even by Kurrawong summer scorcher standards, and far too hot for this time of morning. Lucy guessed it was about 6.30 a.m., maybe quarter to seven if you counted fifteen minutes with the Tiger-cat before it got them into this mess; yet the sun was up above their heads, shining strongly down through the trees. It didn't make sense.

A second later Lucy stopped thinking about anything except the incredible sight opening up before them. There, as they rounded a bend in the track, was a scene from a nightmare.

7

Time Tunnellers

There was the nightmare barbed wire and the nightmare rickety old house – but no nightmare children or soldiers. The fire had turned to ash and the place was as quiet as a graveyard, which somehow made it worse.

An intense memory of crawling like a snake overcame Lucy. She hauled Ricardo down to the ground, and they lay flat and watched. Lucy's mind was racing. Where were they?

Kurrawong couldn't be far away but this place was nothing like Kurrawong, and it was so much like her nightmare it was spooky. The thought that human eyes might be looking out from that house made her tummy hurt. She wanted to turn and run back up the path and along the tunnel as fast as she could, flat torch batteries or not – until she saw a little black dog trotting out of the bushes on the other side of the clearing, white-tipped tail waving like a flag.

'T-Tongue!' squeaked Ricardo. Lucy clamped her hand fiercely over his mouth. What if soldiers came running? A strange piercing birdcall split the silence in the clearing and Lucy had an idea. She risked a soft whistle. T-Tongue pricked up his ears and to her relief trotted obediently over. It was possibly the first time he'd obeyed her in his entire short life!

Finding their faces at licking level, he yelped with pleasure and got on with the job.

'Shhh,' breathed Lucy in his ear, terrified that soldiers might arrive at any moment and bring her nightmare to life.

'Let's get out of here!' whispered Ricardo, but Lucy was staring at a coil of rope near the gate. Just what they needed to get out of that pit.

'Hold T-Tongue,' she said, thrusting the squirming puppy at Ricardo.

She pulled herself forward on her elbows, belly flat to the ground like the soldiers in the TV ads for the Army. The rope was a million Ks away. The sun burned down and her head felt as though it would melt like a candle. Sharp sticks gouged her T-shirt through to the skin but she kept going.

Lucy reached the rope just as a gut-wrenching sound reached her ears: a familiar shouted command.

And marching feet ever closer.

No time to think, let alone crawl. She grabbed the rope, scuttled desperately back to the cover of green and threw herself down, just in time. She lay panting as the smiling soldier and his men marched a column of children into the clearing. She tried to control her breathing. If the soldiers hadn't been yelling at the kids, they might have heard her.

She heard another shouted order and the kids lined up at the barbed-wire gate.

'This is not happening,' Lucy told herself; but T-Tongue, growling low in his throat, clearly thought something was happening. Lucy opened her eyes and gave the hand signal for 'drop' she'd learned at his first and only obedience class (he had failed), and miraculously he dropped down on all fours. He must have known it wasn't a game because he stayed very quiet, quivering, waiting for her command.

Lucy longed to be able to slide backwards up the track, right out of the fix they were in, but the soldiers were too close. She and Ricardo would have to sit it out – if lying with your face buried in the dirt was sitting it out. Half of Lucy's instincts said freeze, the other half said run. She chose freeze, partly because her legs had turned to stone again.

The smiling soldier unlocked a padlock on the gate, barking another order, and the sad parade of children passed through the gate and up the stairs of the rickety house. The heavy door slammed shut behind them.

Then the smiling soldier crouched, examining the ground where the rope had been. Lucy felt sick: there were her footprints in the dust.

A brightly coloured flock of birds burst shrieking from the trees above, and Lucy seized her chance. She began to inch backwards. Ricardo found it harder, as he was grasping T-Tongue, who was starting to make take-on-the-world noises. Semi-Superdog – ready to take on four armed soldiers.

Then a loud, gurgling, throaty cough came from the other side of the clearing. Lucy had an instant over-whelming impression of muscular power and lethal speed. What happened next unfolded so fast, Lucy felt she was still dreaming. A tiger leapt from the undergrowth, knocked the closest soldier to the ground with one mighty swipe of a striped paw, pivoted, and was gone, springing into the trees before the others could even raise their weapons.

The soldier on the ground writhed as blood sprang from the vicious claw marks on his face and neck, but no one moved to help him. The other soldiers just danced on the spot yelling at each other. They were obviously terrified, even though they were armed.

Lucy was struck by the smiling soldier's reaction. He was very still. Then he turned and scanned every corner of the clearing, smiling the whole time. For a few seconds he studied the patch of scrub where Lucy, Ricardo and T-Tongue hid. His hand crept to his face and for the first time Lucy saw the livid scar that snaked down his left cheek to his mouth, lifting his lip in a permanent leer. It was the scar that made him appear to smile all the time.

Then he burst into action, spinning around and firing into the trees where the tiger had disappeared. He shouted at the other soldiers in another language, gesturing wildly. The soldiers fanned out and padded nervously towards the scrub, away from Lucy and Ricardo. At another command they began firing into the jungle.

That was enough for Lucy and Ricardo. They slid backwards as stealthily as they could, staying hidden in the thick bushes. They got around the bend in the track, stumbled to their feet and charged back up the forest track. The crackling of gunfire seemed to go on forever behind them.

They didn't stop until Ricardo tripped over a body on the

path. The body was a little boy. He looked dead. So did Ricardo. He just lay there. T-Tongue began licking the little boy, who opened his eyes and screamed. Like a shadow, a dark-haired girl appeared out of the bush and clapped her hand over the little guy's mouth. All four humans just stared at each other. Lucy saw terror, surprise and recognition flicker over the girl's face like a rapid-fire PowerPoint display. Lucy knew her own face must be doing the same, because she was staring at the girl from her nightmare, the one the Tiger-cat had beamed into her mind a little while ago. Ricardo stood staring at the little kid on the ground, who sat up and stared back in disbelief.

'You got away,' said Lucy and then she thought, *How stupid was that? If the soldiers talk another language, she probably does too.*

'Yes,' said the girl in English.

A fresh volley of gunfire blasted close by and the four kids jumped.

'Quick! Let's get out of here! Can he walk?' hissed Lucy. The other girl didn't answer. Skinny as she was, she hoisted the little guy up onto her back.

'I'll carry him,' said Lucy, but the girl just stumbled off up the track.

'Where are you going?' Lucy asked, running to catch up.

If she knew, she was panting too hard to tell. Lucy and Ricardo looked at each other. They both knew what the other was thinking.

'We know a hiding place,' they blurted out together.

The girl half-dropped the boy and turned to face them, her eyes filled with tears. Lucy grabbed the little boy under his arms and picked him up like a baby. He was much lighter than Ricardo and she could still piggyback *him* around Kurrawong if she had to. There was another volley of gunfire, closer this time, and Lucy took off up the path, Ricardo and the girl following. The path had almost disappeared and if Lucy hadn't noticed the red scrunchie she would have missed the faint track leading to the tunnel.

'Grab the scrunchie,' she hissed to Ricardo.

'Forget it,' he said, but the girl must have known what Lucy was worried about because she grabbed the scrunchie and dived after her through the undergrowth and into the mouth of the tunnel. Lucy had never been so relieved to see a black hole.

Pounding boots getting closer made them freeze just inside the entrance. But the boots charged past and on, and when the kids opened their eyes again, the creepers blocking the entrance to the tunnel were thick and unbroken, as though no one had passed that way for forty years. Lucy didn't quite know how it had happened, but she wasn't arguing. Darkness was just fine with her.

8

The Cubby

'What do we do now?' asked Ricardo

'Walk!'

'Where?'

'I don't know, but we can't stay here.'

Holding the little boy with one arm, Lucy pulled the torch from her pocket and passed it to Ricardo. In the faint beam she could see that the little boy's eyes were closed and he could barely hold his head up. His bones stuck out like chopsticks.

Lucy realised she still had the rope from the clearing coiled over one shoulder. She couldn't remember putting it there. It was as though she had just watched an action video but when she hit Rewind, it was frozen. She tramped deeper into the darkness, the torch barely lighting the ground beneath her feet.

The air in the tunnel got colder and Lucy began to shiver. It had been so hot out there! She could feel the dried sweat and mud on her face and arms. Then the torch batteries finally died. There was no choice but to keep going.

'Ricardo, drag your fingers along the wall so we don't miss the fork in the tunnel,' Lucy said.

And that was how they found the door. If they'd been using the torch, they probably would have missed it.

'Hey, here's a handle! Wonder if it . . .?' Ricardo's wondering was brought to an end by the unmistakable creaking of disused hinges.

Lucy shuffled back towards Ricardo's breathing and felt for the opening with her hand.

'Where's the light switch?'

Exhausted as she was, Lucy started to giggle at Ricardo's question. That got Ricardo going and then they both began laughing uncontrollably at the idea of a light switch halfway to the centre of the earth. A scraping sound and a brilliant flash shut them up. The flash illuminated the face of the strange girl, holding a glowing match. In the brief moment before the flame flickered out, Lucy saw a room with tables and chairs, like a lunchroom, a candle stub in a beer bottle on the table, and cups and a thermos. A second later a match flared again and then Lucy and the strange girl were staring at each in the candlelight. Lucy suddenly realised how thirsty she was. She grabbed the thermos and shook it. Water? Ten-year-old tea? Gross. Hands shaking, she unscrewed the lid, poured some liquid into it and tasted it. Water. She had no idea how many years it had been there but right now it tasted fantastic. She handed a cup of water to the girl, who drank thirstily before putting her arm shakily around the little boy and holding the cup to his lips. He gulped some down and handed the cup to Ricardo.

'We have to get you more water and food,' Lucy said to the strange kids.

'Yeah. We'll get you Cocoa Puffs and red cordial,' said Ricardo.

They looked at him blankly.

'Please don't inform anyone of our whereabouts,' said the girl, turning to Lucy.

'What?' said Ricardo.

'Duh! She means don't tell anyone where they are.'

'As if!' Ricardo said.

'Not as if. You tell Mum everything. You even dob yourself in!'

Lucy turned back to the strange kids.

'We'll be back soon. Come on Ricardo, let's go.'

Together they scraped their way towards the fork in the tunnel, trying not to think about tigers, snakes, rats or soldiers. It seemed to go on forever, much longer than before.

When they finally reached the tunnel entrance, they found the Tiger-cat, perched on top of the pile of rubble, observing them impassively with golden eyes. Overhead, the biggest tree's branches were bent low as though ready to scoop them up into its arms. Lucy just had time to register that the leaves were the right dull green again, before the Tiger-cat sprang out of the pit in one graceful leap and disappeared from view. It was an incredible distance for such a small creature to jump. She began knotting the rope at intervals, the way she had been taught at school camp. Then she scrabbled around for a lump of clay. She squeezed the dense, sticky goo into the shape of a donut, threaded the rope through the hole and flung it over the lowest branch, right at the edge of the pit. The weight of the clay donut carried the rope over and back down to her feet. She repeated the process, looping the rope a few more times and hauling on it to make sure it held. Then she climbed up her home-made ladder, clawing from knot to knot, bouncing off the sides of the pit. Made it! She scrambled over the edge and looked back. Ricardo and T-Tongue seemed a long way down

'What will we do with T-Tongue?' called Ricardo.

T-Tongue cocked his head from side to side, as if to say, 'Yeah! What *are* you going to do?'

Lucy raced down to the clothesline, checked to see Mum wasn't around, grabbed a towel and streaked back up the hill. She tied both ends of the towel to the rope to make a little hammock, and tossed it down. Ricardo tucked T-Tongue in and told him to 'Stay'. Lucy hauled him up before he had time to panic and jump out. Then she dropped the rope and Ricardo climbed up like a little monkey. He swung out of the pit just in time to see Mum charging up the path towards the steps.

'Where have you *been*,' she demanded fiercely. 'I've been calling you for ages!'

'Just exploring,' said Lucy, squinting.

How come the sun is shining right in my face, when at the jungle jail it was above my head?

'Exploring! More like coal mining. You're filthy. Come and have breakfast. I've got an appointment at nine o'clock and it's already eight,' Mum said, coming up to the top stair. 'Gosh! You haven't been down there, have you?'

The kids turned in panic, but the walls of the pit were smooth and unmarked. All they could see was a tree with half its roots exposed. Lucy and Ricardo looked at each other, their mouths open. Then Lucy noticed the plaque where she had dropped it half a lifetime ago and walked down the stairs to retrieve it.

Mum was still scolding: 'You'll break your necks swinging off that rope. I should get someone up to have a look at the hole. I should get it filled in . . .'

'No!' said the kids in unison.

But Mum was already marching down the hill and didn't notice when Lucy and Ricardo turned at the bottom of the path, something tugging at their minds. There, sitting on the top stair washing itself, was the Tiger-cat.

Lucy looked down at the plaque still in her hands. It wasn't telling her anything.

She looked back at the Tiger-cat and met its golden eyes; it wasn't telling her anything either.

9

Late Breakfast

'We're moving out! I've found gold!'

Lucy stared at the plaque in her soapy hands. Where she'd rubbed at the blackened metal it glowed dull yellow.

T-Tongue was thrilled. He tried to climb up on the sink – a brave act for a puppy who hated water.

'I don't think so, love,' said Mum, dryly. 'More likely brass. Let me have a look. Brass goes black when you don't look after it.'

Mum took the plaque to the kitchen door to catch a direct blast of sunlight.

'Yes. It's brass. It doesn't rust, but looks terrible if you don't care for it. This will clean up OK. We'll get some of Grandma's special stuff. Be good as new.'

Then she remembered.

'Now don't go wasting too much time on it. You kids are supposed to be scrubbing the bathroom today. It's just a bit of old junk from the garden.'

'But Mum, it's got writing on it. It could have been

buried for a hundred years. I could use it in a history project or something.'

'Yes – when school goes back! The bathroom needs doing *today*.'

'And the Tiger-cat found it for us,' piped up Ricardo, chomping through his second huge bowl of Cocoa Puffs.

'Shut up, Ricardo!' mouthed Lucy silently. Ricardo opened his mouth again and Lucy realised she was going to have to act fast to stop him blurting everything out. She walked casually to the table, placing herself carefully between Mum's line of sight and Ricardo's bowl, picked up the box of Cocoa Puffs, and poured another huge pyramid of cereal into his bowl, staring into his eyes.

Ricardo dropped his gaze and an incredible sight overwhelmed him: his big sister pouring first one, then two, three – he stopped counting after that – huge spoons of sugar into his bowl without Mum noticing. He was struck dumb with delight. Lucy seized her chance.

'Is Grandma coming today?' she asked. 'Can I ring her and ask her to bring the brass-cleaning stuff?'

It worked. Mum remembered she had to ask Grandma to bring something else, so she rushed off to tell her how creative and cute and imaginative Ricardo was these days. Lucy stayed right where she was to tell Ricardo what a dork and a big mouth he was these days. He was too busy stuffing his face with sugar sprinkled with Cocoa Puffs to care.

By the time Mum got off the phone, they had almost finished the whole box. Ricardo had eaten twice as much as Lucy.

'What is going on with you pair? Look at you!' said Mum, exasperated. 'You're filthy, covered in coal-dust, and

Lucy, you've torn your T-shirt. And neither of you can stop eating. What did you do up there?'

'Just climbed trees and stuff, swung on the rope, looked for enemy bases . . .'

Mum looked relieved. Lucy knew what she was thinking. Good old-fashioned make-believe was better than TV, even if they were filthy.

'Be careful. You can play as much as you like up in the bush but stay away from that hole. The edges will be unstable. We can move the rope to another tree.'

'But Mum . . .'

But Mum wasn't listening, she was shooing Ricardo towards the shower and muttering about how late she was.

Lucy cracked six eggs into the frypan.

'Six!' said Mum, horrified. 'After all that cereal?'

'But they're . . . we're starving,' stumbled Lucy, and was glad to hide her face in the fridge while she looked for the bacon.

'Well, I'll do some more shopping this morning. We might have to be like Grandma and get some chickens of our own. That chook run in the back yard looks all right, it should keep out dogs and foxes.'

'Would it keep out tigers?' asked Ricardo, walking into the kitchen dripping and completely naked. 'Can I have bacon and eggs?'

'What is this, the naked café? Kurrawong's bottomless restaurant?' protested Mum. 'Get some clothes on!' But they were all laughing as Ricardo's bare bum disappeared out the door.

When he returned, dressed, Lucy said they would clean up the kitchen and Mum looked at her as though she had grown the wings of an angel. Ricardo looked at her as though she had gone completely nuts. Then Mum ran out the front door, yelling over her shoulder that Grandma would be over later to check on them. Lucy listened to the Mazda's dodgy engine drive up the street and . . .

'Now!'

She grabbed the bacon and eggs on Ricardo's plate before he could eat them, scraped it with her own into a lunchbox, and hunted in the huge old fridge for apples and oranges. Ricardo grabbed another packet of Cocoa Puffs, bowls and spoons. A carton of milk was next.

What else did they need? Torch batteries. Lucy looked in the second drawer near the kitchen sink. Bingo! How come everyone always kept useful things like batteries and birthday-cake candles and bits of string in the second drawer near the sink? But there was no time for trivia. Lucy darted off to get her school backpack, candles and matches from their bedroom.

Walking between the dragon vases, she saw something was different: the tiger rug. Even with Ricardo's undies and a T-shirt lying on top of it, Lucy knew something had changed. *The tiger corner looked brand-new*. The tiger's stripes were clear and strong and its golden eyes burned out at her. The monkey was still faded and dull, just like before. One more weirdo event to think about. Lucy looked for T-Tongue's lead instead.

Back in the kitchen, Ricardo had packed a bottle of juice and some two-minute noodles.

'How are we going to cook them, goofball?'

'I eat them like that!'

It would have to do. They took off up the path to where

the Tiger-cat still waited, asleep in a sunny patch on the top stair. It opened one eye and then jumped delicately down and began purring and rubbing itself against their legs. It sent no video clips for Lucy but left her in no doubt they were doing the right thing. The only trouble was – the tunnel was blocked. When Lucy peered into the pit, all she saw was a smooth mud wall. She looked at the Tiger-cat. It was sniffing T-Tongue's nose and the puppy had dropped low to the ground, quivering with excitement, or was it fear? Then the Tiger-cat twisted, crouched and leapt, its body soaring in a graceful marmalade curve, then landed efficiently on the pit floor and sprang towards the wall where the tunnel used to be. As Lucy watched, astounded, the pile of wooden dinosaur bones material-ised, with the gaping entrance to the tunnel behind it. No magic commands, no secret machinery – just there again, like a special effect in the movies!

Lucy swung herself down and threw the rope back for Ricardo. He followed and then they realised they'd forgotten T-Tongue. He was whimpering, running up and down the pit's edge. The Tiger-cat growled fiercely from inside the tunnel and that was too much for T-Tongue! With one last desperate, high-pitched bark, he leapt, landed hard, scrambled up and promptly tried to lick everyone, including the Tiger-cat. Lucy snapped his lead on and picked her way carefully over the rubble. The Tiger-cat had already entered the blackness, tail lashing. Lucy switched the torch on, took a deep breath, and for the second time that day entered the unknown, with T-Tongue trotting at her side.

10

Rahel and Toro

It felt safer this time because they were following the Tiger-cat. Reaching the fork, it looked back to face Lucy and Ricardo, its eyes glowing red in the strong torchlight. Then it leapt into the up-sloping tunnel and disappeared. Lucy and Ricardo stumbled on until they reached the door, where the Tiger-cat clawed impatiently at the wood, making a strange yewling growl.

'It's us,' said Ricardo, opening the door and bouncing inside. 'We got you Cocoa Puffs!'

The torchlight revealed the two kids huddled on the lounge, the boy's head on the girl's lap. Their eyes were wide open and scared.

The Tiger-cat padded over and sniffed the boy's face. He shrank away. Maybe he had never seen a cat, let alone one like this, thought Lucy. In the candlelight the Tiger-cat looked even more like a miniature tiger.

'He won't hurt you,' 'She won't hurt you,' said Ricardo and Lucy at the same time.

Neither of the kids on the lounge looked convinced.

The Tiger-cat jumped up on the table where the stubby candle spluttered and began to wash coal-dust from its face and ears. The girl helped the boy sit up. He leaned groggily against her but looked interested when Lucy produced the lunchbox. She gave them the bottle of juice first and they slurped thirstily. The room was oppressively dark with just one candle burning. Lucy didn't like the dark corners. It was bad enough knowing they were this far underground. She took some plates from the bench against the wall and melted wax onto them and lit all six candles from her backpack. That was better.

Lucy served up the food: dry bacon, cold eggs and soggy toast. The kids ate as if it were their first meal in days. Maybe it was. Ricardo poured out bowls of Cocoa Puffs. The strange kids didn't even wait for spoons but drank it like crunchy soup.

Lucy remembered the Tiger-cat and put some milk in a plate on the table. The cat just looked at her and kept on washing itself.

'It doesn't eat, goofball,' said Ricardo, 'it's magic!'

Lucy ignored him and tried to work out what they needed. The kids couldn't stay here without blankets – it was freezing. She remembered all the stuff they'd found in the house that first day. They had put it all in a spare room. There were blankets, mattresses, kitchen things, clothes and pillows – heaps of stuff: everything they needed to hide a couple of kids from the smiling soldier until . . . what? Until she could get them somewhere safe. Like where?

Lucy had a sinking feeling that she was out of her depth. She tried to ignore it, but deep down, she knew something

51

weird was going on, something too weird to wrap her head around. One thing she did understand: these two kids might not be safe at either end of the tunnel.

Like an action replay, something Lucy had seen once on the news at Grandma's flashed into her mind. A boat full of refugees – the man on the news had called them 'illegals' – had been sailing to Australia, but the Prime Minister had sent the Navy to stop them. The Navy had made the boat captain turn around and head back out into the middle of the ocean. Mum and Grandma had had a big fight about it. Grandma felt sorry for the people on the boat because they were running away from a war, but Mum said the government had done the right thing. Lucy still remembered the looks on the boat people's faces. A woman holding a little baby was crying. Some people looked angry and were shaking their fists at the news heli-copter, others sat hunched on the deck with their heads in their hands. There were kids too! They looked really scared.

Grandma said Lucy's mum didn't know what it was like to be in trouble, which made Mum really mad! She said Grandma didn't know what she was talking about and working all night at the hospital for crap money was no picnic. And Grandma told her not to say crap in her house and Mum said Grandma still treated her like a baby. Then Mum turned off the TV and sent Lucy to bed.

'You're treating me like a baby,' said Lucy, but it had no effect.

Now, looking at the two kids in the miners' cubby, Lucy knew she couldn't risk telling anyone about them. She didn't know who they were, or why they were in that horrible jail, but she did not want them to go back there. If Mum found out they'd escaped from jail, Lucy just knew she wouldn't approve. Grandma would feel sorry for the kids but she'd tell all her friends and then it would be all over Kurrawong by lunchtime. And maybe the Prime Minister would find out . . .

Lucy squatted down on the floor and put a candle between herself and the kids. It lit up their faces and made them look skinnier than ever. Ricardo sat down next to her. T-Tongue had given up hoping anyone was going to give him anything to eat and gone to sleep with his nose between his paws.

'Who are you?' Lucy asked the children.

The Tiger-cat jumped down as though it wanted to hear.

'Rahel,' answered the girl. Putting her arm around the boy, she said, 'Toro'. Her voice was soft and accented, but every word was clear.

'I'm Lucy and he's Ricardo and he's T-Tongue and she's the Tiger-cat.'

'I'm Ricardo and she's Lucy and he's T-Tongue and he's the Tiger-cat.'

Lucy glared at Ricardo and turned back to the girl. 'Where are your mum and dad?' she asked. The girl's eyes filled with tears and the boy looked away. Lucy wished she hadn't asked.

'Soldiers got them,' said Ricardo with certainty.

'How would you know?' demanded Lucy.

'Duh . . . the Tiger-cat told me!'

Lucy looked at the Tiger-cat but it didn't say anything, just kept staring at her with those golden eyes. Then, all of a sudden, *that feeling came again*. Her body melted into the cold air of the room, her mind holding tight to the Tiger-cat's mind-rope. Then the Tiger-cat was gone, and in its place . . .

An open door. A man steps out onto the verandah and lights a cigarette. It is the smiling soldier. More soldiers drag a dark-haired woman through the door, onto the verandah and down the stairs. She cries out in a strange language. Lucy under-stands two words: 'Toro' and 'Rahel'. Another soldier appears in the doorway, carrying Toro, who is crying and struggling. The soldier hauls him across the verandah towards the stairs. A blue vase of flowers flies through the door, hitting the soldier and smashing to the floor. The man screams and drops Toro amongst the broken blue china and bright yellow flowers. Rahel launches herself into the open doorway, grabs Toro's hand and tries to run down the stairs with him. But the smiling soldier, calmly smoking his cigarette, simply stretches out a lazy leg from where he stands beside the top stair and trips them. Both children tumble to the bottom. As Rahel and Toro lie helpless in the dust, Lucy can clearly see, on the top pocket of the smiling soldier's brown shirt, a picture: the red-eyed face of a black bull with long yellow horns. Then Toro starts to cry.

Lucy shivered back into her body, chilled to the bone. The scent of the smiling soldier's cigarette was strong in her nostrils. It was so real! She looked around the cubby, but the only smoke came from the candles spluttering on the table. It was her turn to sit with wide eyes and stare at the two children on the lounge in front of her, Toro's sobs still ringing in her ears. The Tiger-cat jumped on her lap and Lucy stroked its fur while she tried to think of something to say. She didn't have to.

'What were you doing in that school?' asked Ricardo.

'It's not a school, Retardo!' Lucy yelled – and then felt ashamed when Toro shrank away from her and the Tiger-cat sat up, startled, sinking its claws into her legs.

'Indeed it is not a school,' Rahel said quietly. 'After they arrested our parents, they sent us to the camp. It is a special prison for the children of the rebels. My mama and papa are rebels. The Bulls despise us . . .'

Her voice trailed off into silence and she hugged Toro closer.

'The Bulls?' asked Lucy, but she already knew the answer.

'Soldiers. They have a picture of a bull on their uniforms.'

'Are your mum and dad bank robbers?' ventured Ricardo.

Rahel looked horrified. 'No! They are rebels!'

Silence.

'What are you doing in Australia?' asked Lucy finally.

Rahel looked puzzled but Lucy didn't give her time to answer. 'C'mon! You can tell me. I'm not going to tell anyone. You're boat people, aren't you?'

'Boat people?' Rahel echoed blankly.

'Yeah, like we're car people,' said Ricardo helpfully. 'We like cars best but some people like boats. Grandma likes buses, so I guess she's a bus person. Then there's bike people. Me, I'm a skateboard person and —'

'Shut up, Ricardo. It's not like that. I saw it on TV. Did you come on a boat and the Navy arrested you? I swear, I won't tell anyone.'

Rahel just looked at Lucy as though she were a weirdo.

Then Lucy saw the flaw in her own logic.

'No, that's stupid, there are no Bulls in Kurrawong. I don't understand any of this. I thought you were just a nightmare until the Tiger-cat sent me a picture of you this morning; and then we found the tunnel, and now . . .'

Her voice trailed off and Rahel finally got a chance to speak.

'We have been dreaming of you too. We watched you washing the rug and your meeting with the Tiger-cat. We have been waiting for you. But you took so long to come to our country.'

'Your country?' Even as Lucy spoke a voice in her head was whispering, *It's too hot at that jail and everyone speaks a different language.*

Rahel looked at Lucy steadily and repeated, 'You came to our country and we are grateful. You saved us from the Bulls'.

'That's OK,' said Ricardo. 'What country?' He didn't seem to have any problem with the idea of another country tucked away at the back of little old Kurrawong.

Toro whispered an answer: 'Burchimo', or that's what it sounded like.

Rahel looked fierce.

'No, Toro! Say its proper name!'

She sat up very straight, dark eyes flashing in the candlelight.

'Toro is doing what the Bulls desire. They insist we call it East Burchimo or they beat us. But its name is Telares. The Bull soldiers came from Burchimo when I was seven and put people in jail. They killed many people and set fire to their houses. They stole many things. They say our country is part of Burchimo, but it is not. They never lived here before the invasion. Toro was only a baby when they came. He cannot recall anything before the Bulls came.'

'But isn't Toro Spanish for bull?' Lucy asked.

Rahel frowned.

'Mama named him Toro because he was born one month too soon. She said he was as impatient as a little bull. But if she had known the Bulls were going to invade, she would never have done it.'

Lucy's head was spinning. *This girl is crazy! Or is she? What about the tiger? We don't have tigers in Australia, except in the zoo . . . and cats aren't supposed to beam video clips right into your brain. And what about those psycho trees? They're all the wrong colour. Maybe it really is another country.*

Rahel's quiet voice broke in.

'We have been in jail for six months. The Bulls came for us on Toro's birthday on the sixth of June.'

'That's slack!' said Ricardo.

'How old are you now?' Lucy asked Rahel, because that, at least, was an easy question.

'Twelve.'

The same age as Lucy. Lucy suddenly felt like a big, dumb elephant next to Rahel, who looked about two years younger, she was so little and skinny.

'How old is Toro?'

'Six.'

Yipes! The same age as Ricardo! Toro didn't have a puffed-up belly like those famine kids on TV, but he looked like a shadow next to Ricardo. And he barely spoke.

'What do you get at your canteen . . . I mean what do they . . . What do you eat?' asked Ricardo.

'Rice.'

'And?'

'Vegetables . . . but not every day.'

'You're lucky! Mum and Grandma make me eat mine *all* the time. What do you have for breakfast?'

'Rice.'

'Rice Bubbles?'

'No. Rice.'

'Lunch?'

'Nothing.'

'Recess?'

'Retardo! They don't have recess! Don't you get it? They're not at school. They're in jail. They don't even have lunch!'

That shut him up big time. He poured another bowl of Cocoa Puffs while he struggled with the concept of rice for breakfast and dinner, with nothing in between. Then he realised what he had done and quickly offered more to Rahel and Toro, but Toro was holding his belly as if it hurt.

'He is not accustomed to this food,' said Rahel.

'I'll have it!' Ricardo said helpfully, then, at Lucy's face, 'What?'

Lucy shook her head in disgust but she felt stupid herself, for not remembering what they'd said on that TV show – that kids who had been hungry have to get used to food again, gradually. She would have to find out more; but right now, time was ticking away and they had to get back to the house, load up all the stuff they needed and get back here before Grandma arrived.

'We have to get more stuff for you. We've got blankets and pillows at home and more food. You can stay here until —' Lucy didn't quite know how to finish that sentence, so she was glad when Rahel interrupted.

'I must locate my aunt!'

'What? Where is she?' said Lucy.

'She fled to the rebel base in the mountains just before we got taken. I must find her. She will know what to do. She is the only one who can help Mama and Papa. She said she would care for us if anything bad happened. I have committed all her maps to memory. I know how to get there.'

'But Toro can't walk. And what about the Bulls? If they see you, they'll just put you back in jail,' said Lucy.

'Toro will recover. It is just that we have not eaten. We *must* find her. If we take food we will be able to hide from the Bulls. We will walk at night and follow her directions.'

Lucy didn't know what to say. Who in their right mind would go out the jungle jail end of the tunnel again?

'At least stay here for a while,' she urged. 'Eat good food for a few weeks and get a bit fatter . . . I mean stronger. We'll bring you food every day, and medicine for Toro. You'll need other things too.'

'I've got a water pistol,' said Ricardo, 'and a Ninja sword'.

The Tiger-cat jumped off Lucy's knee and padded to the lounge. It climbed boldly onto Rahel's lap and began to purr. She looked horrified.

'Pat him,' said Ricardo.

'She won't hurt you,' said Lucy.

Rahel looked at them and then gingerly stroked the cat's

fur. The Tiger-cat purred even more and pushed its head against Rahel's hand as if to say, 'More, please!'

'Scratch between his ears. He likes that,' advised Ricardo, to Lucy's intense irritation.

'How would you know?'

'He told me!'

Purrs reverberated around the cubby. Rahel looked up at the kids and smiled for the first time. It made her look completely different, like a normal kid, not a freaked-out, hungry one.

'Let's go, Ricardo, we've got to get the rest of the stuff before Grandma gets here.'

'See ya,' said Ricardo and took off through the door with the torch, leaving Lucy to stumble along behind until he felt sorry for her and stopped. Once again, the Tiger-cat was waiting, its golden eyes appraising them from its throne of broken wood and rubble, when they reached the pit.

11

The Old Lady's Stuff

Ricardo grabbed the humungous bunch of keys and tried the little silver one. Lucky first go. Clunk, creak; the door opened, and Ricardo staggered back and collapsed on the floor under what *had* been a tower of old lady's clothes. He pulled the pink fluffy nightie from his head and clawed his way to freedom through a lemon dressing-gown and six pairs of massive white undies.

If he hadn't glimpsed the padlocked dragon chest through the pink nightie, he might have given up, but it was irresistible. He clambered up. What was inside? Surely one of the keys would open it? Lucy shouldered past him, tripping on the undies.

'What are you doing? They don't need granny clothes. They need bedclothes!'

She began jamming blankets and sheets into her biggest backpack.

The room was a cross between a treasure trove and a junk shop, full of old magazines, lacy tablecloths, a crystal vase, an old black-and-white TV that didn't work.

'Stop trying to open that chest, Ricardo. Mum told you to leave it alone and you're supposed to be helping me! We have to finish before Grandma comes.'

Ricardo shuffled outside, lugging a bedspread. Lucy threw pillows after him and tried to think what else they needed. She spied a wicker basket by the wall. Perfect. A picnic set. Plates, cutlery . . . everything! Ricardo found a metal bowl with a flower painted on the bottom, big enough to sit in.

'A bath!' said Lucy.

Toxic! He dropped it. Then Lucy found the corner with the camping gear. Airbeds, fold-up chairs, a billy, an esky to keep stuff cold. A heavy tent. A gas bottle and camping stove. Whoever owned the granny clothes must have been an explorer. Rahel and Toro could cook bacon and eggs, and heat water for a bath. They had everything they needed to stay down there forever.

'Ricardo, give up, will you?' She wrestled the keys from him and tried them on the chest herself.

'See,' he said when she gave up, 'it's missing'.

It was so frustrating. The chest was like a magnet.

'It's got Ninja swords in it,' said Ricardo. 'We could give them to Rahel and Toro.'

'Crap. It's got jewels. They could buy a whole new country!'

A loud knock on the front door almost caused Kurra-wong's first recorded dual heart attack. Grandma was early. Parrot poo! They stuffed the bedspread and pillows back inside and locked the door. Lucy sent Ricardo scooting into their bedroom with the backpack, while she let Grandma in.

Except it wasn't Grandma. It was a man in a bright

pink shirt and a shiny tie with pictures of smiling girls in the kind of swimmers that Grandma would *never* wear. Mr Nigel Adams, estate agent.

'Hi there,' he said, smiling.

Actually, he just stretched his lips so you could see his teeth. The girls on his tie were better at smiling.

'Is Mummy home?'

'I don't know. Where does she live?'

His top lip stretched so wide Lucy thought it might split.

'Very funny. Is *your* mummy home?'

'No.'

'Well, I have to pick something up for the owner, so if you don't mind, I'll just —' Nigel Pink-Shirt put one foot on the first mermaid.

T-Tongue thought *not*. He charged up the hallway, with Ricardo in pursuit, doing his best imitation of a Rottweiler. The funny thing was that Nigel Pink-Shirt didn't seem to notice he was being threatened by the canine equivalent of a rug rat. He jumped backwards, and his lips snapped back into a straight line like a piece of elastic.

'Call it off!' he said.

He sounded panicked. Lucy was impressed.

'T-Tongue – *drop*!'

He did!

Nigel Pink-Shirt straightened up and fixed up his tie . . . and then he got nasty.

'You're not supposed to have a dog here. I was only doing your mother a favour because she said you – Linda, is it? – got it for your birthday. But if it bites anyone, the police will shoot it. And if it comes anywhere near me, I will.'

Ricardo bravely came to his sister's defence. 'Her name's Lucy, and T-Tongue doesn't bite people. He licks them.'

'Well, he'd better not lick me. Now, I need to pick something up, so . . .' He tried putting a foot on the mermaid again.

T-Tongue let out one of his Superdog growls.

'Mum told us not to let anybody in while she's not here,' said Lucy loudly.

'Very sensible, but I'm not just anyone. I'm the agent. Look, all I want is an old box. It's got dragons carved on it. Have you seen it?'

'No,' said Lucy.

'Nuh,' said Ricardo.

'Grrrow,' said T-Tongue.

'What the hell's *that*?' said Nigel Pink-Shirt, as something fierce and ginger clawed up his leg and onto his bald head.

Then he said things much worse than Mum ever said, even when she was really mad. The Tiger-cat, eyes blazing, made some impressive noises too, and then streaked across the shaky old verandah and around the side of the house.

'Nobody said anything about a cat,' screamed Nigel Pink-Shirt, then winced as he touched the blood-red clawmarks on his skull.

'It's not ours. It's feral,' said Lucy.

'It's a feral tiger,' said Ricardo, then looked really worried.

'GrrrFFF!' said T-Tongue.

Nigel Pink-Shirt backed away down the stairs.

'Tell your mother I'll be back for that chest.' He marched back to the car, muttering to himself. He slammed the door and began examining his scratches in the rear-vision mirror.

'We'd better get the Ninja swords out of the chest,' said Ricardo.

He had a one-track mind.

'Grrrow,' said T-Tongue. So did he.

Then Nigel Scar-Skull opened the window and yelled, 'And I'm going to tell the Council to set poison baits for that feral cat before it claws someone's eyes out'.

He drove off in a cloud of dust, revving the guts out of the engine, and the smell of burning rubber wafted onto the verandah.

12

The Octopus Information Exchange

'Yoohoo! I've made something delicious!'

Lucy and Ricardo had just had time to dump all the blankets and picnic gear into the pit before a familiar voice called out to them from the house. They walked panting into the kitchen. On the table was an enormous chocolate cake, a colour telly and a sewing machine. Grandma never travelled light, even on the bus.

It was a particularly huge chocolate cake with cream in the middle and about three hundred Smarties on top: a Grandma special. One piece was already gone because she'd made Joe, the bus driver, turn the engine off and have some.

Grandma had Joe wrapped around her little finger. She proudly told Lucy and Ricardo how he had kept the passengers waiting while he helped her aboard with her sewing machine, telly and chocolate cake.

'Then he drove me all the way up here, even though the last bus stop is at the bottom of the hill.'

She lowered her voice: 'I think he was breaking the

rules, just quietly, but I was the last passenger, so no one will know. You won't tell, will you, Ricky?'

Ricardo was on his second slice and by the time he could speak he had remembered there was something he had to ask Grandma.

'Do you know the old lady who lived here before us?'

Grandma and her friends were like a secret society with X-ray vision and bionic tongues. Lucy remembered when Mandy Hoffman told everyone she was going to Disneyland and Lucy rushed home to ask if they could go too and Grandma already knew about it. She knew how much it had cost and which credit card the Hoffmans had used to pay for it and the strain it had put on the marriage because Mr Hoffman had wanted to go to Euro Disney instead of America.

Grandma's old friends were *formidable*. Dad said Grandma and her gang added up to one giant old octopus. If you just tugged on one of its arms and asked a question, sooner or later one of the other arms would tickle you under the chin with the answer. What's more, they'd tell you why you were asking in the first place. Dad called Grandma's bingo club the Octopus Information Exchange.

Grandma acted all innocent at first.

'How would I know? And how do you know it was an old lady?'

Ricardo looked at Lucy.

'I don't,' he said slowly, looking as if he didn't know what to say.

Then he did what he always did when he didn't know what to say. He ran around the room, squealing the same word over and over again, 'Lady, lady, lady,' until Grandma told him to cease and desist.

Lucy thought she had better say something.

'I think it was an old lady too,' she said.

'Why, Lucy love?'

'Because of all the mermaids and it's got an old lady's garden, like your one, Grandma, with all those roses.'

'Well, it was your grandpa, rest his soul, who planted all my roses, Lucy, but I think I know what you mean. I can ask at bingo, if you're really curious. Beryl Shepherd used to live up this way when her Bill worked in the mines. I'm sure she'll know. Now, show me this horrible old rug you're all so excited about, and if you stop prancing about and look in my bag, Ricky, you'll find something special for that dreadful dog.'

Ricardo's eyes nearly popped out of his skull when he saw how bright the tiger was, but for once he kept his mouth shut. Luckily Grandma hadn't seen the rug before, so she didn't notice anything different. Lucy was caught between pride at hearing Grandma say how beautiful and exotic the tiger must have been when the rug was new, and really wanting her to get out of the room in case the rug decided to get even newer. Hang on, what was that between the tiger's front paws? It looked like . . . oh no! Lucy quickly sat on the tiger's head, covering its paws with her feet.

'Get off him, stupid,' said Ricardo, shoving her.

'She's a her, you idiot!' and Lucy shoved him back.

'Now, if you two are going to fight, I'm going to make a cup of tea.'

Lucy shoved Ricardo again and he tried to get her in a neck lock.

Grandma shook her head and walked out.

'Look at this, you dingbat,' said Lucy, wriggling easily out of Ricardo's grasp and getting up to show him what she had been hiding.

'Oh.'

It was very faint, but there was no doubt. The image of a snake was woven into the rug. Its disturbingly large head was between the tiger's front paws. It certainly hadn't been there before. Maybe it was a trick of the light, but as they stared, the snake seemed to get even clearer, its body twining along one entire side of the rug before tapering to a pointed tail.

Ricardo had gone pale.

'First the tiger in the rug, then the Tiger-cat in the tunnel, and then the tiger in the jungle. Do you think . . . ?'

'Yep,' said Lucy.

'Then I'm not going.'

'We have to. They need more food!'

Silence.

'How long does a packet of Cocoa Puffs last?'

13

Feline Flashback

Grandma had set up her sewing machine in the kitchen and said she was going to make them both a pair of cargo pants with lots of pockets. Ricardo asked her for a pouch to hold a Ninja sword. She said she'd see what she could do.

'What's a Ninja?' she whispered to Lucy.

'You know. Martial arts.'

'Oh! The chaps in the white pyjamas.'

Grandma didn't watch enough action videos. It didn't matter. It meant Grandma had the afternoon sewn up and Lucy and Ricardo were free. Grandma thought it was great they wanted to go on a bush walk and said it was terrible that they hadn't had lunch. She pulled heaps of food out of her bottomless bag – bread rolls, cheese, muesli bars, grapes. Grandma took food wherever she went, just in case war was declared or the stock market crashed while she was at the hairdresser or something.

They formed a production line in the kitchen, making cheese and salad rolls. Grandma cut them each another slice of chocolate cake and asked when they'd be back.

'Midnight?' she grinned. They nodded. Grandma cut them even more cake and said, 'Actually, six o'clock would be better because I'll have to try your new pants on you. If you leave me alone until then, they might be ready.'

OK, they said, and disappeared.

Charging up the hill, they met the Tiger-cat and, this time, Lucy abseiled into the pit even as the Tiger-cat was leaping at the solid wall. She landed like a professional and raced over the freshly materialised rubble and down the tunnel – until she remembered all the blankets and picnic gear. Oops.

Then she remembered the snake in the rug. When they finally arrived, both Lucy and Ricardo were thoroughly spooked and charged in the door without knocking. Rahel and Toro jumped.

'Sorry! We've got some more food and blankets for you.'

'Thank you,' said Rahel, and shoved Toro.

He looked at them with big brown eyes and said, 'Fank you'.

'My grandma's making me Ninja pants,' Ricardo said importantly.

What could you say to that? Lucy handed Rahel and Toro a blanket each and began getting out the food. They all sat at the table, the Tiger-cat too, with Rahel and Toro wrapped up in their new blankets. T-Tongue sneaked onto the lounge.

Then Ricardo said the fateful words, 'I have to go'.

'You'll just have to wait,' said Lucy, exasperated. But Lucy realised she hadn't thought of the most basic thing! Rahel and Toro couldn't stay down here without a toilet.

Rahel's announcement was even worse: 'We must return to the jail'.

'What? What about your auntie?' exclaimed Lucy.

'It is my duty to assist the other prisoners. Mama and Papa would expect it of me.'

Why did she always talk like that, as if she were giving a school speech? And she couldn't be serious about going back!

'How are you going to do it? The Bulls will shoot you!'

'The four of us will sneak back under cover of darkness. Two of us will distract the guards and two will assist the children to escape one by one. We will deliver them here and then later trek across the mountain to my aunt.'

'Cool,' said Ricardo.

'*Crap!*' thought Lucy.

The Tiger-cat padded over, looked into Lucy's eyes and . . .

'Here we go again,' thought Lucy, as she began to shiver and felt the tug of the Tiger-cat's mind-rope.

She's inside the jungle jail, behind the gates! Kids are marching right past her, as if she doesn't exist. Some of them are so little! They should be in kindergarten . . . They look so scared and unhappy. The smallest, a tiny girl with dirty, tangled curls matted into dreadlocks, is turning, looking directly into Lucy's eyes as though she alone can see her. She's wrapped in an old sack, like a Roman toga. It's the little girl from Lucy's first dream, the one taken away from her mum when the smiling soldier's men stormed the park.

Lucy blinked and found herself back in the miners' cubby, gazing at the Tiger-cat, which started washing itself as if nothing had happened. She looked at Rahel and Toro.

'OK, if you have to, then I'll come too.'

'Fank you,' said Toro.

'What day is it?' said Rahel.

'Saturday.'

'Then we go tonight.'

'Good!' said Ricardo, 'Grandma should have my Ninja pants ready by then.'

14

Peanuts

Grandma did have his Ninja pants ready by then; and Lucy's; and her own. She'd gone a bit wild and made a pair of pink ones for herself: bright pink. Ricardo's and Lucy's were jungle green and they said they liked them so much they wanted to wear them to bed. Grandma said OK – 'just this once'.

'We'll cook dinner, Grandma,' said Lucy.

'*You* can!' complained Ricardo, and then he looked thoughtful and agreed. Grandma was happy.

'That would be lovely, kids. I did get rather carried away on those pants. All those pockets! Think what you could keep in them! Clothes pegs, tissues, packets of biscuits for bingo . . .'

She kept chattering while Lucy chopped up spuds. It was ages before Grandma noticed how huge the pile was.

'Stop! You must have chopped up five kilos. Who wants to eat baked spuds on a hot night like this? And your mum isn't even home for dinner . . . oh, that reminds me. Your mum had to fly to Sydney. A little girl is sick and they needed a nurse to look after her in the plane. She'll stay the night up there. Lucy, do stop! We'll never eat them.'

'Mum always does this many baked potatoes,' Lucy said airily. 'Then we eat them in the morning and for lunch the next day.' But she stopped chopping and slid her mountain of potatoes into the big old oven.

Ricardo was checking out the freezer. He spirited twenty-four cheese and spinach pies into the oven while Grandma was still going on about the potatoes and hospitals and the dangers of flying in small aeroplanes.

Then she said something Lucy wanted to hear.

'By the way, I've got that brass-cleaner you wanted Lucy, love. You just wipe it on and rub it off with a soft cloth. What are you trying to clean?'

'Just something I found in the garden.'

Grandma raised her eyebrows, holding the can out of reach.

Lucy thought quickly. She didn't quite know why, but she wanted to keep the plaque to herself.

'Look at the time, Grandma, *Brain Bank* is starting. The antenna's in the lounge room. Do you want me to set up the telly?'

Grandma dropped the can, and was out of the kitchen before Lucy had even finished the sentence.

Lucy and Ricardo were always trying to get Grandma to enter *Brain Bank*, because she rattled out the right answers like a machine-gun before the real contestants even opened their mouths. But she always laughed and said she wasn't going to make a fool of herself in front of Australia. The kids didn't see how Grandma making them lots of money or winning a car and a holiday was making a fool of herself, but she wouldn't be persuaded. She just sat there every night winning wads of virtual money, virtual vacations to tropical islands and virtual vehicles. *Very frustrating!*

Lucy wandered into the back yard with the brass-cleaner and began rubbing at the plaque. A word emerged, letter by letter. 'T…E…L…

TELARES!

She had never seen the word written down, but recognised it immediately. It was where Rahel and Toro came from.

'I don't get it,' she thought. This was crazy, and not even proper crazy – it all felt real and unreal at the same time. It felt like a weird daydream, but there was the plaque, solid and real in her hands, and today she had seen real soldiers and heard real guns and seen kids who were really frightened.

She didn't want to think about tonight. She wanted to jump into bed with T-Tongue and go to sleep. She was scared, so scared she felt sick.

Lucy heard a rumbling purr, and felt soft fur against her legs. She met the Tiger-cat's golden eyes. Instantly, she knew what the creature was thinking. She didn't get any pictures this time, just a strong sense of anticipation and excitement . . . and something else? Hunger? Gazing into the animal's eyes, Lucy felt her own pulse quicken. In a split second, she was eager for action. And in a weird way it made her feel peaceful.

Lucy hurried back into the kitchen. Ricardo was filling his backpack with everything he could get his hands on: peanuts, sultanas, dried apples. If he had any fear about tonight, he wasn't showing it. His hair was spiked up again and he looked like a crazy little soldier himself, in his new Ninja pants and black T-shirt; a commander in an army of lunatic midgets. He was singing a little song while he packed.

'I am the Ninja of the peanuts . . . Oh, peanuts are my friends . . . The peanuts think I'm great . . . They jump into my bag . . . I'm going to take them for a walk . . . The peanuts are my friends . . . They say eat me, eat me, eat me . . .'

Lucy *knew* she had not been like that when she was six years old, not even once; but if it made him happy . . .

'OK, Ninja,' she said, 'just remember you have to clean up after dinner so we can get all the leftovers without Grandma noticing'.

Grandma got the shock of her life when Ricardo jumped up after dinner to wash the dishes and Lucy began putting the food away. Grandma started yawning and said she wanted an early night. Good idea. Lucy started yawning too.

'Looks like we all need to turn in,' Grandma said.

Normally Lucy would have ranted that Mum always let them stay up late, but not tonight. Grandma got another shock when Ricardo agreed meekly to a bath. She went off to run it, which gave the kids just enough time to smuggle the leftover baked spuds and pies into their backpacks.

Lucy still had that strange peaceful feeling she had soaked up from the Tiger-cat, even though they were probably about to get shot or be human-burgers for a tiger or sausage rolls for a giant python. She still didn't understand anything and it still felt crazy but suddenly it was also simple: if Rahel was going to risk rescuing that little girl and the other kids, then Lucy had to help. That was certain, even if she didn't have a clue how.

It was comforting to do something she did understand. Something easy, like stuff her bag with food no one was ever going to eat because they would all be dead soon. *Crazy*. The peaceful feeling evaporated. Why was she going to get out of bed in the middle of the night? Come to think of it, why was she letting Ricardo come? *Because he would tell if she didn't*. He might tell anyway, but he would definitely tell if she went without him. Well, that was easy, she wouldn't go either. She'd just stay in bed.

Then the image of the little girl wrapped in that horrible sack flashed into Lucy's mind and she remembered her nightmare. What had the mother said? 'My little girl is yours now, you must look after her until you find . . .' Until Lucy found what? And why Lucy?

As if to answer her, suddenly, like a PowerPoint show, Lucy saw all the faces of the little kids from the jungle jail. When she thought about the looks on their faces she felt . . . what was the right word? Urgent. That was it. She was needed urgently. This was an emergency. If she didn't help them, no one would! And she couldn't tell anyone, not even Grandma. She'd never believe it. How could she? Lucy was having trouble believing it herself. It was way too weird for grown-ups. And she'd said she would help. It was up to her and Ricardo and a weirdo feral cat – armed with a whole lot of baked potatoes.

Later, in bed, Lucy tried to think it through, make a plan, but she had to admit in the end she had no idea what they were going to do. Ricardo wasn't much help. He just lay there and sang his peanut song over and over again. Lucy checked her watch one more time. She had to stay awake until Grandma went to sleep. When she heard the snoring, she would wake up Ricardo and they would sneak out. After that . . . maybe the Tiger-cat or Rahel would think of something. Because all Lucy could think of was peanuts.

15

Ninja Pants
in the Night

'Lucy! Wake up!'

Lucy gazed blankly at the spiky-haired Ninja by her bed, Rahel's face still swimming before her eyes.

'Get up! We're late!' urged Ricardo.

Lucy looked at her watch: 2 a.m. She hadn't meant to fall asleep. How could she have slept through Grandma's snores? Now Rahel would think she'd chickened out. They only had a few hours before sunrise. She jumped out of bed and grabbed her torch. Then she got a good look at Ricardo. He had his Ninja pants on, and what looked suspiciously like a plastic sword stuck into the pouch Grandma had made. A scarf was tied around his forehead. He looked like a dork.

Lucy bent to pick up T-Tongue, and paused. The rug had changed again. The snake coiled between the tiger's front paws had distinct diamond patterns, pale yellow on grey scales. Her eyes followed the pattern, from the head resting between the tiger's paws, to the tip of the tail, much too far away in the other corner of the rug.

'Come on,' hissed Ricardo. Lucy tore her eyes away and padded after him, with T-Tongue in her arms.

They opened the creaky back door. Grandma stopped snoring. They froze. After a long pause she started again, and they crept outside. Lucy glanced up and saw the full moon marching towards the western cliffs. It gave the back yard an eerie glow, but petered out when the path met thicker rainforest. Then the Tiger-cat materialised in the torchlight, to lead them up the path to the stairs. It faced them at the top, eyes fierce and tail whipping and made a strange, throaty sound, halfway between an ordinary miaow and a growl, eyes blazing red in the torchlight.

'Sorry we're late,' gulped Ricardo.

Lucy shone the torch into the pit and caught her breath as, once again, the Tiger-cat sprang straight at the wall, its body forming a perfect arc in the torchlight. Just when Lucy was sure the Tiger-cat would smash against solid earth, the clay wall dissolved before her eyes and the Tiger-cat landed gracefully in the yawning mouth of the tunnel and turned to look at her, tail lashing. T-Tongue made an urgent growly whimper. Lucy put him down and he launched himself into the pit without hesitating, his lead sailing out behind him. Lucy and Ricardo flew down the rope and then stumbled to keep up, as T-Tongue disappeared with the Tiger-cat into the mountain.

Lucy wished she had cats' eyes and could throw the torch away. It seemed to take forever to reach the door. Lucy gave a warning knock this time and Rahel wrenched it open.

'We believed you were not coming!'

Lucy felt terrible.

'Sorry. We slept in. We brought you some food.'

'We will eat as we walk,' said Rahel, taking a baked spud in one hand and a pie in the other.

Her face was a mask. Lucy couldn't tell what she was thinking. She didn't look scared. She looked as if she did this all the time. Toro was up and ready for action too, looking much better than he had this morning. His limp wasn't so bad. He checked out Ricardo's sword and the two boys grinned at each other. Obviously they didn't have a clue what they were in for.

'We can't take these guys with us,' said Lucy. 'What if something happens to them?'

Rahel's expression didn't change.

'Toro is required because he is small,' she said simply.

Lucy thought that was a great reason to leave him behind, but Rahel marched out the door after the Tiger-cat, already darting up the tunnel with T-Tongue in pursuit. Ricardo and Toro ran after her and Lucy found herself stumbling in the rear. It wasn't a position she was used to. She caught up, shouldered past the mini-Ninjas, and asked, 'What are we going to do when we get there?'

Her voice was shaking and she knew she sounded scared. Rahel touched her arm but didn't stop or say anything. Lucy tried to speak, but her voice had gone back to bed. By the time she'd woken it up again, they had rounded the bend at the end of the tunnel.

'Stop,' said Lucy, panicking. 'We can't just go marching in and tell the Bulls to open the gates!'

Rahel's eyes flashed in the torchlight.

'Do you believe I am stupid? There is a hole in the back fence. We have observed it through the bars. Toro and

Ricardo will climb through. The guards neglect to check the fence or the back of the jail. They think we cannot get out. Besides, they sleep in a room at the front of the building and believe everyone is too intimidated to defy them.'

'What about the ones near the fire?'

'They are supposed to stay awake. But it is Saturday, the night they consume much alcohol. The Bull Commander travels to Telares City every Saturday and does not come back until late tomorrow. The guards, they enjoy it when he is away; they buy wine. They do not stop drinking until late at night, even the guards who are supposed to stay awake near the fire. The ones sleeping inside are the worst. Besides, on Saturdays, only two guards stay on duty at the fire.'

'My dad says soldiers aren't supposed to get drunk in uniform,' Lucy said.

'But these guards are not professional soldiers. They are just militiamen.'

'Milisha-what?'

'Militiamen. They don't even have uniforms,' said Rahel.

'OK, but who's the guy who smiles all the time? He's got a uniform.'

'That is the Bull Commander,' said Rahel. Abruptly, she changed the subject.

A scene from the morning's drama at the jungle jail played back in Lucy's mind. Rahel was right. The smiling soldier did wear a brown uniform with that ugly picture of the horned bull on it. But this morning, at the jungle jail, the other guards had looked kind of mixed up. Their pants were all different colours, and some of them just wore T-shirts. One even had a long ponytail.

83

Rahel was still talking softly.

'We will avoid the clearing at first, go around the back and Toro and Ricardo will climb through the hole and then open up the entry . . .'

'What entry?'

'The jail, it is rotting. They have put us in the strongest section but some of the wood in the walls was loose and my friends Carlos and Pablo have aggravated it but the guards don't know. They extracted all the nails so the wood slides out. Toro can slip through with Ricardo's aid. When he is inside, Ricardo will conceal himself and wait. Toro will help the smallest children climb out and Ricardo will hide them. Meanwhile, you and I will survey the guards in the clearing . . . and respond to any emergencies,' Rahel finished abruptly.

Why did she talk like that? She used all those big words but she still made it sound as if they were just going shopping.

'What do you mean, emergencies? They'll kill us. They can run faster than us and they have guns!'

'We will create a diversion.'

Rahel spoke calmly, with absolute confidence, and then, as though the conversation were over, walked on. Lucy watched, stunned, as the Tiger-cat leapt past Rahel, through the thick creepers and vines blocking the mouth of the tunnel. The creepers seemed to melt away. Lucy couldn't think straight after that. She clicked out the torch and followed the others into the nightmare night.

16

Night Eyes

Lucy glanced at the night sky. It was splattered with a million stars and the luminous full moon hung poised above the cliffs, ready to drop down out of sight. How did that happen? They must have spent a lot more time arguing than she'd thought. Then a bank of cloud washed over the moon and Lucy could barely see the track. The Tiger-cat padded forwards, the children keeping close behind so they wouldn't lose each other in the shadows. Lucy kept T-Tongue on his lead.

In a few minutes she saw a glow through the trees and ducked down beside the others, lying on their bellies at the edge of the clearing. Below, two figures huddled near the blazing fire. One was sitting, the other lay curled on the ground. Neither wore a brown uniform.

The air suddenly grew brighter as the moon sailed out from a blanket of cloud. Rahel signalled to Toro. He moved like a silent shadow, sideways, away from the path. Ricardo didn't have to be told to follow. Lucy was amazed. He didn't look scared. He looked as though he was having a great time.

Lucy had seen him look like that before, playing with his friend Dario. Dad used to give them tea-towels for capes and called them the Caped Crusaders. Lucy called them the Crappy Crusaders: Derango and Retardo. They could play soldiers and pretend wars and super-heroes for hours but they were always incredibly noisy. Lucy could hear them miles away, even when they were supposed to be stalking each other. Now, as Ricardo melted into the jungle after Toro, Lucy wondered where elephant-feet little brother had learned to walk like a cat.

The Tiger-cat had vanished. Rahel stood cautiously and Lucy, not knowing what else to do, crept after her around the edge of the clearing, and circled the house, keeping well under cover. T-Tongue walked obediently on his lead, apparently understanding the gravity of their mission. He was behaving like a very grown-up puppy. No growling, no jumping around like a canine lunatic.

Rahel moved excruciatingly slowly, making hardly a sound. Lucy was trying desperately to copy her. She imagined she had padded paws, instead of feet, which did exactly what she wanted and landed softly in the right places. Was this how the Tiger-cat did it? In a moment of clarity she recognised what the Tiger-cat had felt earlier. She had thought it was hunger and it was – the hungry anticipation of a skilled hunter. Suddenly, Lucy was having fun. Fear melted. Hunting stirred in her bones.

Rahel halted abruptly. Ahead Lucy could just see the wire of the fence and a darker shadow looming up behind it. They were right beside the rickety old house. The boys were already at the fence and Toro slipped through the narrow opening, Ricardo on his heels. T-Tongue wanted to go after them but Lucy held him back.

Rahel gestured to Lucy. Time to go. On a sudden impulse Lucy tied T-Tongue's lead to a tree and in a low voice told him to stay. He sat quivering but made no sound. Lucy followed as Rahel pushed further into the jungle, creeping right around the back of the building and along the other side. Then Lucy saw a blaze of light through the trees and realised they had reached the far side of the clearing, where the tiger had prowled earlier. Rahel, dropping low to the ground, inched relentlessly forward. Lucy was drawn after her, despite the rock of fear that had dropped into her guts.

They crawled as close as they dared to the edge of the clearing and lay in the grass and shrubs, watching the roaring fire. Massive trunks blazed, sending out a blast of heat that even they could feel. The guard lying down was snoring.

The one sitting up took swigs from a bottle, in between gazing into the fire, eyes narrowed. Lucy was close enough to see his expression: morose. Now and again he would mutter something to the guard asleep next to him, or perhaps to himself. He reminded Lucy of Uncle Fred, when he'd had too much of Grandma's fruity Christmas punch and couldn't get out of his armchair. He would watch TV, *even if it wasn't turned on*, but he would think he was watching the cricket and start swearing at the umpire.

The guard was watching the fire as if it were TV. He kept muttering to himself as though he were swearing at an umpire too. Lucy could see something next to him, glinting in the firelight.

A gun.

Suddenly the guard lurched upright and staggered

towards Lucy, then tripped and spun back to face the fire. He was swaying drunkenly, only a few steps from the girls. He had a long ponytail. He began muttering to himself in a strange language. Then he started singing. It was about as good as his walking.

Lucy could feel a giggle welling up, about to burst out loud enough to wake every guard in the camp, drunk or not. Then something happened that drove away all thought of laughter. The guard, still singing, lurched around towards them. He blinked, closed his eyes, opened them wider, blinked again . . . and began to stumble towards them with arms outstretched like a zombie.

17

Diamond Necklace

Lucy and Rahel ran, plunging back into the jungle, creepers whipping their faces, not daring to look behind. After only a few steps, they heard a thud, followed by a horrified gurgle and a thrashing of branches . . . then silence.

Lucy forced herself to look back.

Illuminated by the fire, the frighteningly still figure of the guard lay near a tree at the edge of the clearing. A thick dark scarf was wrapped around his neck and upper body. As Lucy watched, transfixed, the 'scarf' began to move, like a living noose. A massive python. The guard had had his last drink, sung his last song.

Lucy turned to run but crashed into Rahel. Lucy couldn't speak. She pointed at the guard and his deadly necklace. Rahel's sharp in-breath told Lucy she understood, but she didn't move. An awful fascination held them frozen as the python began to ponderously uncoil from around the guard's body. It was as thick as Lucy's leg. She stopped breathing. The snake slithered towards them.

'This is it!' Lucy thought. '*Run!*' But her body would not obey.

She stayed frozen, even when the snake slithered smoothly over first her feet, and then Rahel's. Taking its time, the long, sinuous form disappeared into the night, giving Lucy enough time to note the unmistakable gold diamonds on its back, glowing in the firelight.

Rahel held Lucy's gaze for a long moment and then shook her head, as though to clear it. Then she was Action Woman again, darting into the clearing to crouch over the still-snoring form of the second guard. In one smooth movement, Rahel stood up holding a bunch of keys. In her other hand she held the gun. Simultaneously Lucy heard a rooster crowing in the jungle. She checked her watch: 3 a.m. That rooster had insomnia.

Rahel jogged over to the big gates. She found the right key, undid the padlock and slipped through, with Lucy on her heels. They crept up the stairs, onto the rickety verandah. Close up, it was somehow familiar. Why? Something tugged at Lucy's memory. Then she saw something else that stopped her in her tracks – a naked mermaid adorning the battered front door. But she had no time to think about that. Rahel had turned the key in the lock and the heavy old door creaked open. In the hallway were two armed guards, sound asleep on the floor.

There was something about grown-ups lying on the carpet in the hallway, slumped on top of each other and snoring as loud as trains, that made Lucy want to crack up, no matter how scared she was. The sight of them, rolled on top of each other, still holding bottles of wine, with eyes closed and mouths open, was too much!

Rahel was already tiptoeing around the sleeping sentries and up the hall. She opened the first door on the right. Dodging the guards, Lucy just had time to notice the faint outline of a mermaid in the hall's threadbare carpet before stepping into a scene that took her breath away. She was standing in a shabby replica of the ballroom in the mermaid house. The chandelier was gone, replaced by candles in wine bottles near the door and on the other side of the room, near a barred window. They cast pools of light over the floor and Lucy didn't have to scrape too much dust away with the toe of her runner to see the faded blues and greens of a familiar ocean scene.

Then Ricardo stepped from the shadows, plastic Ninja sword raised importantly. 'Put it away, doofus!' Lucy spoke sharply without thinking. Rahel shook her head warningly. At the same moment, two boys moved into the light near the window; both were around her age, with tense, thin, dirty faces. The taller one had sharp, clever features. He was staring intensely at the gun cradled in Rahel's arms. The other boy came close to Rahel and never took his eyes off her face. Lucy guessed they were the ones who had made the hole in the wall.

The insomniac rooster crowed again, and simultaneously Lucy became aware of a dull glow through the bars. The room was still dark, but outside the sun was coming up – hours and hours too early. Rahel said something quickly in her language. Both boys answered at the same time, and from the look on Rahel's face Lucy guessed she wasn't happy about the answer.

The tall one stopped staring at the gun and moved closer to the window. Something about the way he held his body, peering through the bars at the dawn light, reminded Lucy of a catapult, stretched tight, aching for release.

Then Lucy realised what was wrong: where were the other children she had seen being marched through the gates? In a rush, that urgent, hunting feeling was strong again. Instinctively, she headed for the door and down the hallway towards where her own room would be if she were at home. No dragon vases stood guard but the door at the end was unmistakable. She opened the door – and then saw why no one had bothered to lock it.

An enormous wooden contraption, like a picture frame, took up one whole wall of the room. Sleeping children lay curled together like puppies on the bare floor in front of it, each wearing a collar around the neck. With a jolt, Lucy saw they were chained to the bottom of the frame.

Only one was awake, standing in the centre of the room, as close to the open door as her chain would allow. She had intense dark eyes and matted dreadlocks, and was wearing a sack like a toga. Suddenly, as a shaft of sun lit up the room, a tiger appeared next to her. A tiger rug, just like Lucy's, was stretched tightly across the wooden frame – but it wasn't finished. Only half the rug was there. The rest was just a series of criss-crossed threads, ready for wool to be woven through them. Lucy stepped towards the little girl and saw that in her tightly clenched fists she held gold, red and green threads.

She also saw the distinctive diamond pattern of a python winding between the tiger's paws; and beside it, the bright gold of a monkey, much, much brighter than the monkey on their rug at home.

Rahel appeared at her side.

'Give me the keys,' hissed Lucy.

She saw a flash of acknowledgement leap like a spark between Rahel and the little girl, before Rahel turned back to Lucy, holding out the keys. As Lucy's hand closed on them, Rahel didn't immediately let go. Her gaze held Lucy's for a long moment. In her dark eyes, Lucy suddenly saw something she hadn't understood before: a vast, sad knowledge, and a kind of emptiness, as though Rahel had hollowed herself out to make room for everything she knew.

'See,' her look seemed to say as she held out the keys to Lucy, 'this is what I know'.

She let go of the keys and Lucy dropped her gaze and fumbled, looking for the right one. The little girl touched Lucy's arm. Her skin felt like paper. She pointed to a key. The padlock snapped open, letting the chain rattle to the floor. Lucy bent to shake the closest slumbering child.

'Wake up!' she hissed. 'We're getting out of here!'

But the little boy didn't stir. Lucy felt a touch on her arm again and met the little girl's eyes. She was shaking her head.

'They will not wake,' hissed Rahel. 'We must come back again. We have run out of time!' Still holding the gun, she moved to pick up the little girl but Lucy got there first. Holding the tiny body close, she felt the sack, harsh and scratchy, on her skin. She gave the sleeping children another desperate glance, made a silent promise – and ran.

18

Ponytail Zombie

When Lucy reached the hall, Rahel was standing outside, pointing the gun at the slumbering bodies of the soldiers, beckoning Ricardo and Toro and the two strange boys to come past. The tallest hesitated for a few seconds, looking longingly at one of the guards' guns, but he must have decided it was too risky to grab it from its holster. He kept going. Lucy followed them down the hall, clutching the child in her arms, dodging bodies and bottles. She plunged down the stairs into a pale, eerie dawn.

Ricardo and Toro were waiting at the gate.

'Ricardo! Get T-Tongue! I left him at the hole in the fence.' Ricardo looked wonderingly at the girl in her arms, but obeyed her. That was a first. Rahel arrived at the gate and began to padlock it but, on a sudden impulse, Lucy stopped her. She put down the child and pointed at the remaining guard, still snoring near the fire, with empty wine bottles scattered about him.

'Let's lock him in.'

Rahel's eyes widened and she nodded. She signalled the

two bigger boys and they all walked back to the guard. Rahel put down her gun and they grabbed his arms and legs. He was out cold. He didn't stir, even when they accidentally dropped him as they dragged him through the gate.

Lucy picked up the little girl and turned to see Rahel pocketing the keys, the guard locked behind the fence and the gun safely back in her possession. She flashed an unexpected grin at Lucy and then they ran for their lives across the clearing as the sun burst into full light, as bright and clear as a diamond.

From the safety of the jungle, Lucy dared to look back. Staggering to his feet, face pressed incredulously into the wire fence, was a guard about to have the worst hangover of his life. A hangover, but no gun. And no keys. He looked as if he were seeing a ghost: a white-faced ghost in Grandma's green Ninja pants, carrying a small child. Suddenly elated, Lucy grinned at him and he slid back onto the ground.

But Lucy's elation was short-lived. On the other side of the clearing, a stumbling figure crashed through the undergrowth. He stood swaying, looking from Lucy to the guard locked up behind the fence, and back again. His eyes locked on Lucy and, as he advanced towards her, arms stretched out like a zombie, Lucy saw clearly a ring of black bruises on his neck. After what that snake had done to him, maybe he *was* a zombie: one of the walking dead. Except he was more like the wobbling dead. He kept staggering off at a tangent and then would turn around in circles until his eyes locked on Lucy again and he kept coming.

Lucy took off and caught up to the others almost straight

away, crashing into a bruising tangle of arms, legs and skulls. Ricardo, in the lead, had ground to a halt because the Tiger-cat had leapt out of the jungle directly into his path, forcing a people and puppy pile-up. Bodies were sprawled everywhere, much to the delight of T-Tongue, who was licking Ricardo's face.

'Get up! Zombie!' Lucy screamed. But the only one who seemed to understand was the Tiger-cat, who, tail lashing, sprang off the main trail, onto the overgrown track leading to the tunnel. Lucy would never have found it on her own. She heard a crashing and stumbling from the clearing.

'He's coming!'

Lucy, still holding the little girl, grabbed Ricardo's hand and dragged him to his feet, then plunged into the jungle after the Tiger-cat. Branches whipped at her face but she didn't stop, desperate to keep up with the Tiger-cat, her eyes locked on the two distinct white spots on the back of each feline ear. If she lost the Tiger-cat, she was sure she would never find the tunnel.

Then heavy raindrops began to fall. Within a few seconds, the bright sun had dimmed and the jungle steamed as rain teemed down. Lucy slid to a halt, struggling to see the tunnel. She heard a low growl and suddenly, there was the Tiger-cat, sitting calmly out of the rain in the black entrance. Lucy skidded gratefully inside and finally let go of Ricardo's hand. Panting hard, water streaming down their faces, the rest of the ragged party piled in. When Lucy looked back the entrance was closed again. All she could hear was the driving rain, falling just in time to wash away their footprints. All she could smell was the pungent jungle air.

19

Dracula

Lucy found her torch and scanned the assembled company. The new boys' muddy faces revealed exhaustion and fear. That was understandable. They were standing in a big black tunnel to nowhere. The little girl was clinging to Lucy's leg like a baby koala. Only the animals seemed unconcerned. The Tiger-cat was fastidiously washing itself, licking a paw and rubbing it over ears and face. T-Tongue had finished shaking water over everyone and was sniffing excitedly around the tunnel.

The Tiger-cat stopped cleaning itself, padded up to Lucy, and began rubbing against her legs, purring loudly. The little girl shrank behind Lucy, pressing fearfully against the wall of the tunnel. The Tiger-cat was being affectionate, but nothing could change the fact that it looked like a miniature man-eater. Lucy glanced at Rahel and surprised a smile. She at least looked happy, even though she was wet. And she still had a good grip on that gun.

There was no point standing around. Lucy hoisted the little kid up and began walking. Wet, the sack was even scratchier, and the girl's hair smelt strongly. She had only taken a few paces, when the black air erupted. Lucy felt a rush of wind and something nameless and horrendous whooshed past, touching her head. She dropped to the ground, her cry bouncing off the walls. The tunnel reverberated with screams from the others, but the child in her arms still didn't make a sound.

Lucy shone her torch up. What she had thought was a solid brick roof was in fact a huge cavern. Her beam picked out the flapping wings of several huge black bats, before they swept away into the darkness.

'Great. That's all we needed. Dracula!'

'Those creatures touched my head,' said Rahel's voice from behind Lucy.

'Me too!' yelped Ricardo.

The torch revealed a honeycomb of smaller caves in every corner of the main cavern. *Don't think about what might be hiding in there*, Lucy told herself. Resolutely, she stood and marched on the main track towards their den. All she could hear was her own ragged breathing and several pairs of scuffling feet. She felt herself calming down. Gradually, her heart stopped pounding. After a while, the sound of their steady footfalls was oddly soothing.

'Wait for me,' Rahel's voice called out, from a long way behind. Lucy stopped and shone the torch backwards. Rahel trudged slowly out of the darkness.

'I am extremely exhausted,' she said, as if to excuse herself. 'It is hard to keep up.'

The dank tunnel air pressed close as the little party moved off again. *Just put one foot in front of the other,*

Lucy told herself, as the weight of the little kid began to tell on her arms, but the rhythm was almost hypnotic and Lucy felt her mind drifting. Then something crystallised in her mind: *time and the weirdo things it was doing*. This morning the moon had set too soon, and the sun had come way too early at the jungle jail. And early yesterday morning, when they first came through the tunnel, the sun had only just started to come up at home but it was already broad daylight at the jungle jail, with the sun shining down strongly on her head when she crawled out to get the rope. And it had been so hot! It didn't add up. Lucy stopped suddenly and Ricardo stomped on her heels.

'What are you stopping for?' he said. 'It's morning and Grandma will be getting up. And I'm hungry.'

'Actually, the sun's not even up,' Lucy said. Her torch showed the door to the cubby and suddenly the little kid in her arms felt hugely heavy. She put her gently down on a chair and lit all the candles again. The little girl just sat there silently with her big dark eyes fixed, first on Lucy, then on the matches, the candles and the Tiger-cat, washing itself all over again.

The two new kids stole inside too, silent shadows – but not Toro. He had the hang of things. He pounced on the Cocoa Puffs before Ricardo had a chance. Rahel was on the case too. She grabbed plates from the picnic basket and Lucy got out all the spuds and spinach pies. There was silence while everyone looked at the loaded table. Then, as though the food referee had blown a whistle, everyone started eating, even the little girl.

Lucy watched their faces. She decided the little kid looked about three years old, the same age as her nephew

Jamie, but remembering how small Toro was for his age, maybe older.

Rahel touched her arm, leaning backwards in her chair to look at Lucy's face.

'I must thank you for your presence,' she said, in her strange formal way, as though she was picking words out of the dictionary. 'I, too, was very intimidated by the soldiers.'

'You didn't look it!' said Lucy. 'I thought I was going to wet myself when the Wobbling Ponytail Zombie started chasing us.'

'Wet yourself?' Rahel sounded puzzled.

Lucy realised she had blundered and went red.

'You know, pi— Oh, forget it. I was really *intimidated,* anyway,' she finished lamely.

Rahel was undeterred. 'What is a zombie?'

'When someone dies but they can still walk,' said Ricardo helpfully. 'They're all over the place. We've got two down the road at the graveyard.'

Toro looked horrified and Lucy promised herself she would never tell Ricardo really big lies ever again, no matter how much she wanted to scare him into sub-mission. The trouble was, he didn't seem to be scared. He held his Ninja sword in one hand, while stuffing his face with the other.

'Zombies aren't real, Retardo.'

'Yeah, right!'

'No they're NOT,' she blasted, then felt terrible when everyone froze.

The little kid stopped eating and her eyes got bigger and bigger in the candlelight.

'Sorry,' said Lucy quietly, and was grateful when Rahel saved her.

'What is a ponytail?'

Lucy could answer that one. She flicked her own long, dark ponytail, and Rahel's face brightened. She reached up and began fiddling with the dense pile of hair coiled on top of her head. In a few seconds she had unwound the longest plait Lucy had ever seen.

'Wow! It must go down to your knees when it's out!'

Rahel grinned at Lucy's stunned face.

'Undo it!'

Rahel shook her head.

'We have had no water to wash in, or soap, and no brushes and combs. For the first few days I kept plaiting it to keep it neat but then I became too tired and just kept tying it in a knot. It is matted together like a carpet. I may have to cut it off.'

'I'll do it,' said Ricardo enthusiastically.

Lucy glared at him. 'What?' he said, but Lucy turned to Rahel. 'Don't cut it. Come back to my place and we'll wash it and put loads of conditioner on it and Grandma can comb . . .' Lucy's voice trailed off as she realised the impossibility of what she had just suggested. It was strange: after everything they had gone through this morning, why did Rahel's hair seem such a tragedy? But it did.

'Don't worry. We'll bring everything you need down here,' Lucy heard herself assuring Rahel.

Suddenly she was struck by how weird their meeting was. Normally when she met a new girl they checked out each other's hair and clothes *first*, not the next day. Then they talked about sport and what music they liked and their favourite foods. If they really liked each other, they stayed over at each other's houses and watched videos and showed each other their special things and their Barbies (even if they *had* grown out of them) and if they *really*, *really* liked each other they talked about boys. But as for Rahel's clothes, well, there wasn't much to say about a ragged T-shirt and shorts, was there? And as far as Lucy could see Rahel owned only two 'special things': a box of matches and a stolen gun. Maybe she had a heavily armed Barbie somewhere, but Lucy didn't think so.

Then she noticed something.

'Where's the gun?'

Rahel's face went blank.

'It has been disposed of,' she said, expressionlessly.

So *that's* why she had fallen behind in the bat cave . . .

'Awww,' from Ricardo was drowned out by a furious exclamation from the boy with the sharp face. Lucy was left in no doubt of his feelings, even if the speech he launched into was entirely in Telarian.

But all of a sudden, Lucy wasn't listening. She felt falling-over tired; collapsing-on-the ground tired. The little girl must have felt the same, because she crawled into Lucy's lap and went to sleep, thumb in mouth. Her hair, brushing under Lucy's chin, was matted with dirt, and the scratchy sack toga was filthy. Baths. She would have to get the old lady's big metal tub and the gas bottle down here. But what was she going to do about water? Run a hose from the back-yard tap all the way down the tunnel? Yeah, right!

Someone began coughing and Lucy realised how cold

it was. At the jungle jail it had been warm before the sun came up. It was even warm when it was raining. The only reason those guards had a fire was because they hoped it would scare away the tiger. The kids were going to need clothes to replace the rags they were wearing, and blankets. And there was another problem: they couldn't all stay down here. They wouldn't all fit on the lounges.

Just then Rahel began speaking in her own language. The two new boys, who had been talking urgently but quietly, fell silent. Rahel gestured at Lucy and said her name, and did the same for Ricardo. Then she pointed at T-Tongue and then at the Tiger-cat, washing itself on one of the cupboards near the sink. She seemed to say a lot about the Tiger-cat and then began stroking its back and rubbing the wide velvet band above its nose. Lucy loved that bit. It was deep orange and soft, just before the black stripes on its head formed a sharp arrow shape. A magnificent rumbling purr filled the room. The new kids watched. The tallest boy was frowning and the other one looked worried. The tiny girl slept on, shuddering in Lucy's arms now and again, and making little crying sounds. They were the first sounds Lucy had heard her make. Lucy remembered the other little kids, chained up to the second tiger rug. They had been so deeply asleep! As if they were dead.

The Tiger-cat leapt down and trotted over to the new boys and rubbed against their legs, purring loudly. They sat as though ready to catapult through the ceiling but slowly relaxed, even tentatively rubbing its head. Then it padded over to Lucy, gazing at the tiny sleeping child, its amber eyes unblinking. It reached up an insistent paw and touched her leg. The child sat up – and froze. The Tiger-cat's burning eyes held her black ones – then Lucy heard the best sound of that long night: a tiny giggle, more like a splutter really, but definitely happy. Lucy didn't know what picture it had beamed into the little girl's mind, but it had worked. Maybe a cartoon. She fell asleep again, smiling, relaxing into the warm curve of Lucy's body.

Rahel was talking to the new kids in her language. Lucy's attention was drawn to the tallest boy, the one with the sharp face, the one who'd got angry about the missing gun. He had a strange face, half-sad, half-fierce. He had shoulder-length hair and was as tall as Lucy. His name was Carlos. Pablo had shorter hair, and he was a bit smaller than Lucy. He was thin too, but his face was rounder, and broke into a dimpled smile when he was talking to Rahel.

Pablo smiled at Lucy when Rahel introduced him, but sharp-featured Carlos just glanced at her and then looked away.

'We have all known each other since we were small children,' explained Rahel. 'My papa taught them to speak English too.'

'Is he a teacher?' asked Lucy.

Once again Rahel's eyes filled with tears. She just shook her head and pointed to the little girl.

'This is Angel.'

'I have dreamt about her,' Lucy blurted out. 'The smiling soldier told the others to take her mum away. And she had a beautiful dress but she never speaks . . .' Lucy's voice trailed away.

'That is correct!' Rahel sounded excited. 'She has been

with us for many weeks now, but she has never said a word – not in the daytime anyway. Sometimes she will cry in her sleep and call out for her mama and papa, but when she is awake – nothing. She has never smiled for us.'

'How come she was awake and the other kids weren't?'

'Drugs,' Rahel said simply, 'the militia give them a drug to make them stop crying and sleep.'

'What about Angel? Why wasn't she sleepy?'

'Sometimes she would spit it out without the guards seeing. She hated it . . . and maybe she knew something special would happen tonight.'

Lucy was about to ask why all the kids were chained up to the tiger rug, but Ricardo got in first.

'If she can't talk, how do you know her name is Angel?' he asked.

'When she came to the camp she had her pretty dress on and the guards stole it and left her naked. We tore up a rice sack and tied it on her. She had her hands like this . . .' Rahel clenched her fists tightly, 'and I noticed something the guards had not seen.'

Rahel opened her box of matches again and removed a tiny square of folded paper, about the size of a postage stamp. She handed it to Lucy, and then looked at her thoughtfully, head on one side. Lucy unfolded it gingerly. The paper was dirty and creased, as though many fingers had unfolded and refolded it.

'I dreamed about this too,' she breathed, and Rahel nodded slowly, as though this had confirmed something. Lucy moved closer to the candle and read aloud the words written in English: 'I am Angel. I am four years old. My mama and papa love me very much. If you find me, take me to my grandpapa and grandmama at 15 Pasadena Square, Telares City'.

There was silence in the cubby. Lucy watched the candlelight flickering on the little girl's sleeping face.

'We can take Mum's Mazda,' said Ricardo.

20

Where on Earth
Is Telares?

When Lucy finally clambered out of the pit into the Kurrawong night, and turned to haul T-Tongue up, she couldn't resist shining her torch back down into Ricardo's face. Flabbergasted, he was gazing up, taking in the stars and the full moon, its belly just grazing the tallest cliff in the west. Not even a smidgen of light breached the eastern horizon. Stepping off the stairs, Lucy noticed that the ground was bone-dry. No way had it rained here.

They stumbled down the path and inside. Lucy's watch said 4.30 a.m. So did the clock in the kitchen. They tiptoed in without disturbing Grandma's snores and into their bedroom. Lucy shone her torch on the rug and noticed that the diamond-backed snake had grown, extending its reach around another corner of the rug. Its diamonds were a startling gold and its scales were almost black. Its head . . . well, Lucy still didn't want to look too closely at its head but she could see it was much more distinct than before. Definitely the kind of snake you didn't play with. She shuddered as she remembered the monster in the clearing, slithering over her feet. She'd hated that feeling of being turned to stone. But, on the other hand, she had definitely got a better deal than the Ponytail Zombie.

The sun was high in the sky by the time T-Tongue woke them up, whimpering to be let out to do doggie doings. Grandma had already finished one crossword, started another and drunk three cups of tea.

'You two look like you danced the night away. You must have really needed that early night.'

'We might have another early night tonight, Grandma,' said Lucy, thinking on her feet. 'I'm still tired.'

'So am I,' said Ricardo, yawning theatrically.

'Well, your mum will be exhausted by the time she gets back. She'll be going straight to bed herself. Probably hardly had any sleep after that trip. She'll be a nervous wreck, and I wonder how that little girl she was looking after is? And by the way, Lucy, I couldn't find any of those extra spuds you cooked last night. You cooked enough to feed half the town. I was looking forward to having some fried up with an egg on toast for breakfast. I had to make porridge. Where did you put them, dear? Maybe that rotten dog of yours . . .'

Lucy opened her mouth to defend T-Tongue but, luckily, Grandma broke off to concentrate on a tricky clue.

Lucy served a bowl of porridge from the steaming pot. Then she had an idea. She hurried into the hallway, where all their books were stacked in boxes. She was looking for the atlas Auntie Alice had given her for her tenth birthday. Auntie Alice was a teacher and always gave her educational presents. Lucy had thought at the time that it was the most boring present *ever*. She was about to open it for the first time in living history when the book under it caught her eye. It was deep green and when Lucy ran her finger along its spine it was smooth and shiny – old leather. Lucy was certain she had never seen it, even though it had been her job to pack up all the books from their old house.

Curious, she picked it up. Its leather cover was worn about the edges, as though many hands had opened it. It was embossed with an old-fashioned map of the world, in heavy gold. In one corner was a compass; in another an old sailing boat. On the first, yellowing page was one word in curly lettering: **ATLAS**. It must be Grandma's.

Lucy took both books back to the kitchen table. In between mouthfuls of porridge she checked out the index of Auntie Alice's atlas. How did you spell Telares again? She looked under everything starting with T, but couldn't find it.

'Grandma, have you heard of a place called Telares?'

'Never heard of it, dear, is it that new housing estate out near the shopping centre? Beautiful houses out there, Beryl says . . .'

That settled it. If Grandma hadn't heard about it, no one had. Except maybe Dad. Before he came to Australia he had travelled all over the world. Then a dog bit him while he was bushwalking and he showed up at Kurrawong Hospital. Mum had to give him a needle in his bum. That was how they had met. They never really explained how they had fallen in love and got married because everyone would always crack up at the beginning of the story and that was that. Mum and Dad used to laugh about it together, which felt nice.

These days, though, Mum made grim jokes to her friends about how she should have let him catch lockjaw, the old-fashioned name for tetanus, because it made your jaws lock like cement and you couldn't talk about science, morning, noon and night. Lucy hated it when she said things like that. On the other hand, if Ricardo . . .

When Lucy was little she'd asked what an astronomer did. Dad had said he looked for dead and dying stars.

'A star doctor,' Lucy said, and everyone laughed. Dad was so clever he found stars no one had ever seen before. Once he even went to Hawaii to look through a huge telescope. Other scientists said he was famous. In his family, he was most famous for forgetting to eat, sleep and keep the lounge room sort of tidy – so you could walk from the kitchen to the television without having to take out life insurance. He just didn't notice.

He was always so tired from working that he looked grey – but happy. He never yelled at them. He always stayed up late to watch international soccer matches, and let the kids stay up too. They *did* have to ask him things four times before he even heard them, but then he would smile, say sorry and do whatever they wanted – even let them drink Coke for breakfast. Mum went psycho when she caught him.

Then the fights started. He became grey and worried. Grey like a ghost. Mum shouted one day that she was sick of living with a ghost. She wanted someone who was married to *her* and not to some star he hadn't even found yet. She said Dad loved whatever he saw at the end of his telescope more than the people in his own lounge room.

Lucy was terrified then and wanted to throw up or cry, but she didn't do either. She just yelled at Ricardo.

Now, holding the strange book, Lucy wished he would hurry home from China.

Grandma's voice snapped her out of it.

'That's a beautiful old book, dear! Where did you get it?'

'In the hall.'

Well, the strange green leather atlas wasn't Grandma's. Lucy kept looking in the index of Auntie Alice's one. She tried B for Burchimo. Bingo! There it was: a cluster of red-brown islands with a big fat one in the middle. They were in the Pacific Ocean, way up to the north-east of Australia.

Lucy looked in vain for Telares. She looked carefully at the cluster of red-brown islands that made up Burchimo. Then one caught her eye. It was the same colour but sat like a lonely seagull in the ocean, much further east. It had no name but a distinctive shape: two halves joined like the outstretched winds of a soaring gull. It was right near a dotted line called – Lucy had to squint to read the tiny writing – International Date Line. But it wasn't Telares. According to the map, it was definitely part of Burchimo.

Just then, Grandma looked up and said: 'What was that suburb you asked about, Lucy, love?'

'Telares, and it's not a suburb, it's a country.'

'You're a good girl doing homework in the Christmas holidays. A country, eh?'

Lucy didn't bother trying to explain to Grandma that you didn't get Christmas holidays homework, especially when you were never going back to primary school again. She knew it was useless because Grandma had got that thinking look on her face. Lucy imagined a little ticking clock on her forehead, like the icon on the computer when the hard drive was busy. But Grandma didn't have the right software installed. She shook her head.

'Telares. No. I don't know it. It's ringing a bell, only I can't remember why. Strange.'

And she went back to her crossword.

Lucy closed Auntie Alice's atlas and opened the mysterious old green leather one. When she turned the heavy, yellowed pages to the index, the name Telares jumped out immediately. She turned to page 17 and there it was, the nameless, lonely seagull of an island that she had seen in the other atlas, massively enlarged. She could clearly see the two 'wings', joined like a V at the bottom. The surrounding ocean was beautifully painted in glowing greens and blues. Dolphins and whales cavorted in the water, and schools of fish swam close to the sandy shores. The island was ringed with golden beaches. At the top of the page, in gold writing, was a date: 1600 AD. Faintly, on the left of the page, was the rough ink outline of a familiar cluster of islands: Burchimo. Telares had pride of place in this atlas!

As Lucy stared at the map, a rushing and roaring filled her ears. The solemn greens and browns of mountain ranges, valleys and plains rippled, and the black dots of cities and towns shook and shifted. The sea boiled and frothed, surging onto golden beaches, swamping plains, roaring through the valleys, flooding all in its path, until only the tallest mountains remained. The island was sinking under the sea! The roaring intensified, like a giant shell held to Lucy's ear. Suddenly she realised that her head was so close to the atlas she was almost lying on it. As she lifted her head, the sound of the sea retreated and she watched the map resolve itself again into ordinary greens and browns. The sea resumed its innocent calm blue.

Lucy shook her head. She couldn't escape the overwhelming sensation that Telares had almost disappeared before her eyes.

Lucy flicked back a few pages. There was Telares again, that same unmistakable stretch of wings and golden beaches. But the date was 1300 AD! And the name of this island was Za Zu. Lucy looked in vain for the cluster of islands that made up Burchimo. But what she saw instead on the left of the page was the undeniable shape of the east coast of Africa. Za Zu looked like Telares but it was off the coast of Africa!

Lucy looked back further. There it was again: an island called Akala, shaped just like Telares, but parked off the coast of South America and dated 900 AD. Another called Guan-zhi, near China, dated 500 AD, with fierce dragons painted in the sky around it. What was going on?

She turned to the first map in the atlas. The same shape again, up near the North Pole. There was no date on it. She turned the next page . . . and the next. Each showed the same island, only in a different part of the world. There was one right near England! Lucy counted back. The dates started at the third map and kept rising, sometimes 100 years, sometimes more.

But after a while, the pages became blank. Disappointed, Lucy turned another, and another – all blank, about twenty of them, until she reached the index. In fact, Telares, on page 17 was the very last map.

Lucy picked up Auntie Alice's atlas again and looked for

islands shaped like Telares near the North Pole, Africa, South America, England and China.

Zero, zilch and zip.

Where had they gone?

All of a sudden, the full import of it hit Lucy. She was clearly going nuts and should just go back to bed for the rest of the holidays. She dropped the atlas and went to her bedroom, with T-Tongue trotting cheerfully at her heels. She jumped into bed and pulled the covers over her head. T-Tongue wasn't having any of that. He nuzzled his way under the blankets and tried to lick her neck.

Lucy sat up and examined the rug morosely. It didn't help. What she had thought, at first glance, were fresh signs of another snaky growth spurt, was something quite different. She was gazing at a faint but unmistakable trunk. The trunk of a beautifully dressed elephant, with a jewelled headdress and what looked like a little caravan on its back. And that dark smudge next to it. Was that a . . . bat?

Lucy pulled the blankets back over her head.

21

Calling All Chickens

'Are you OK, Lucy?'

Grandma knew something must be wrong if Lucy was in bed in the holidays.

'Yes, Grandma. I'm just a bit tired,' she mumbled from under the blankets.

'You might be getting sick. You'd better stay inside today. And no more homework! Just read a book or something.'

Lucy sat bolt upright.

'I'm fine, Grandma. Really! It's the holidays. No one gets sick in the holidays. I can't stay in bed. I just didn't want to do the dishes.'

That was feasible enough to get Grandma off the scent. Phew. She bustled off to see if Ricardo had similar ideas. Thankfully, she didn't have her glasses on so she hadn't noticed the new additions to the rug.

Lucy followed her outside to where Ricardo stood near the old shed. It had a big yard around it, fenced with tall wire and completely overgrown with grass and vines.

'Can we get chickens, Grandma? Today? Please?' Ricardo begged.

'Come and wash up and we'll talk about it. Does your mum want chickens? I always like having a chook or two around myself. At least you know they're not being locked up in those horrible little battery cages. And the eggs taste so much better. We'll get the kind Grandad liked: silky bantams. Fluffy ones. We'll go down and see Joe's friend at the produce store, but you've got to wash up first . . .'

Lucy would never tell him, but she secretly admired Ricardo for thinking of the chicken plan. They could at least feed the kids eggs. Next, they needed clothes. She made an excuse not to go to the produce shop, even though she liked the idea of choosing chickens. As soon as Grandma and Ricardo left, she rifled through her clothes. Between her and Ricardo, they had heaps of shorts, T-shirts, jumpers, jeans and tracksuits. They would have to do. Everything would be too big for Angel, but anything was better than an old sack. Next she raided the old lady's room and filled a big backpack near to bursting with blankets.

Lucy knew she had time for one quick trip down the tunnel before Ricardo and Grandma got back. She grabbed whatever she could from the kitchen and flew up the path. She could see the Tiger-cat on the top stairs but it jumped into the pit when it saw her coming. Swinging down that rope was getting so much easier, even with a heavy pack on her back. And T-tongue didn't freak out at all. Despite the smiling soldier and everything weird that was happening, Lucy suddenly felt fantastic. So what if she didn't understand? This was fun.

She made double-quick time down the tunnel, even though the batteries in her torch were getting weak again. It was as though her feet knew the way and the dark air didn't seem so oppressive. Her eyes seemed to penetrate its velvety blackness better. Maybe she just wasn't so scared.

When she opened the door, Angel and Toro were huddled asleep on the lounge. Rahel, Carlos and Pablo looked as though they were holding a council of war around the lone candle on the table. They stopped talking in their language when Lucy appeared and she felt awkward . . . the odd one out. Their expressions were very severe, as if they'd been arguing. In that instant, framed by the doorway, they looked like adults. Small and skinny, yes, but their faces looked just like people on television, talking about wars and elections and the stock market. The boys wore that same expression Lucy had noticed on Rahel near that horrible frame Angel had been chained to – as if they knew too much: serious and old.

'I've brought clothes and blankets and food.'

'Thank you,' Rahel and Pablo said at once.

'Personal jinx!' said Lucy.

'Personal jinx?' asked the same two voices at once.

'Personal jinx! You say it if someone says something at exactly the same time as you.'

Rahel and Pablo looked puzzled, then they both smiled. It was amazing how different they looked. But Carlos was looking at her as if she had crawled out of a long dark hole in the ground. Well, she had really. But so had he.

'Well, I've got to go. Mum's going to be home soon,' Lucy said, unpacking her bag. Rahel and Pablo called goodbye as she headed for the door but Carlos ignored her. With a quick glance at Angel fast asleep on the lounge, Lucy was out of there.

22

Expert Assistance

'Ricardo, get into that room *right now* and *mess it up!*'

'NO! Grandma didn't say!'

'I didn't say clean it up, I said *mess it up!*'

Lucy had called in an expert. She propelled Ricardo into the room and showed him the new additions to the rug menagerie. The batty smudge was now clearly a bat, and the elephant was even brighter than before. Gold chains secured a large red jewel in the middle of its forehead, it was wearing a fancy coat and the little caravan on its back was painted brightly.

Grandma was outside telling the new chickens exactly how many eggs they had to lay. Lucy was desperate to get the zoo covered up before she came back inside. She knew she could rely on Ricardo. By the time he had finished you couldn't tell the room had a floor, let alone a rug. It was a remarkably simple procedure.

1 Block doorway with dirty washing and several soccer balls. Adults unable to enter room without falling

over. (Discourages clean-up attempts while child is eating or at the movies.)

2 Tip out all Lego.

3 Get all stuffed toys; stand in middle of room and throw in air.

4 Get all gaming magazines (see above).

5 Get all pyjamas. Place over elephant's head and trunk (pyjama leg), tiger's face, snake, bat and monkey.

6 Get all undies. Throw at big sister.

7 Run away from big sister, avoiding soccer balls and dirty clothes. Throw soccer balls at big sister if necessary.

Ricardo fled to the chook pen and safety with Grandma, with Lucy chasing him. Grandma was proudly displaying twelve chickens that looked like two-legged Persian cats. They had weird fluffy heads and some were black, some white and others tabby-coloured. Silky bantams. They were scratching around happily in the long grass and Grandma was telling them about the Great Depression when poor people who had chickens and vegie gardens in the back yard did OK and everyone else went hungry. The silky bantams didn't seem to be listening, but then, they didn't seem to have ears either.

Lucy picked up her favourite soccer ball, the one Dad had given her, and decided to get Ricardo back the best way she knew: beating him at soccer. They played until Mum's Mazda sputtered into the driveway, sounding worse than ever. Mum looked tired but very pleased to see them and they couldn't stop talking.

'Mum, I went with Grandma and we've got fifty

chickens . . .'

'Did the little girl die . . .'

'Did the aeroplane crash . . .'

'We've run out of food . . .'

'Grandma says they always crash . . .'

'Grandma says we're both having growth spurts and we need more food . . .'

'Can we go to the movies after we buy more food?'

'Grandma made us Ninja pants . . .'

'And she made some for herself!'

Mum headed for the safety of the kitchen and a cup of tea before she tried to answer anything. No, the little girl hadn't died, she was going to be OK, fifty chickens sounded a lot, but if Lucy and Ricardo were eating as much as Grandma said they were, then maybe they needed them . . . oh, it was really only twelve chickens . . . no, the aeroplane had not crashed and she'd been in lots of planes and they usually didn't . . . and yes, they were both growing quickly and the movies did sound like a good idea, maybe this week . . . and we can't possibly be out of everything . . . the cupboard was pretty full . . . how many spuds did you say they ate? . . . yes, I will come and look at the new chickens . . . yes, your pants are great, especially Grandma's pink ones . . . T-Tongue, get off me . . . was it you who ate all those extra spuds?

Lucy was *going* to tell Mum about Nigel Scar-Skull's visit, but she thought she would let her have a sleep first, and by the time Mum woke up later in the afternoon Lucy had other things on her mind.

23

Carlos the Zombie

When Grandma had caught the bus home and Mum had fallen asleep, Lucy, Ricardo and T-Tongue went back down the tunnel with the Tiger-cat, where they found all the kids wearing warm clothes and wrapped up in blankets, except Carlos. He was still wearing his ragged T-shirt and shorts, even though it was freezing. Lucy thought he looked more relaxed when she walked in but he began scowling again as soon as he saw her. Well, whatever his problem was, it wasn't hers. She ignored him.

Angel was asleep again.

Rahel was shocked to know it was 2 p.m. She had completely lost track of time in the permanent night of the cubby. Then Lucy repeated her theory about time doing different things at each end of the tunnel.

'I think the sun comes up earlier at your end,' she said.

'And I looked Telares up in an atlas – two atlases! I couldn't even *find* it in one of them – well, I could, but it didn't even have a name. It was just this weird blob, way out in the ocean. But then I found this other book – this really, really old book – and it had a map of Telares and . . . and . . . it was still really way, way out in the ocean . . .'

Lucy's voice trailed away.

'It is really way, way out in the ocean,' said Carlos, as though she were really dumb, 'but it is most definitely not a blob. It is our homeland'.

Rahel took in Carlos' scowl and Lucy's glare. Her next words cut them both off.

'I have come to a decision. We go back tonight and fetch the others.'

There was a stunned silence.

Then Carlos said bitterly, 'I agree. And on this occasion we do not give up until we have everyone'.

Lucy stepped forward.

'What do you mean, give up? We didn't give up – we just couldn't carry them all. Anyway, how come you didn't offer to help? And how are we supposed to wake those little kids up?'

'There are more prisoners who will not be drugged,' Rahel said calmly. Lucy remembered the long line of kids marching through the gates yesterday morning. But there'd been only five little ones chained to the tiger rug.

'Where were the others last night?' asked Lucy slowly.

The other boy, Pablo, spoke shyly.

'After Rahel and Toro escaped, the Bull Commander was filled with fury. He did not realise Rahel and Toro had escaped until yesterday morning, when he brought the night shift back from the workshop.'

Lucy was completely lost. Workshop? Night shift?

Pablo went on, 'When he saw two were missing, he went crazy. He took all the bigger children back to the workshop. But Carlos and myself were detained for questioning in the jungle house because he knew we were friends with Rahel'.

Pablo paused, and shot Carlos a strange look, almost like an apology, before turning back to Lucy.

'It was fortunate you came for us when you did! He had just started the interrogation when his mobile phone rang. It must have been something important, because he left immediately for Telares City. He ordered the militia to question us but they consumed too much alcohol. But when he got back he would have beaten us very badly.'

'That's so slack!' said Ricardo.

Pablo looked a bit puzzled, but carried on.

'That's why we were the only ones in the jungle house last night, apart from Angel and the little ones.'

'Hang on!' Lucy wanted to go back a step. 'What workshop?'

'Near the jungle house is a workshop. We work there. That is what we are engaged in from morning to night.'

'You're all engaged? Yuck! Who to?'

'Ricardo, he means they work there. Engaged in work.'

'Naa! He said they —'

Carlos' bitter voice cut through the argument. 'We make toys for rich children like you, and rugs for you to walk on.'

'We're not rich!' exclaimed Lucy and Ricardo together.

As if! Not like Mandy, who had her own laptop and flew on aeroplanes all the time and owned every single Barbie that had ever been made. And Mandy's mum piled on about seven necklaces and big earrings just to buy milk. Lucy's family wasn't like that.

Carlos' brain had clearly died. He was a zombie!

There was an angry scrape as Carlos the Zombie moved his chair, but Rahel spoke to him sharply in Telarian before he could reply. He shrugged his shoulders but remained silent. Rahel turned to Lucy with the same empty expression she had worn in the carpet room with the little kids.

'It is true,' she said simply, holding Lucy's eyes. Something in her gaze made it impossible for Lucy to turn away. 'We do make things. We have small fingers.' She said it as though that explained everything.

Lucy searched Rahel's face and all of a sudden felt dizzy. She had a vivid picture of Angel's little hands, grasping those brightly coloured threads. She suddenly felt as if she was a computer connected to the Internet. Rahel had just downloaded way too much information to her hard drive. Now it was Lucy who knew too much. Her system was about to crash.

With a deep breath, Lucy rebooted her brain.

'You mean Angel and those little kids have been weaving the tiger rug? And you guys all work for the Bulls too? But why? Kids aren't supposed to work until they're fifteen.'

Pablo answered her: 'They make us work for them so they can get rich,' he said simply. 'The Bull Commander's friends, the ones with ribbons and medals on their uniforms, make all the money. The Bulls have factories for children all over Telares.'

He didn't sound angry, just sad.

'And they hate us because we are all children of rebels.' Carlos hissed.

'That is *so* slack!' said Ricardo.

Lucy still didn't understand.

'But what about Angel and the other little kids? Why don't they go to this workshop?'

Everyone started babbling until Carlos shouted over the top of the others, 'I was in the camp the longest, I will tell her'.

Lucy watched his intense, gaunt face in the candlelight.

'Before, the prisoners all stayed in the workshop. I heard the guards talking about it in the army truck when they drove me from Telares City the day I was arrested.'

Carlos' voice dropped a register. 'Everyone in the village said the house was haunted; they just left it to rot and the jungle took it over. But the Bull Commander forced his men to go inside, and when he found the tiger rug in the very back room, still on its loom but not finished, he grew very much excited and ordered that it be completed. From now on, he said, the prisoners would sleep in the jungle jail. But the guards are terrified. That is why they get drunk.'

It was as though Carlos could not stop once he had started talking. The story poured out of him.

'But at first no one knew how to complete the rug because no one could find the old pattern. It was not in the house. Then the Bull Commander sent the militia to question the villagers but they said bad things would happen if they even spoke of it. Then the Bull Commander said bad things would happen if they *did not* speak of it. He would burn down a house a day until the pattern was found.

'The next day, the pattern appeared mysteriously beside the rug – well, half of it. It had been torn in half. The Commander cursed about that, but at least there was enough to start making the rug again. Now, whenever the Bulls bring in a new truckload of children, he picks the smallest, because their fingers are tiny. He makes them follow the pattern exactly. Soon they will be finished and he will start looking for the second half of the pattern. He is very cruel to the children. He only lets them outside once a day. Otherwise, they are chained to the tiger loom, day and night. That is where they eat and sleep.'

'. . . and dream,' thought Lucy.

Rahel broke in. 'Enough explanation of this. We must make a very good plan to rescue the others.'

'But there must be about twenty of them,' Lucy said, 'We can't fit anyone else in here. It's hard enough feeding everyone as it is.'

Carlos didn't seem to notice what Lucy had said.

'Yes, Rahel, the Bull Commander will be very much angered because we have escaped. He will not let the militia drink wine. He may get extra guards. We will have to take them by surprise.'

'Let's ambush them,' said Ricardo.

'Yes. An ambush,' said Pablo, as though Ricardo had just suggested a chocolate milkshake and a trip to the movies.

Rahel mused aloud: 'We need a decoy . . .'

This was all going too fast. Lucy did not like the feeling that the whole world had begun taking Ricardo's words much more seriously than her own.

'Please listen,' she pleaded. 'Even if we *can* rescue everyone, how can we possibly fit everyone in here? And you can't stay in the dark for very long. You'll turn into bats . . .' her voice faded out.

Carlos uttered a phrase in his own language which

sounded suspiciously like 'What a loser'. Lucy knew the bit about the bats wasn't true, but she did remember reading something about how kids needed sunlight or they got sick. If you got too much you got skin cancer, but not enough and you got something else. Something about a vitamin you needed from the sun. Vitamin D, that was it.

Pablo's soft voice broke her train of thought. 'You will think of some way to keep them safe,' he said simply. 'You have to.'

Lucy felt her system was going to crash again. This was too much.

'Look, we'll talk about it later. Ricardo, we have to go. Mum will be looking for us. Here, T-Tongue!'

Trudging up the tunnel, Lucy was relieved to be gone. Maybe she wouldn't go back. They were all crazy (except Angel)! And Carlos the Zombie was worse than crazy. He could make toys for the rest of his life for all she cared. They were probably really dumb toys that no one wanted to buy anyway.

She was so glad to be out of there, it was easy to ignore the little voice that said: *You made a promise.*

24
Hiding Place

Mum was awake but still a bit dopey and she kept yawning. Lucy decided to forget about the kids in the tunnel and do something really normal, like make her mum baked beans on toast. Ricardo tried to make Mum a cup of tea but left the kettle sitting in the sink with the plug in and the tap running and then decided to clean T-Tongue's teeth and began chasing him up and down the hall. The kitchen flooded and Mum made him mop the floor. Then she suggested a bush walk.

'Come on. It will be lovely in the rainforest. I haven't explored this place properly and you kids know all about it. Where does that path go? Can you get past that big hole?'

Lucy led the way, detouring around the pit. She could see where the path started again on the other side but you had to bush-bash to get to it. They emerged above the pit, looking down into it. No sign of the tunnel. Phew. It still gave her a funny feeling in the stomach, though. Mum shuddered.

'You kids haven't been down there again, have you?'

'No.' Personal jinx.

They walked up the steep path, winding steadily into the rainforest. With each step the forest got cooler and darker. It smelt spicy, like those oils Mum burned in her room. The path zigzagged between enormous trees with twisted, tough bark, some hollow right through and big enough for a family picnic. Then the trees thinned out and changed. The new ones had smooth, red trunks and grew at crazy angles, like twisted bones, out of the rocks, straining towards the sky. There were great sandy rocks, some piled on top of each other, others hollowed out into caves big enough to camp in. They kept walking and the forest grew denser and darker.

'Listen!'

Lucy could hear a gurgling, splashing sound, off to their left.

'Can we look for it, Mum? I'm thirsty.'

They branched off, following the sound. Lucy ran ahead. After a short, steep climb, she squeezed through two large boulders and stood on a flat rock platform, with a tantalising glimpse of sunlight on water only a few steps away, just behind a boulder covered in green lichen. Lucy edged around it – and stopped just in time to avoid plunging off a roaring waterfall. She gazed down, a long way down, at a deep pool, with rocks and towering trees surrounding it like a fortress. She saw a narrow sliver of sandy beach on the closest side, where the creek formed an elbow. On the far side was a clearing big enough to play soccer in, though maybe not with a whole team.

It was a secret valley – you couldn't see it from home and not from the road either.

Lucy heard Ricardo behind her.

'It's a waterfall,' she said warningly.

'Cool! I'm jumping!'

Mum grabbed him just in time. Then Lucy saw the way down: behind the towering boulder were a series of rocks like gigantic stepping stones, tumbling down to the sandy beach below. She picked her way down, the others behind her.

'Well done, Lucy, this is fantastic!'

Mum splashed her face in the pool, exclaiming how clean it was. Then she threw herself down on the soft sand with arms outstretched and pronounced it 'heavenly'.

Lucy and Ricardo waded into the pool. It got quite deep quickly. It was warm on top but icy-cold at their feet, and a few metres out it was way over their heads. After that hot climb it was like eating an icecream. They dived and splashed and then Ricardo dared Lucy to jump off the waterfall. Lucy turned and looked. How deep was the pool? She swam closer, until the spray was in her eyes and then dived as deep as she could. Cold closed like a vice, but she still couldn't touch bottom. When she swam back up, still with her eyes closed, she heard her mother cry out 'Lucy! Lucy!' with a note of panic.

Opening her eyes, she realised why. She had surfaced behind the waterfall itself. She glanced behind her and saw a cave heading back a surprisingly long way, completely hidden by the curtain of water. She just had time to register a shaft of sunlight spearing down a hole in the rock platform above, revealing a sloping sandy floor well above water level, before her mother screamed again. She dived and swam under water, surfacing on the other side in time to see Mum wading into the pool, fully dressed.

'Don't do that to me! I thought you'd drowned.'

'Just practising holding my breath for the swimming carnival,' Lucy said blithely and dived again.

Surfacing behind the waterfall, she scrambled up into the cave and back towards the shaft of sunlight. The cave was much bigger than she'd first thought, big enough to camp in . . . in fact, she'd stumbled on the perfect place to hide an army of feral children.

She swam to the beach.

'Got any food?'

Mum unpacked treats from Sydney: spicy Lebanese pastries, shish kebabs, Turkish delight and sweet baklava.

Everyone ate in contented silence.

Then Ricardo blew it.

'Can we bring Dad here?' he asked hopefully.

Lucy kicked him. Just mentioning Dad could make Mum mad these days.

There was a moment's tense silence before Mum spoke.

'You can bring him here, Ricardo, but it's probably better if I don't come.' She didn't sound mad, just sad. 'We seem to fight all the time these days, even though we don't want to. We'll be friends again one day, I guess, but right now, we're not.'

Ricardo looked thoughtful.

'I had a fight with Leo, but it only lasted till lunchtime. Could you make up with Dad by tonight?'

Mum laughed and said she didn't think they could make up properly by tonight, and adults often were just not as smart as kids, so their fights lasted longer . . . and no, she didn't know why that was.

Lucy sat silently, kicking a rock, thinking about Carlos the Zombie. Why was he so rude? She couldn't imagine ever being friends with him. But it didn't mean she wouldn't help the other kids. And now that she'd found the cave and the campsite, she *could* help them.

She plotted and planned as they scrambled back down the mountain, making a long list in her head. What did Dad pack when they went camping? They wouldn't need a tent, but they would need sleeping bags, pillows, cooking things, matches, newspaper, plates, spoons, food . . . heaps of stuff. They were going to have to raid the old lady's exploring collection again. They couldn't until Mum went back to work tomorrow, but Lucy could sneak out tonight and tell the others her plan. This morning she hadn't wanted to go back at all, but the secret place had changed everything. She could tell Pablo she had thought of something after all.

'Is Grandma coming tomorrow?' she asked.

'Not until after lunch. You'll be on your own from when I leave at eleven. Will you be OK for two hours? I don't really like leaving you, I'm away so much, but you're pretty sensible these days, Lucy – and Ricardo, you have to do what Lucy says.'

They had reached the path above the pit.

'Even if she tells me to jump in that big hole?'

'Lucy isn't that silly,' said Mum.

25

Soaking in It

After dinner Lucy said she was going to read in bed. Mum made Ricardo go too. Lucy whispered, 'We'll hide the kids at the waterfall. We'll sneak out tonight and tell them, then we'll raid the old lady's stuff tomorrow'.

Mum came in to say goodnight.

'What happened in here?' She sounded as if she'd just seen something gross at the hospital. 'Actually, I don't want to know. Just get it cleaned up in the morning. Goodnight.'

Ricardo fell asleep straight away but Lucy watched the candles flicker, and heard the music from Mum's meditation tape drift down the hall. It was a goofy lady with an American accent telling you to imagine yourself by a river. Lucy thought it was better to jump in a real river, like today. That always felt good. But Mum was always sound asleep by the time the tape finished.

Lucy closed her own eyes and felt sleep wash over her.

Some time later, she opened her eyes and met the Tiger-cat's golden gaze. She looked at her watch. Eleven p.m. Time to go. Lucy poked Ricardo but he wouldn't wake up.

Too bad. The Tiger-cat leapt out the window impatiently. Picking up T-Tongue, Lucy went softly down the hall and out into the moonlight.

Only when she landed in the pit did she realise she had left her torch behind. The Tiger-cat padded into the tunnel and Lucy knew she would have to feel her own way. Her stomach lurched as she stepped into the dark tunnel. Then she noticed something odd. She couldn't actually *see*, but she seemed to sense where the walls were.

Lucy concentrated. It was as if some part of her mind was stretching like a piece of elastic, reaching out to find the way. It was like . . . *listening*. And she was *a hunter* again, alert and ready, like a cat. The feeling was even stronger than before.

Lucy knew she was at the door before her questioning hand slid along its wooden surface and grasped the handle. She walked in so quietly, she startled everyone. Three candles burned on the table. Everyone smiled at her in relief, except Carlos the Zombie, and Angel. Angel just looked at her out of those big dark eyes. She was sitting on Carlos' knee. He was cuddling her. Poor thing. The Tiger-cat went straight up to Carlos and began rubbing against his legs. Traitor. Carlos smiled and stroked the Tiger-cat and little Angel giggled.

'I have found somewhere to hide you and the other kids,' announced Lucy proudly. 'You're going camping.'

'Camping?' said four voices at once.

'Personal jinx,' said Pablo and Rahel carefully, and Lucy laughed.

'I have found a safe place up on the mountain.' She

gestured at the air above her head. 'No one goes there and there's lots of clean water and vitamin A, I mean D, and I've found a cave for you to sleep in and we'll bring you food so the little kids can get strong. Then you will be ready to find your auntie and take Angel home . . .' Her voice trailed off.

Angel climbed down and trotted over to Lucy with arms outstretched. Lucy picked her up, just as someone knocked at the door. Everyone else froze, then shrunk back into the shadows. When she opened the door, a gun was pointed at her head.

It was Ricardo, dressed up in his mini-Ninja costume, with his biggest Super Soaker aimed at Lucy's forehead.

'What did you go without me for?'

'You were asleep, goofball.'

'No, I wasn't. I was awake all night.'

'Well, how come you didn't notice me go?'

Ricardo's answer was to squeeze the trigger but Lucy, still holding Angel, ducked and Carlos copped a faceful.

'Cool,' thought Lucy, ducking and weaving around the cubby. But Angel was clinging to her neck, making a strange sound in her throat.

Ricardo tried again, but Rahel snuck up behind him, snatched the gun and threw it to Pablo.

'Can't you see you are scaring Angel,' she scolded. 'She thinks it is a real gun!'

Ricardo had the grace to look ashamed. 'I didn't mean to.'

'Well, you did,' Lucy said brusquely. 'And I'm supposed to be looking after her. Her mum told me to, so cut it out!'

'You have never met her mother,' Carlos said scornfully, wiping water from his face with his sleeve.

'I told you, I dreamt about her,' Lucy protested, turning to Rahel for help. It came from an unexpected quarter.

'Yeah. I dreamed about her too. And her mum said we had to babysit her. But I don't think we get paid. That sucks!'

'You suck, Ricardo!' But Lucy was grateful for the interruption and for what Rahel said next in her quiet voice.

'They speak the truth, Carlos. Remember what Lucy said the other day. She had information about Angel that she could not have known otherwise. She knew about her beautiful dress and about her mama. We must stop arguing and co-operate.' Lucy wouldn't have quite put it like that, but couldn't agree more.

And so a council of war ensued. Everyone drew up a chair to the table and sat around the spluttering, smoking candles.

'I think this campsite is the best place to go,' said Lucy. 'Mum knows about it, but she's too busy to go up there without us, and we could always warn you in time and you could get into the cave. No one can see it from the road and, anyway, I think you have to go through our back yard to get there.'

Everyone thought about Lucy's words for a minute and then Rahel made up her mind.

'If it is safe we will go to this campsite in the morning,' she said firmly, 'We will prepare everything for the new ones, then, in the night we will return to the jungle and free them.'

No one said anything.

Lucy looked at their faces, shadowed in the candlelight. Suddenly, she'd had enough.

'Look, I'm going back to bed. Mum doesn't sleep as well as Grandma and she might wake up. Ricardo probably woke her up as he was leaving and she's called the police already.'

'I did not!' said Ricardo, outraged.

But Lucy was already regretting the line about the police because everyone at the table was looking really tense.

'Only kidding. Look, you guys should all get some sleep. Mum will go to work in the morning and we'll get all the camping stuff together and fetch you. Come on, Ricardo. See you all later.'

She strode out the door. When Ricardo caught up she realised he had also forgotten the torch.

'How did you get here without the torch?'

'I've got magic powers.'

'Oh yeah, right!'

The Tiger-cat was waiting in the pit for them, its purr reverberating off the walls.

Later, lying in bed, Lucy couldn't stop thinking. She knew what Dad would say if she told him what was happening: he'd say it wasn't. He'd get Auntie Alice's atlas out and show Lucy it was impossible. He was a scientist, after all. He didn't say a star existed unless he could prove it. But he would congratulate her on her vivid imagination.

Grandma would tell her she was the best big sister in Kurrawong for including Ricardo in her imaginary world, and offer her about six chocolate biscuits. Mum would tell her to write it down and enter it in a competition, and say how pleased she was that Lucy was getting on better with Ricardo. And how glad she was that Lucy was only making up all that stuff about sneaking out at night.

T-Tongue whimpered in his sleep. Lucy stroked his soft black fur until he relaxed. Then she was asleep too, dreamlessly for a change.

26
Playing for the Bulls

Lucy stumbled out into the kitchen.

'You slept in, Lucy love!'

Mum was making pancakes with the first eggs from the new chickens. Lucy ate six with lemon and sugar and Ricardo asked for ten but ate nine. Mum said she could see what Grandma was talking about and left for work an hour early to go to the supermarket. She said the groceries would be delivered at about lunchtime and did the children think they would starve before then? She got in the car muttering darkly about having to ask Dad for more money to feed them.

Lucy waved until the car disappeared in a cloud of exhaust fumes and then ran inside and made hardboiled eggs for the kids. Then she grabbed the keys to the room with the old lady's stuff. The first thing she saw when the door swung open was the dragon chest. What was in it? Why did Nigel Scar-Skull want it? Staring at the carved dragons, Lucy suddenly felt dizzy. For a few seconds that feeling swept over her again, as though information had just been downloaded into her brain. And suddenly she knew what she had to do. Nigel Scar-Skull must not get his hands on that chest. She didn't know why, but she was certain. Even if she couldn't open it, even if she didn't know what was in it, she had to hide it. And the best hiding place was the tunnel.

She looked at the chest carefully. It had two brass rings, one at each end, for handles.

'Come on, Ricardo, help.'

It wasn't as heavy as it looked. They left it at the back door then rushed back to find airbeds (a double and two singles). The fold-up chairs would have to wait. Ricardo filled the esky and backpack, while Lucy kept looking. Bingo. A whole crate full of cooking gear. A wire grille for making toast on the fire, a frypan, a heavy black pot with a lid. There weren't enough things to sleep on, especially with more kids coming, but they could use bedspreads. Then Ricardo found a sack with a picture of a lady in a hammock, drinking from a funny-shaped glass with a little umbrella and a cherry in it. In it was – surprise – a hammock. Then he found three more. The old lady who owned the house really did come from a happy camping family. They had everything. Last of all Lucy grabbed the big bowl with the picture of the flower in the bottom. It made an enormous stack at the back door. It would take them ages to get everything up that track.

'Toro will help.'

Retardo had actually had a brainwave! Lucy looked at her watch: 10.30 a.m. It would take them half an hour to get all the kids out of the tunnel. But Ricardo was right. With Mum and Grandma gone, they could come right down to the house and help carry everything up to the campsite. Lucy and Ricardo could get home by 1 p.m. to meet Grandma. If they needed to go back up they could tell Grandma they were setting up a secret base on the mountain or something.

It wasn't a *lie*.

Lucy swung down the rope and trotted along the tunnel, Ricardo behind her. Again, there was that strange feeling as the dark enveloped her. Her eyes couldn't see but *she* could. Weird. She didn't bother turning on the torch.

When they got to the den, the Tiger-cat was sitting on the table next to a last sputtering candle, the size of a thumbnail. In the pool of light it cast, Lucy could see the children had packed up the picnic basket and blankets. No one said anything.

'Hi,' ventured Lucy.

But Rahel just looked right into Lucy's eyes and then suddenly stood up and blew out the candle. There was a collective gasp and bodies milled about Lucy, heading for the door, but she stood stock still, rocked by Rahel's expression. For an instant, fear had flared on Rahel's usually calm face. The enormity of what Lucy was doing suddenly struck her. These kids were putting their lives in her hands. They had left one life behind, without knowing what lay in front of them. They were walking into Lucy's world, with no choice but to trust her.

She opened her mouth to call out but Rahel was gone. Someone bumped into Lucy.

'My apologies,' breathed Pablo.

'Here, take the torch. I don't need it,' Lucy said, loping into the darkness of the tunnel. It was a relief. Not quite natural, like breathing, but welcome anyway, like diving into the pool in the clearing yesterday. It was as if she was holding her breath underwater. Her sight was holding its breath as some other sixth sense stretched out and swam in the darkness.

Lucy saw Rahel's silhouette at the end of the tunnel and the next minute the ragged little party gathered in the bottom of the pit, blinking in a shaft of sunlight.

Rahel's gaze went from Lucy to the Tiger-cat, washing itself on a broken beam, and back again. Once again Lucy saw that flicker of fear. The others shifted uncomfortably until Ricardo broke the ice, charging at the side of the pit, swinging up the rope like a monkey. He jumped up and down at the top, threw down the rope and called out excitedly, 'C'mon, Toro!'

Toro didn't move until the Tiger-cat stood up, stretched, sauntered over and began rubbing against his legs, purring. Then, in a flash, she leapt in one graceful curve to the top of the pit.

'C'mon, Toro!'

Toro finally grinned and trotted forward to grab the rope. He hauled himself up, Ricardo offering advice the whole way, and then threw the rope at his big sister. Rahel caught it, hesitated, and then passed it to Lucy.

'You will go first,' she said, quietly intense, her dark eyes searching Lucy's.

Lucy took the rope and lunged at the wall, bouncing up the smooth sides. At the top, she tossed the rope to Rahel.

'You can do it,' Lucy said.

Rahel wore the same determined expression Lucy had noticed before the raid on the jungle jail. Seconds later, she was clambering out of the pit.

'Put Angel in the towel,' called Lucy, throwing the rope down to Carlos. Angel snuggled into the towel, hanging on as if she were on a ride at Luna Park. At the last minute T-Tongue whined to be let in too. He put his big paws on Angel's little knees and her face broke into a smile. Even Carlos laughed as he lifted the puppy in next to her. Lucy hauled them up, straining to take the weight of both puppy and child, conscious of Carlos' critical gaze.

Carrying Angel, Lucy walked a few steps down the path. Ricardo and Toro were already almost at the back yard and Lucy was afraid they had made too much noise. What if Grandma came early?

She looked back and saw the others still gathered on the stairs. They weren't going anywhere. Pablo wore an anxious frown but managed a weak grin for Lucy. Carlos shot her a deadly glance and scanned the trees as though expecting an ambush. He got one, but it was only the Tiger-cat, leaping from a branch, startling everyone, and then rubbing soothingly against their legs, each in turn.

Rahel spoke. 'We are afraid, Lucy. We have danger behind us and danger in front. We want to trust you, but where we come from people are betrayed to the Bulls every day. And we don't know what danger awaits.'

'Look, I know you'll be safe. You'll feel better once we get to the campsite. It's the perfect hiding place.'

The silken fur of the Tiger-cat rubbing against her calves caused her to glance down and in an instant she was lost in those golden eyes.

. . . *only they have turned blood red and Lucy is gazing into the eyes of a bull. She is looking at a heavy gold ring with a large black stone set in the centre, cleverly carved in the image of a bull. Red stones for eyes, vicious horns marked in gold. Then she sees the ring-wearer's face. The Bull Commander! He stands in the shadow of a laneway. An old lady sidles up to him. Furtively, she points across the road where a lone teenager stands in a pool of sunlight, kicking a soccer ball against a wall. The ring-wearer opens a wallet. The old woman does not take her eyes off the notes being counted out. She snatches them, looks furtively about, and melts back into the dark lane. The ring-wearer steps briefly into sunlight and Lucy sees the familiar brown Bull uniform. Then he is stalking, shadow to shadow, doorway to doorway, moving closer and closer to the teenager. Suddenly Lucy understands but her warning shout comes too late.*

'Pablo!' Lucy shuddered back into her body, and by his frantic reaction realised she had shouted out his name. 'I saw you,' she said, looking straight into his eyes. 'The Bull Commander gave an old lady money to find you, then he was stalking you . . .'

Pablo shrugged resignedly.

'It was the day I was arrested. The old lady, she was my neighbour.'

'Your neighbour? Why?'

Carlos did not give his friend time to answer. 'Traitors! They are traitors,' he hissed. 'They betray people to the Bulls for money. And as for the militia, they are the biggest traitors. They have given up the right to call themselves Telarian. They have no country.'

'The militia?' Lucy was horrified. 'You mean they are Telarians?'

Carlos nodded angrily.

'So the Ponytail Zombie is Telarian too?' It was incomprehensible to Lucy. As unthinkable as going for the other side in the Grand Final.

Pablo tried to explain.

'My Papa told me that when the Bulls first came, many people were scared and hungry. Bulls went into all the villages and took many young men and gave them wine and cigarettes and food if they joined the militia. They made them say where the others were hiding. If they didn't, the Bulls would beat them, sometimes shoot them . . .'

'Cowards!' spat Carlos. Lucy wasn't sure if he meant the militia or the Bulls.

'My aunt says some may change their minds now because the rebels are getting stronger,' whispered Rahel, as though she didn't quite believe it. Carlos just laughed.

'My mama said we could not trust people any more,' Pablo said sadly. 'She said some helped the Bulls because they were poor. But some just told the Bulls you were a rebel, because they didn't like you. My friend's father was arrested and the person who told lies about him got their house!'

As usual, Pablo didn't sound angry. Even when he was talking about the most horrible events, he just sounded sad.

'Well, you're safe now,' said Lucy firmly, 'but if we don't get a move on Grandma will find out about you and all of Kurrawong will know by dinnertime!'

That shut them up. Rahel considered Lucy, standing there with Angel snuggled into her shoulder trustingly. Then she nodded and her face broke into a smile.

'I know you will help us,' she said, 'and so does Angel.' She headed down the stairs. Pablo glanced up from petting the Tiger-cat and a brief smile lit up his face. The Tiger-cat rolled onto its back in the sunlight and stretched luxuriously, showing off its striped belly, purring loudly. Pablo scratched its chest, then followed Rahel down the stairs.

As Carlos came past Lucy, he muttered darkly, 'We have no choice but to trust you'.

'Suit yourself,' said Lucy.

27

Tale of Two Rugs

Lucy made everyone wait behind the chook pen while Ricardo checked that the coast was clear. Angel stared at the chickens as though they were some great TV show. At Ricardo's signal, they crept stealthily towards the back door.

It was all too much for T-Tongue. He began to bark furiously, even though he knew them all. He didn't stop until the Tiger-cat stalked up to him, eyeball to eyeball and made an extraordinary sound. It started as a low growl, which seemed to paralyse T-Tongue, then reached a screaming crescendo that made the hairs on Lucy's neck stand up. T-Tongue tore his eyes away from the Tiger-cat, and ran yelping under the house. Everyone laughed except Angel, who shrank up against Lucy's side and clung to her leg. When Lucy opened the back door, the Tiger-cat stalked inside, tail lashing.

Lucy strode up the hallway to her bedroom. But when she turned, no one had moved. They were huddled at the door, staring at the mermaid carpet in consternation.

'Come on,' Ricardo said impatiently, 'I told you, no one's home.'

No one moved. Then the Tiger-cat reappeared and began twisting and purring around their legs. Lucy saw every tight face relax into a smile and the group stepped into the hall.

Lucy had been going to show them the rug first, but the Tiger-cat had other ideas. It streaked up the hall and jumped daintily up at the handle of the ballroom door, releasing the latch. It swung open and Lucy, curious, followed. She felt the vibration of several pairs of feet coming down the hall and then heard a united gasp as they walked in behind her.

The room looked even more like an underwater world since Mum had made them wash every wall. The painted floor shone. Angel struggled to be let down and stepped onto the floor, as though she were walking into a swimming pool. She tried to pick up a crab near her feet and everyone laughed at the look on her face when she realised it was a drawing.

'Come and see our tiger rug,' said Ricardo and charged out of the ballroom and back down the hall, T-Tongue and Toro in hot pursuit.

'Don't break the dragon vases,' Lucy yelled.

Angel cried out at the golden eyes that smouldered up at her when the clothes and soccer balls had been cleared from the rug. She tried to climb up Carlos' leg. He picked her up and she hid her face in his shoulder.

By the looks on everyone's faces, Lucy had some explaining to do.

'We found the rug the first day we moved in and it was

really old and grungy. Then it just started to grow itself new again! And now we have to keep it covered up so Mum and Grandma don't notice. It's really weird. First it was just the tiger and a monkey—'

'My monkey!' interjected Ricardo.

'And that's the other weird thing: Ricardo and I have been having the same dreams, always about you guys. When we dreamt that the tiger helped Rahel and Toro escape, our tiger became *much* brighter.'

Rahel knelt to run her palms over the carpet tiger.

'This is very much what happened,' she breathed. 'The man-eater came and we took our opportunity and ran into the jungle.'

Lucy shifted undies off the snake's head.

'Then this appeared!'

It was more impressive than ever. Muscular coils studded with shiny gold diamonds, winding from one edge of the rug to another.

'Ponytail,' Rahel hissed.

'Pardon?' said Carlos.

'I informed you,' she answered absently, not taking her eyes off the carpet snake, 'the ponytail militia stopped chasing us because of a snake just like this one.'

Lucy revealed the monkey. Its golden mane was brighter than before. Angel made a strange sound and Lucy looked at her with concern. But the little girl was smiling.

'I don't know about this one. Maybe we're going to meet a monkey. Would you like that, Angel?'

'I would,' said Toro.

'I already have,' said Ricardo importantly.

Rahel looked at him sharply. 'Is this true?' she asked.

'Yes. I talked to him. It was the night before we found the house. I dreamt about him and then I dreamt I got turned into a monkey. It was great! I chucked mangoes at Lucy!'

Everyone burst out laughing, especially Carlos, and even Lucy had to smile.

'But it is true. Monkeys like this do throw mangoes. I have seen them throw mangoes at the Bull Commander,' Rahel said. 'It was the day they took me to the jungle jail. The truck broke down in the jungle and the militiamen had to call on the radio for help. They tied me to a mango tree so I couldn't run away. I was very hungry and thirsty and then I heard a sound and a golden monkey like this,' she gestured at the carpet monkey, 'picked a mango and dropped it right down next to me. It was the first food I had had in many days. Then the Bull Commander came in another truck and told the militia to put me back inside, but the monkey pelted them with ripe mangoes. One struck the Bull Commander in the head! He was filled with rage and began to shoot into the tree. But the monkey was too quick for him.'

Lucy was still gazing thoughtfully at the carpet.

'I reckon the animals show up when we need them,' she said firmly. 'Think about it. Has a tiger ever hurt one of the kids at the camp?'

'No,' said Rahel firmly.

'But the Bulls and the militia get attacked, don't they? I bet that's how the smiling soldier got his scar!'

'This is true,' said Pablo, quite pleased about the whole idea.

'And that snake – how come it didn't get us that night?

We were crawling around in the jungle for ages. And then it just crawled across our feet and left us alone.'

'What are you saying?' demanded Carlos impatiently.

'Something weird is happening and I don't know what it is, but it's got something to do with this carpet and the one that Angel was making. It is the same pattern, isn't it? And what's going on with the two houses? They're almost exactly the same, only yours got turned into a jail.

'And what's with the Tiger-cat? How come it can beam video clips into our heads? And time's doing all these wacky things. And that weird old atlas. If you get too close, you feel like you're drowning. And every page has a different Telares, only they're all over the world and they're called different names. But when I look in Auntie Alice's atlas, they're not even there!

'And then there's the dragon chest and Nigel Scar-Skull and he really wants it, but I *know* he's not supposed to get it. Don't ask me how I know.'

Rahel considered the tiger rug, head on one side.

'Yes, and why is the Bull Commander so determined to make Angel and the others finish the rug? Did the guards ever explain that, Carlos?'

'He says that the rug is worth much money, and they will be rewarded when it is finished. But the guards say the rug has made the Commander crazy. He thinks about nothing else.'

In the silence that followed, Lucy suddenly remembered the time.

'Cockatoo crap! We've got to get out of here. Help mess up the room!'

The Telarian kids looked at her blankly but Toro got

into the swing of things as soon as he saw Ricardo doing what he did best. He looked delighted. They were doing such a good job that no one heard the knock at the door.

No one, that is, except T-Tongue, who charged up the hall and threw himself at the front door in a frenzy of barking. Lucy froze, thawed, then rushed to the bedroom door and closed it. The Telarian kids shrank against the walls as a loud voice boomed, 'Shut up, you stupid mutt!'

'Nigel Scar-Skull!' hissed Lucy, and her desperation communicated itself instantly to the others. The boys dived under the bed and Lucy had to pull Ricardo out by the ankle.

'You don't have to hide, doofus, you live here!'

'I forgot,' said Ricardo and scrambled out. Rahel took his place under Lucy's bed and Carlos headed for the wardrobe with Angel. Just as Lucy closed the door on them, she caught the look on Carlos' face: 'I knew you would let us down,' it said.

She didn't have time to worry about his paranoia because Nigel Scar-Skull was pounding on the door, shouting, 'I know someone's home, so open the door!'

Lucy stepped out of the bedroom, clicked the door shut as silently as she could and saw the Tiger-cat padding down the hall, body slung low to the floor. It crouched, ready to spring, at the bedroom door, hidden between the dragon vases.

Lucy grabbed T-Tongue's collar and opened the door to reveal Nigel Scar-Skull holding a Super Soaker, even bigger than Ricardo's. The clawmarks on his head were still clear.

He pointed his weapon at T-Tongue and then looked warily over his shoulder and back up the hall. He barely glanced at Lucy before he started talking: 'Well, Louise, I was just in the area and thought I'd drop in to see if you'd found that chest yet. You asked Mum about it, like a good girl, didn't you?'

Lucy was painfully aware she was not a good girl and that the dragon chest was in full view at the back door.

'Uhhmm,' was all she could manage but then Ricardo materialised beside her, armed with his Super Soaker. Would Mum understand if they soaked the agent? Probably not.

'It's OK, Ricardo,' she said, 'I don't think we're going to need that, it's only Nigel Sc – I mean Mr Adams.'

Nigel Scar-Skull took in Ricardo's triple barrels and bared his teeth in a lip-splitting smile.

'No, young man, you won't need that. Now just – ' But his mobile phone rang and he answered it clumsily, juggling his Super Soaker.

'I'll hold it,' said Ricardo helpfully.

He glared at him and swung away. 'Yes. Are you sure? This'd better not be a false alarm again. She's had turns like this before. OK, OK, I'll be right there!' He hung up and looked irritably at Lucy.

'Now, Linda, have you found this chest? I don't have much time. I have a sick relative to think about.'

Lucy shook her head.

'Nuh,' Ricardo said.

Nigel Scar-Skull frowned heavily. 'Look, I don't want to have to say —'

But his phone rang again. 'Adams,' he answered irritably. Then his entire expression changed.

'Great to hear from you, mate. No, it's going like a ripper

at this end. What's that? It means everything's great! Look, I'm a bit tied up right now. What's that? No, I'm not really tied up! I'm busy, mate, I'm busy. Look, I'll call you back. OK, bye.'

Nigel Scar-Skull disconnected the call, shaking his head and his stretchy smile snapped back into a thin line.

'Listen, I'm not wasting any more time here. You can see I'm a busy man. I've got people calling me from all over the world. You get your mother to ring me. It's urgent! Your lease says you have to facilitate house inspections. If this goes on much longer, I will have to assume you are obstructing an inspection and reconsider your lease.'

He strode down the stairs but then seemed to remember something. Raising his Super Soaker, he looked nervously about, then jogged to the car and drove off in a screech of tyres.

Lucy slammed the door shut. When her heart stopped pounding, she went back and told the others they could come out. Rahel looked gratefully at Lucy and said, 'We appreciate what you have done'.

Lucy shrugged her shoulders, embarrassed, and told them what Nigel Scar-Skull had wanted.

'We have to get out of here. He might come back. I reckon he wants that dragon chest as much as the smiling soldier wanted the pattern for the rug. Come and look.'

She led the way to the back door and moved the bedspreads off the dragon chest. Carlos looked thunderstruck and began talking excitedly.

'There was one just like this in the jungle jail! The Bull Commander took it for himself. He was very angry because he could not find the key. Of course he could smash it open, but the militia say it is far too valuable. These old carved chests are worth much money. He has probably sold it in Telares City.'

'Well, we can't open this one either but we have to get it into the tunnel before we go to the camp or Mum might hand it over to Nigel Scar-Skull,' said Lucy. As soon as she looked at the chest she got that same dizzy feeling as she had last time. And when the dizziness passed she was left with an overwhelming sense of urgency, as though every cell in her blood was saying, 'Hide it *now*!'

Carlos surprised Lucy by stepping forward to help. They each grabbed a brass ring, and again Lucy was struck by how light the chest was.

'Ricardo,' she called as they struggled awkwardly across the yard, 'make sure nothing gets left behind'.

Halfway up the path, Lucy noticed the Tiger-cat trotting along behind them. At the top of the stairs the Tiger-cat loped forward. Carlos looked stunned when it did that Open Sesame leap and the tunnel entrance appeared behind the pile of rubble.

Lucy hauled up the rope and tied it to the brass rings. They lowered the chest carefully, and then clambered down to drag it into the tunnel.

By the time Carlos and Lucy climbed out of the pit, the other kids were almost at the stairs, laden with camping gear.

'We got everything,' said Ricardo.

Wrong. They'd forgotten the hardboiled eggs. Grandma would be here any minute. Lucy raced down to get them and caught up with the others on the track above the pit.

Ricardo and Toro complained about how heavy their

loads were until Rahel told them to shut up, in two languages. They did. Lucy was impressed.

Finally, with Carlos carrying Angel, they stumbled through the passageway between the rocks and clambered down into the grassy clearing by the creek. No time to show them the cave. Lucy and Ricardo ran for home, flying into the yard exhausted just as the bus appeared. And the shopping had been sitting in the sun on the step for so long that the icecream had melted and Grandma was mad at them for not putting it away. Then she saw just how good a job Toro and Ricardo had done on the bedroom. Oops.

28

'Girls Can't Play Soccer'

Finally they escaped, after putting the groceries away, doing the dishes and promising to get the room tidied up tonight. Grandma relented when they told her they had urgent business at their secret base.

'Much better than watching TV,' she said, waving them goodbye, but they only got as far as the chook pen, before she called them back.

'You can't go without food. Here, take this, and this, and you'll need some fruit too, and . . .'

When their backpacks were full she asked, 'Where are you going again?'

'This cool place we found with Mum.'

'Well, that's OK. So long as your mum knows about it.'

Finally they escaped *again*, with about thirty sandwiches. Lucy remembered to grab a soccer ball and as many swimmers and boardshorts as she could find, while Ricardo grabbed a hammock he'd left sitting at the back door. Lucky Grandma hadn't seen that!

As they neared the rocky pass, they smelt smoke. They

stepped into the sunny clearing, to find Pablo tending a simmering pot under a shady tree. A large flat rock made a kitchen bench for the cups and bowls and pots hung from the tree. He looked delighted to see them.

'I am making tea,' he said proudly.

'Where did you find tea?'

Pablo pointed underground.

'Yuck. It must have been down there for about ten years,' Lucy said.

'Ricardo!'

Toro's call came from the big rock on top of the waterfall. He was jumping up and down and waving his arms. Ricardo took off after him, clambering over the rocks like a two-legged goat.

Angel was asleep in a hammock slung in the trees, and Rahel and Carlos the Zombie were standing knee-deep in the pool.

'Hi,' said Lucy.

'Welcome,' said Rahel.

Carlos nodded. Maybe he was going to be less of a zombie.

He noticed the soccer ball under her arm. 'Do you play soccer?' she asked.

He was scornful: 'Of course!'

'So do I,' Lucy said.

'Girls don't play soccer.'

'Well, that's funny,' snapped Lucy. 'I don't know who was playing in last year's Grand Final if it wasn't me and my friends.' Zombie.

'What good is a girls' team?'

This was war!

158

'We play in mixed teams! There were boys in our team and on the other team!'

'Boys who have to play with girls are no good.'

'Crap, only the good ones get in our team. You have to go through selections and everything. I'm in because I can run fast and tackle hard and I'm good at penalties.'

Lucy would never find out what Carlos was about to say because Rahel poured a pot of pond water on his head. Lucy's burst of laughter was cut short by the same treatment.

'Both of you will desist! Carlos, just because girls aren't allowed to play soccer at home doesn't mean they don't play soccer here. Lucy is helping us and you are discourteous to her all the time. Lucy, you must stop fighting with Carlos. He doesn't mean it. He . . .'

She looked as if she wanted to say something else but didn't know if she should.

Carlos looked stormy.

'I do mean it. We don't need her help. I don't need any of you. If you would tell me where you hid that gun, I would shoot the Commander and rescue the others myself.'

He stormed off, vanishing up the creek.

'What is *wrong* with him? I haven't done anything to him but he hates me!'

'Ask Pablo,' Rahel said.

The three of them sat around the fire, Pablo drinking his antique tea. Rahel spoke softly.

'Carlos has been in the jail longer than any of us – for more than a year. We grew up together. His mama and papa and mine were friends before . . . before . . .'

Pablo whispered.

159

'Before the Bulls killed them.'

The clearing was terribly quiet. Suddenly a crow cawed in the trees like a warning, and Lucy shivered. She didn't know what to say.

'Carlos' papa used to coach the Telares Tigers,' Rahel went on, 'the best soccer team on the island'.

Pablo interrupted. 'The best in the Pacific! They thrashed Burchimo the year before the invasion 4-0, in front of the Tongan royal family. My papa said they invaded to pay us back!'

Rahel jumped in again.

'After the invasion, they didn't stop people playing soccer but they made the Tigers change their name. They passed a law against speaking our language and we all had to speak Burchimese at school. We weren't allowed to mention the word "Telares". You could be sent to the jail just for saying it in the street.'

Pablo broke in again. 'You're supposed to be telling her about the Tigers.'

'I am! They made Carlos' papa change the Tigers' name to the Burchimo Bears. Everyone hated it. At home nobody ever called them the Bears, but in public we had to. So at the big matches in the stadium we would have to chant out "Bears, Bears, Bears", but in our hearts we knew we were going for the Tigers. And they were still the best team on Telares.'

Pablo took over the story. 'The best? They were the greatest. The Tigers won every game. They defeated the garrison team three times! Three times!'

'What's a garrison?'

'It's where all the Bull soldiers live in Telares City. They

160

had their own soccer team called the Burcho City Bulls – they changed the name of Telares City to Burcho City but it is the same thing – and the Bulls played in the All-Island League. Everyone hated them and would hiss when they scored –'

'Which was hardly ever!' said Pablo.

'. . . and they knew everyone hated them and it made them play worse than ever. But the Bull referees would give all our players red cards – for nothing! – and send them off. Bull soldiers would come to all the games with their weapons because they feared a riot. It was indeed frightening!'

Pablo took over again.

'And at the last Grand Final it became very serious. Almost everyone on the whole island went to the match. People from the mountains walked for days to get there. The crowds flowed up the streets for hours. There were more Telarians in one place than the Bulls had ever seen. And everyone hated them! They could feel it and they were scared!'

'It did not feel like a soccer match,' said Rahel, 'and deep down everybody knew it was much more. Papa said it was a chance to show the generals that they had not won, that we were still undefeated. They might have taken over the country but not our hearts. But Mama would not let me go to the game. She said people would get hurt. She didn't want Papa to go but he did anyway.'

'My mama would not let *me* go but I went anyway,' said Pablo. 'With Carlos. At half-time the score was Tigers two, Bulls zero. It should have been much higher but the referee disallowed a Tigers' goal. The crowd hissed for about five minutes and the Bull soldiers went onto the field and pointed their rifles at the crowd.'

Rahel jumped in, 'Then, in the second half —'

'How would you know? You were not there,' complained Pablo.

'Everyone knows. Papa told me this story so many times. In the second half, three Bulls players tackled our striker and knocked him out. He was carried from the field but they did not even get a yellow card. Then, ten minutes from the end, when everyone knew the Tigers had won, the referee gave our goalie a red card –'

'A red card!' said Lucy. 'What for?'

'For stopping a penalty.'

'That's what he's supposed to do!'

'Not that day! The referee found some excuse to give him a red card and that was that. He was off the field.'

Pablo went on, 'And that was when Carlos' papa picked up a megaphone and stood on the sideline facing the crowd and began to chant "Tigers, Tigers, Tigers". There were Bull soldiers all around him, but he did it anyway. Then everyone stood up and began to chant with him. The soldiers fired into the air but everyone kept chanting.'

'What about the ref?' asked Lucy.

'You could tell he wanted to run away but he blew his whistle and the game started again. But they still could not score. The Tigers defended like, like . . .'

'TIGERS,' said Rahel. 'From home we could hear the roar from the stadium. We could hear "Tigers, Tigers, Tigers", and it sounded like ten thousand tigers growling. We heard the shots and Mama panicked. We were listening to the radio and the commentator said the Bulls had only fired in the air, but we were really scared.'

'Then the Tigers scored again!' said Pablo, his eyes sparkling.

'Rafael, our best player, tackled a Bulls player in midfield, got the ball, and just . . .' Pablo stood up, swung his leg back and executed a perfect blast which sent Lucy's ball careering into the bush on the other side of the creek. 'The ref just stood there with his mouth open. And then the full-time siren sounded and the crowd went mad.'

'It was like a hundred thousand tigers! That night there were parties all over town, but the biggest one was at Carlos' house. All of us went. And that's when it happened.'

'What?' said Lucy nervously.

'The Bull soldiers came and arrested the entire Tigers team, including Carlos' papa. They hated him for starting that Tigers chant. But they took Carlos and his mama too! The next morning, Carlos was taken to the camp, and the day after that his parents' bodies were dumped in the street outside their house. It was a warning to everybody else. But it didn't work! That is when my mama and papa joined the rebels. They had lost their best friends. Just for winning a soccer match.'

'They did the same thing all over the city,' said Pablo. 'Many people died that night. And after that, no one wanted to see soccer matches. The All-Island League was dead.'

There was a cough behind them

'Talking about me?' said Carlos. He was holding Lucy's soccer ball.

No one answered.

Carlos looked challengingly at Lucy: 'Penalty shootout?'

They picked two big trees for goalposts. Lucy was to be in goal for five shots, then Carlos. Carlos tried to send his first shot whizzing close to the left-hand tree but Lucy was onto him, diving spectacularly. A heavy frown descended on his face and he marched, muttering, back to the penalty spot. Whatever he said to himself must have worked. Lucy did her best but couldn't stop him pounding the next *four* home. *He might be skinny but he was good!*

Lucy's turn. She bent to take her runners off, because Carlos wasn't wearing any.

'Leave your shoes on,' Carlos said and his condescending tone made her even more determined to take them off. And a few seconds later Carlos got his first shock. Lucy dummied and slammed the first goal home. And the second. But Carlos, frowning as he walked back to the goal line, must have have cottoned onto her technique because he stopped the third triumphantly. Now the pressure was on! If Lucy missed again Carlos would be king of the camp. That's how it felt, anyway. And it really hurt, kicking without shoes!

'Think like an iceberg,' she told herself. That was what her very first coach, Mrs Morias, used to say when she was teaching them to kick penalties and boys from other teams stood on the sideline, jeering and laughing.

'Get cold and icy,' she would say. 'If you let them turn you into a puddle of water, you will miss. Think like an iceberg!'

At first Lucy hadn't known what she meant but once, when the goalie was grinning and pulling faces at her as she lined up the shot, whispering, 'Girls can't kick' so only Lucy could hear, she tried it. It worked! She let his grins and taunts bounce off her ice-hard skin and pounded the ball home before he knew what hit him.

Lucy took a deep breath, went icy and *bamm* – the ball shot through the gap on Carlos' left. Carlos frowned. She lined up the next shot, felt the ice – and booted the ball to his right. Four all! Game over.

Then, to their own surprise, they both started laughing. Rahel made Carlos and Lucy shake hands and then raised both their fists in the air while Pablo cheered. One minute they hated each other, the next they were planning a full-on match with everyone playing and Ricardo and Toro had scrambled down off the rocks and wanted to start *now*. But then Carlos began to cough. Lucy watched, shocked, as his thin frame shuddered, as though coughs had taken over his whole body. And when he finally stopped coughing he looked angry again and walked off on his own.

Rahel and Pablo had gone very quiet.

'He should go to a doctor,' said Lucy. Then she remembered how complicated this all was. Suddenly the pool looked great. She dived in without another word, swimming underwater until it hurt. Surfacing behind the waterfall, she climbed up into the cave, towards the shaft of sunlight at the back. The hole it shone through in the rock platform above was quite large, and she could haul herself up, and then clamber out, above the waterfall.

'We can use this to get the bedding into the cave without getting it wet,' she said aloud.

They'd have to watch it when it rained, but most of the cave would stay nice and dry. Lucy dropped down and swam back to tell the others. Carlos was back, and still grumpy, but he cheered up when he saw the cave.

'There is room here for many people,' he said.

Everyone got excited then, but it still took ages to get the cave set up because they had to haul everything up over the rocks and across the creek. Toro and Ricardo weren't much help because they kept jumping off the waterfall instead. Lucy heard Rahel going off at her little brother. She didn't understand the words but wondered if it was anything like what she had just finished saying to Ricardo, most of which Mum wouldn't have liked. Rahel rolled her eyes at Lucy and they both laughed.

They swam again and sat on the hot rocks to dry off, devouring the contents of Lucy's pack. Then Rahel reminded them they were supposed to be planning a jailbreak. Ricardo suggested they give the guards notes from their mothers telling them they had to go home because they had forgotten their lunch.

Carlos said he thought they shouldn't do anything on a Saturday night ever again, because the Bull Commander would probably be there next time. Pablo agreed the guards would be more wary now. They wouldn't be drunk any more.

Carlos got grumpy again. 'If you would give me that gun, I could shoot some of them and scare the rest off.'

Rahel shook her head impatiently. 'Don't you see? There should be no guns on Telares. We were happy before the Bulls came with their guns.'

'Yes, and now we have to take their guns from them,' Carlos said ominously.

But Rahel just shook her head again. 'Besides, one gun against so many is not enough. If we start to shoot at them and hurt one of them . . .' Rahel cut her own throat with a pointed finger before saying in a deathly voice, '*Reprisals*! They will kill the others'.

'But then who would make their stuff for them?' asked Lucy.

'They have lots of children at the workshop,' said Rahel.

'How many?'

'Perhaps a hundred,' said Carlos.

'A hundred! I thought you said there were only about twenty more. And why don't they sleep with you at the mermaid house?'

'We sick make their thoughts,' said Toro.

'Huh?'

Rahel explained:

'The other children are from the local village, near the camp. Their mamas and papas are not rebels, or if they are, the Bulls don't know yet. So the children are allowed home at night but their families know they must deliver them every morning or they will be arrested. But they don't let us talk to the village children.'

'They tell them we have rebel germs,' sneered Carlos, 'a sickness, so they will not answer if we do succeed in speaking to them'.

Rahel cut in before Lucy could respond.

'Tonight we go scouting. We will follow the Bull Commander. He does not sleep at the jungle jail with the others. We must find out where he goes.'

'Then we will ambush him,' said Toro happily.

Lucy looked at her watch. 'We've only got three hours before sunset, which means it's almost dark in Telares.'

'We must go now!' Rahel jumped up.

'We cannot all go,' said Pablo slowly, nodding towards Angel.

He was right. But who should go?

'Penalty shootout?'

Which was how Carlos and Lucy ended up going down the tunnel with only the Tiger-cat at their heels.

29

Reprisals

Once again, Lucy didn't need a torch. She was definitely getting better at this. She strode confidently ahead of Carlos until her questing mind listened and *felt* the tunnel fork. A little later her mind stretched into space. The bat cave. They hurried towards the dim light at the end of the tunnel. Lucy felt a disturbance in the air as the Tiger-cat flew at the obstructing greenery. Carlos gasped as the creepers dissolved, and then he stood staring at the last light of a Telarian sunset.

In no time they were at the clearing. They crept around the back of the house, passing close to the fence where shiny strands of wire marked hasty repairs, and then Carlos turned into the jungle. After a few minutes, Lucy spied a clearing very like the one they had just left, but with a corrugated iron building. Carlos crept forward, too close for Lucy's liking.

They heard a shout and dropped to the ground. Two huge doors at the front of the building swung open, as though a hungry metal beast had opened its metal mouth to eat. Instead, the beast poked out its tongue as two columns of marching children emerged, flanked by rifle-wielding guards. They kept coming and coming, endlessly. Lucy counted and was up to ninety when a voice cried out and the children froze. At another shout they swung right, and headed into the jungle. Lucy could see the exhaustion on their faces. Then she saw something unexpected: a gang of silent adults standing in the disappearing light at the edge of the clearing, as if waiting. They gathered the children close and disappeared into the gloom of the trees.

Another order was barked from the building and another group of children marched out of the metal mouth. Lucy counted seventeen. They were more frightened than the others. Cowed. They kept their heads down and scrambled quickly out under the accusing eyes of two guards.

Then in the last seconds of the day, another soldier stepped out: the Bull Commander. He stood alert as the children went by, eyes following every move, his mouth fixed in that gruesome smile. Then he glanced sharply up to where Lucy and Carlos lay hiding at the edge of the clearing.

Something about the Commander really chilled Lucy. There *was* something different about him. He wasn't like the militia. He was looking up into the jungle as though he knew someone was there; as though he could smell them. Dad had told her that dogs smelled fear. The smiling soldier was poised and alert like a hunting dog.

Lucy held her breath. She prayed he couldn't see them in the semi-darkness. Her prayers were answered. The Commander shut the doors of the building and jogged after the guards and the second sad, crooked line of children. Lucy could see them stumbling up the path, the little ones only just keeping up.

Lucy and Carlos waited a few minutes and then retraced their steps, creeping through the undergrowth back to the rickety old house and their vantage point overlooking the clearing.

Just as night fell, flashing torches and shouted orders signalled the arrival of the seventeen children. The small, weary figures were marched up the stairs and into the dark house.

The guards gathered around the fire pit and coaxed some coals into life, while the Commander stood apart, smoking.

Then a figure stepped into the firelight – a stooped old woman, carrying a stick over her shoulders, with two buckets hooked over each end. She lowered her burden, removed bowls from one of the buckets and filled them with some kind of food from the other. The Commander took his without a word.

The guards ate eagerly. The woman spoke to the Commander, pointing first at the old building and then at the bucket of food. He shook his head, making an angry, dismissive gesture. Lucy heard Carlos' sharp intake of breath as the old woman hoisted the buckets back onto her shoulders and hobbled away,

Lucy knew what the scene below meant, without being told. Reprisal. These kids were not being fed because the others had escaped.

Lucy felt fury rise but then it turned to fear as a light swung towards her. The torch on the Commander's helmet glared at her. He was walking straight towards her.

Lucy pressed her face into the ground, which shook with each heavy step. *Crunch, crunch*, closer and closer! A few more steps and he would be upon them. Lucy tensed, ready to run – then heard a distinctive splashing sound.

False alarm.

Even Bulls had to go!

Lucy dared to lift her head. Watching the Commander's retreating back, she noticed she could still feel his steps with every muscle in her body. She felt the vibration, even as he reached the fire. Had fear made her senses sharper?

The Commander barked an order, the guards jumped to their feet and saluted, and then he marched out of the clearing, in the same direction as Bucket Lady, his rifle at the ready.

Carlos touched Lucy's shoulder and they stood up and crept sideways. The Commander had a head start *and* a head torch.

Lucy loved the moonlight. That hunting feeling swept over her and she padded lightly after Carlos, all her senses stretching to find the way. When the workshop loomed in front, he led her around the back, and about thirty paces into the jungle.

Had the Commander slipped past? No. Lucy felt a vibration in the ground, swelling up through the soles of her feet; a steady excitement, like a beating heart. Then Carlos pointed. A light bobbed in the darkness. A minute later, she heard the stealthy crunch of boots, their rhythm matching the vibration under Lucy's feet. Again, she had *felt* him coming before she saw or heard him!

He went past and they watched until night swallowed

the beam of his torch. Carlos slipped among the trees, careful not to walk on the path itself, but staying close to it. All the time Lucy felt the Commander's weight on the earth, shifting and shaking under her feet. She was following a tremor, not a soldier.

There was a sharp crack as Carlos stepped on a branch. Lucy felt the Commander stop dead. She grabbed Carlos' hand and pulled him to the ground. With her chin in the dirt again, she felt a stronger shuddering under her body. He was coming back! A beam of light bounced off the trees above them. And then – the forest cracked open!

The thunder of his weapon brought branches crashing down around Carlos and Lucy. They huddled together, as the Commander's helmet light swung crazily, ripping the shadows apart, and his gun blasted the trees to pieces.

In the stinging silence that followed, Lucy lay like a stone. She tasted dirt. The Commander shouted once, hoarsely, then she felt his stampeding feet heading away down the track.

'The tiger . . . he is afraid. He thought we were the tiger.' Carlos' voice was shaking.

Lucy felt her pounding heart gradually slow. She concentrated. She could still feel the Commander's feet, and even sense what direction he was heading.

'I can feel him running,' she breathed to Carlos. 'Come on!'

She padded down the path, letting her feet do the listening. She would know if he stopped again. It was Carlos' turn to follow.

The path swung to the right, onto a long flat stretch, before twisting downhill. Soon they saw the first lights of the village. Shouts wafted up. They crept closer and saw a circle of huts on stilts, spaced around a central clearing with a fire in the middle. Lucy smelt smoke and something else familiar . . . They were near the sea!

They went as close as they dared to the first round hut, clinging to the shadow of a mighty tree. The Commander barked harsh orders to a crowd gathered around the fire. Carlos translated.

'He is saying a tiger is about, and is telling everyone to get inside their huts . . . but first they must make the fire bigger.'

Lucy saw, on the far side of the clearing, someone who didn't seem to share the alarm: a young woman, squatting on the top step of her hut, wearing a bright sarong. Long dark hair fell over her shoulders. The Commander swaggered over to her.

'What is he saying?'

'He boasts he shot one tiger and wounded another.'

'Liar, liar, pants on fire!'

'I beg your pardon?'

But the Commander was speaking again and the young woman answered. She got up and went behind the curtain, the Commander following.

'She asked where was the body if he had shot a tiger? He said he would bring the body tomorrow and make a rug for her bed.'

Lucy and Carlos crawled back to the path and began walking. Part way up, Lucy's feet began to tingle. The sensation grew stronger.

'There's someone ahead,' she hissed.

Carlos listened, then shook his head. Lucy lay flat on

the ground. That was better. A rush of energy, then, not exactly a picture, but an impression formed. One person, creeping slowly as though they didn't want to be heard. A guard disturbed by the gunfire?

They moved forward cautiously on the twisting track and along the flat stretch. Just before they reached the workshop Lucy grabbed Carlos' hand and dropped to the ground.

'He's stopped,' she whispered.

The moon sailed out from behind a cloud and Lucy suddenly had a clear view of the clearing – and the Ponytail Zombie! He was so close Lucy could see the expression on his face. He didn't look like a zombie, he looked alert and watchful. He stood in the clearing for about a minute without moving.

Then Lucy felt a tremor in the ground from the other direction. Someone else was coming! Someone smaller and lighter than the Commander. Whoever it was gave a low whistle, and the Ponytail Zombie stiffened, and slipped into the jungle towards the sound. Lucy felt his steps and that of the stranger fade into the night.

It was nearly dusk when Lucy and Carlos climbed out of the pit. Lucy was relieved to see Ricardo step from behind a tree with T-Tongue. There was no sign of the other kids, thank goodness. It was dangerous near the house with Grandma around. She'd invite them in for chocolate cake and have their whole life story out of them in fifteen minutes flat, even if they pretended not to speak English.

Lucy swung out, checked Grandma wasn't around and signalled all clear.

'See you in the morning,' she said to Carlos.

'Yes, I will see you,' he said, in that formal Telarian way.

Suddenly Lucy knew something had changed between them. They had barely talked to each other, but down there in the jungle, they'd been on the same side.

Carlos melted into the bush.

30
Angel's Revenge

Ricardo woke up early and jumped on Lucy. He wanted to know again what had happened last night, even though she had told him up at the pit. He couldn't believe the bit about the kids in the jungle jail not getting fed.

'I'll tell you again when we get up the mountain,' she said, trying to smother him with her sleeping bag.

After breakfast, they hurried to the clearing. Pablo was making ten-year-old tea again. Lucy made a mental note to get fresh teabags. Angel was building a mud castle under a tree near the creek, Carlos was practising tricks with the soccer ball, and Toro was jumping up and down, trying to tell Ricardo about some mission he had been on early in the morning with Pablo. Rahel shushed him.

'First we require a full report from Lucy and Carlos.'

'You go first,' said Lucy to Carlos. His face darkened as he described the old lady with her buckets and how she had gone away without feeding the children.

There was silence.

'Reprisal,' hissed Rahel. 'I told you . . .' She had that look on her face, the one she'd had when she first told Lucy they were going back to rescue the others: extremely calm, *extremely determined.*

Lucy told them about the Commander firing at the 'tiger' on the way to the village. Toro and Ricardo made her tell it three times. Finally she got to describe the village and how the Commander seemed to be staying in Sarong Lady's hut.

Then they got to the bit about the Ponytail Zombie and the stranger in the dark. Toro and Pablo both started talking at once about their own mission. They said they had been lying in the jungle near the clearing when something big came crashing towards them. Just when they thought they were about to get trampled by an elephant, it fell over and started singing. It was the Ponytail Zombie. He was clutching a bottle of wine and every now and then he muttered to himself about having to catch the 'girl ghost'. He kept saying the 'girl ghost' had turned into a snake and chased him and how he was going to squeeze the 'girl ghost' around the neck. He made so much noise that the guards 'on duty' around the fire woke up.

Toro looked at Lucy and said very carefully, 'I almost wetted myself'.

'No,' said Ricardo helpfully, 'You almost wet yourself'.

'I almost wet yourself,' said Toro perfectly.

'Great,' said Lucy, much embarrassed, as everyone started to laugh – but she didn't feel great about Ponytail Zombie wanting to *strangle* her.

Pablo kept going.

'Then the militia arrested the Ponytail Zombie!'

'Arrested him?!' Mass personal jinx.

'Yes!'

Everyone cheered.

'The guards said the Commander had ordered them to arrest the Ponytail Zombie on sight,' Pablo continued. 'He had been missing since the breakout and the Commander blamed him for it. Besides, bottles of wine kept disappearing from the Commander's own supply. They looked at the bottle in Ponytail's hands and handcuffed him. Then the Commander arrived. He yelled at Ponytail so loudly, that we got very frightened.'

'Yes, I almost . . .' Toro said, but everyone shushed him.

'But the Ponytail Zombie just kept muttering about the 'girl ghost' who had turned into a snake and pointing at his own throat,' Pablo said. 'And when the Commander *examined* his throat and saw all the bruises from the snake he told the guards to release him. But he really screamed at them all and said if they let one more rebel child escape they would be shot. They were really scared!'

Then Pablo dropped a bombshell: 'The last thing the Commander said was that proper Bull soldiers would arrive soon to take over the jungle jail. He said he was sick of the militia and their carelessness and stupid superstitions. He said proper Bull soldiers would laugh at ghosts and not be afraid of tigers. Proper Bull soldiers would shoot the tiger and never let any children escape.'

That shut everyone up.

After a minute, everyone began arguing. Carlos was still going on about the gun and Rahel was still ignoring him. Lucy got sick of listening and looked about for Angel. She was playing under the tree, silently absorbed.

Lucy wandered over, and was surprised at how clever Angel had been. She had made a family of stick people out of twigs lashed together with vines, with gumnuts for heads, and she'd built a castle from creek mud. Three stick people, two tall, one small, were 'standing' on the mud castle's roof. Nearby, were two more mud buildings, each surrounded by a stick fence. One was empty, the other had big stick people standing outside the fence and many tiny stick people on top. Lucy was amazed at the detail.

'Cool, Angel! Can I play?'

But Angel gazed intently at her handiwork and didn't reply. Then she picked up two big stick people from outside the first fence and 'marched' them to the mud castle, making harsh sounds in her throat, as though she were issuing orders. She climbed them up the castle wall and when they reached the top, charged them at the two other big stick people waiting there, making rumbling sounds in her throat. The attacking stick figures rolled their victims off the castle, into the dirt.

Angel pushed the two fallen stick people over to the empty mud building and 'locked' them both behind the fence. She took the smallest stick prisoner to the mud building where all the other tiny figures stood on the roof. She made a little stick prisoner jump from the roof and begin to gouge a hole in the mud wall. Then she picked up all the prisoners and charged them at the fence. They broke through and Angel directed a series of battles, holding a prisoner in one hand and a guard in the other. The fights lasted a few seconds each and the stick prisoners always won.

The game wasn't over yet. Angel walked her victorious stick people to the second fence and knocked it down. She released the two fallen stick people inside, then picked up all the escapees and marched them to the castle, up the walls and stood them on the roof. Then, very carefully, Angel dismantled the fences and put them around the castle instead. Wearing an expression of profound but silent satisfaction, she examined the completed fence, then she picked up the defeated stick guards and trotted towards the fireplace.

'Angel!'

Angel stopped, turned to look at Lucy, and then kept going, faster. Lucy ran. When she caught up, Angel was staring at the stick guards as they writhed and curled on the red coals, then burst into bright flame.

31

Blue Elephants

Angel's game had been freaky. Once, when she was little, Lucy had tied up Mandy's Barbie and cut its hair – she couldn't remember why now – but she could remember the look on Mrs Hoffman's face just before she rang Lucy's mum to come and take her home. But Lucy had *never* staged a mass jail breakout of prisoner Barbies and then *burned* the guard Barbies! That was way over the top.

Ricardo had let her tie him to the clothesline once, after Dad had made them watch a movie about a German concentration camp. Ricardo was supposed to be a Nazi guard who Lucy had captured, except he kept getting it wrong and saying, 'I don't want to be a Nasty any more. Why can't you be the Nasty?' Mum had come out and said Lucy was being *really* Nasty and to untie him straight away.

Carlos' raised voice distracted her.

'. . . And the old lady who feeds them – if she was on *our* side she would *poison* all the guards.'

Rahel looked upset.

'She is just an old lady! The Bull Commander *makes* her bring the food!'

Pablo looked anxiously from Rahel to Carlos and back again.

'The old lady fed us too,' he said. 'We would be dead without her. And the others will be dead if the Commander does not let her feed them soon.'

Carlos drew an angry cross in the ground with his toe, but didn't reply.

'I have been thinking,' said Rahel. 'The drugs the guards give to the small children – if we could steal them and give them to the guards instead . . .'

Everyone began talking at once.

'Bucket Lady,' said Lucy. 'We'll get the drugs and put them in her buckets of food.'

'The Commander keeps the drugs with him at all times,' said Carlos. 'I heard the guards talking about it.'

'Then we'll just have to get them from him,' said Lucy.

Everyone went very quiet.

Then they all started arguing again.

By Telarian sunset, they had a plan. Ricardo and Toro had given up complaining about being chosen to mind Angel while Carlos, Pablo, Rahel and Lucy went back to the jungle jail. Rahel and Pablo were going to find out where Bucket Lady lived. That left Carlos and Lucy to check out Sarong Lady's hut and try to steal the drugs.

When they trotted down the track to the pit, the Tiger-cat was waiting on the stairs. Lucy checked Grandma wasn't in the back yard and then they swung down. As soon as she entered the tunnel Lucy was aware of that strange heightening of her senses. She stretched her mind and *listened* to the dark.

It was almost dark when they reached the end of the tunnel. Lucy decided to try something. She padded lightly, trustingly, towards the greenery, and it fell away, parting cleanly to let her pass. She shivered and grinned back at the others. Then the Tiger-cat took off, leading them into the gathering night. Close to the edge of the clearing they began to crawl.

Familiar sounds broke the peace – stamping boots, harsh words. The gang of kids stumbled in and were locked up. Again the Commander smoked a cigarette, while the militiamen stoked the fire.

Pablo and Rahel slipped away to hide on the other side of the clearing near the path, ready for Bucket Lady's arrival. Lucy's eyes were fixed on the Commander. Every now and again he glanced up into the jungle. Again she was reminded of a hunting dog, a predator. She shivered. When Bucket Lady hobbled into the clearing, bent nearly double under the weight of her buckets, he took his meal without a word. Once again Bucket Lady pointed at the second bucket and at the locked gate. Once again the Commander waved her away.

Lucy and Carlos slipped deeper into the jungle, behind the rickety old house. Every few minutes, Lucy would stop and place her palms on the ground. Somewhere up in front she felt the heavy, slow tread of Bucket Lady, followed by the double tremor of two lighter pairs of feet: Rahel and Pablo. When she checked again, further down the track, she felt a tremor behind, and whispered to Carlos, 'The Commander has finished eating. He's coming'.

He didn't question her instinct, but led her deeper into the jungle, on a twisting path, until the lights of the village beckoned through the trees below. They waited a few minutes, listening and then Lucy heard a sound above and, looking up, saw the Tiger-cat in a tree. It was draped on a low branch, apparently completely relaxed, its eyes gleaming. Without thinking, Lucy sprang lightly up and climbed onto a strong branch with a good view.

In the centre of the circle of huts, a fire blazed. There was a flash of colour and Sarong Lady appeared on the steps of her hut. At the sight of her, the Tiger-cat uttered a low growl and padded along the branch, bending it until Lucy thought it would break.

The Tiger-cat growled again, concentrating fiercely on the scene below and Lucy suddenly felt as if her whole being was swept up in its feline intensity. A hot current pulsed through her and she felt charged and brightly connected to the Tiger-cat. She imagined herself lit up like a Christmas tree.

The Tiger-cat crouched lower, still staring at the young woman below and Lucy's charged mind reached fever pitch. It was as though her breath itself flowed into the Tiger-cat's bright gaze. At the same instant, the subject of the cat's attention looked up in surprise, as though someone had called her name. She scanned the trees and an image flashed into Lucy's mind, just before Sarong Lady turned, hurried back to her hut and climbed the stairs, urgency in every step. At the same time, the Commander appeared on the other side of the clearing, heading for her stairs.

The Tiger-cat relaxed and Lucy flopped against the fork of the tree, exhausted. Slowly the sweat on her body cooled. But she could not shake the image from her mind of a candle-lit room, and Sarong Lady placing a dark bottle on a table near a window, with the spreading branches of a tree just outside.

Lucy knew with absolute certainty that the Commander's drugs were in the hut and that the tree was her ladder up. It was as if the Tiger-cat had plucked the image from Sarong Lady's mind, like a goldfish from a pond. She felt the silken brush of the cat's fur as it slipped past her, and after a while she gathered the energy to climb down, to find an irritable Carlos.

'Why did you take so long? What did you see?'

'Shhh! Sarong Lady was there again. And something weird happened. I can't really explain it. It was as if the Tiger-cat used me to call her. I don't know why, but I think she's important.'

'Call her? You didn't call out.'

'No, I know. It was something different. I can't really explain it. But the Tiger-cat showed me where the drugs are. They're in Sarong Lady's hut, near the window and there's a tree we can climb up. But the Commander is there. We're going to have to get rid of him somehow.'

Lucy and Carlos padded back up the track, and soon the dark mass of the workshop was upon them. Lucy felt a double tremor in the earth again. Pablo and Rahel? She hoped so.

Carlos' low whistle cut like a knife into the night's inky skin. Silence. Then a wobbly return whistle came from the clearing in front of the workshop. Carlos whistled again and first Pablo, then Rahel stepped from the trees.

'We found Bucket Lady's house,' Rahel whispered. She was holding the bunch of keys she had taken from the drunken soldier the other night.

'And I think I know where the Commander keeps his drugs,' breathed Lucy.

'Shhh! Let's get inside,' said Carlos.

Rahel unlocked the workshop's metal mouth and it gaped open. Lucy tried not to imagine she was walking into the belly of a metal monster, about to be digested.

'Torch!' whispered Carlos and Lucy flicked it on to reveal a series of frames along one wall, holding half-finished rugs. They all had the same distinctive, brightly coloured pattern, mostly scarlet, black and gold, but none was as beautiful as the tiger rug.

Lucy took a step forward to see better – and something snaky whipped against her face. She reared back, choking with fear. Carlos grabbed the torch and and swung it around to reveal a lifeless rope hanging from the ceiling beams. As if to prove she wasn't afraid, Lucy reached out and yanked on it, just as the three others hissed, 'Don't!'

There was an unrecognisable noise and Lucy fell beneath a rain of missiles. Some kind of huge blindfold wrapped itself around her face, as blows landed on her head and body. She fought back, arms flailing wildly. She scrambled to sit up, clawing fabric off her head . . . *and found her favourite soccer ball in her lap!* Scattered at her feet and rolling out of the range of Carlos' torchlight, were about three hundred more.

If any guard had ventured out he would have heard sounds previously unknown in that workshop. Four kids trying desperately to stifle their laughter, mirth bouncing off the tin walls.

They collected themselves, and the balls. Each bore the same stamp as Lucy's one at home – a blue elephant in a circle of ten stars – and the brand Ten Star Jumbo. No doubt about it. They were the same as her bestest, bestest soccer ball, not the daggy old one they had been kicking around the clearing, but the one Dad had given her the last time she saw him.

The fabric that had blindfolded Lucy was like a big hammock. They piled the balls back in and Carlos winched it back up to the rafters.

On a bench nearby Lucy saw thick needles and heavy black thread, plus sheets of leather: white, blue and gold. She went closer. Some of the blue and gold sheets had been cut into six-sided shapes, with holes punched around the edges. There was another heap of white leather shapes, five-sided ones: white pentagons, stamped with a blue elephant in a circle of ten stars.

As Lucy picked one up, she felt someone behind her.

'See the toys we make for people like you?'

The acid in Carlos' voice burned away all laughter. It was as though he blamed *her!*

She turned on him hotly.

'You don't make them for peop—' Her words petered out as she looked down at the blue elephant pentagon in her hand.

Carlos turned sharply away.

Clutching the pentagon, Lucy watched in furious frustration, as Carlos left the workshop. Last night they had felt like a team, but that feeling had vanished like a drop of water on a fire. How unfair was that? He was just blaming her because she wasn't Telarian and she didn't have to make her own soccer balls. Zombie! Except she did own one of these balls. But that wasn't her fault either. The argument went around and around in her head.

'Come, Lucy, it's time to go,' said Rahel. Was that sympathy in her quiet voice?

As hot tears threatened, Lucy lingered only long enough to pocket a handful of blue elephant pentagons.

32

Never Again

Lucy woke up staring at Ricardo's bed. Empty. She swung her feet out of bed and half-heartedly kicked some more undies over the tiger. She felt the pile of the rug between her toes, plush, luxurious.

Grandma bustled in before she could check it out.

'Any washing, Lucy, love? Where are those pants you wore yesterday? Good heavens! I can't even walk in here. You'll have to tidy this room.'

'Ricardo messed it up,' Lucy grumped back, even though she knew that was really unfair.

'Never mind, you can both help. There they are . . .' Grandma headed for Lucy's pants, lying crumpled on the floor.

'*No!*' The elephant pentagons in her leg pocket! 'I mean yes! I mean I'll bring them out with the rest of my stuff.' She dived out of bed to get there before Grandma could pick a path through the chaos.

'All right! Keep your pants on!'

When Grandma had gone, Lucy ran her hand gently

over the tiger's stripes. It was definitely softer and more luxurious than before, but it didn't cheer her up. She felt the pentagons and thought about last night. It didn't help, so she hid them under her mattress and wandered into the kitchen to eat a desultory breakfast. For once, Cocoa Puffs were tasteless. She plodded disconsolately outside. Ricardo wasn't around and neither was T-Tongue. Even he had deserted her.

Last night they'd locked up the workshop and crept back to the tunnel, parting without a word at the stairs. The others had gone their way and she had gone hers.

That was fine by Lucy. She was never going to the clearing again. She would organise food, but Ricardo would have to be delivery boy. She looked over her shoulder and saw the tunnel closed, walled up with red and brown clay. Good.

Lucy gazed bleakly down the path. It wasn't her fault. She hadn't bought the stupid ball. Dad had, and he wouldn't have if he'd known about the kids. Carlos was a zombie. He didn't even *know* she had a Ten Star Jumbo.

Yet.

He was going to love that.

No, he wasn't. He was never going to find out, because she was never going anywhere near him again.

It wasn't her fault his life was bad. Her life wasn't great either. She hardly ever saw Dad any more. She knew that wasn't like Dad being murdered, but that didn't make it feel any better. She missed playing soccer with him and watching the World Cup replays on TV. Lots of things. Coke for breakfast. And it wasn't her fault the stupid Bulls took over Telares. Carlos could go on missions on his own from now on. With any luck he might get caught. Maybe a tiger would eat him.

A velvet head pushed insistently on her kneecap. The Tiger-cat. At least it hadn't deserted her. It purred and rubbed against her calves as Lucy traced the markings on its head. Then it did something very un-cat like. It jumped lightly onto her lap and put both paws on her shoulders. Lucy knew what was coming and closed her eyes. She wasn't in the mood.

Ow! A padded paw whopped her on her cheek. She opened her eyes . . . and was caught in the spotlight of the Tiger-cat's golden gaze. After a suspended, shuddering moment, the stripy feline face melted into the lined and wrinkled one of the old lady the Tiger-cat had beamed at her that very first morning on the steps. But she wasn't crying in this video clip. She was saying the same words over and over again, looking directly from those tawny eyes, deep into Lucy's: 'Little flower, little flower, little flower'.

The words were still ringing in Lucy's head when she shuddered back inside her skin. They echoed as she watched the Tiger-cat stroll down the path, tail flicking, and disappear into the bush. Great. What did that mean? She was still wondering when Ricardo jumped on her and almost toppled them both into the pit. He saw the look in her eye and hurtled down the path, bursting into the kitchen with Lucy, murderous, behind. Grandma and Mum were both there.

'Stop it, you two.'

Adult personal jinx.

'What's up, Lucy? You don't look very happy.'

Double adult personal jinx.

Mum and Grandma didn't agree on politics but they seemed to share the same brain about everything else. Especially Lucy.

'Nothing. I'm fine.'

'Well, get dressed, then, I'm taking you to the movies.'

'Well, get dressed, then, Grandma's taking you to the movies.'

See?

33

Science Meets Soccer

An hour to kill before the movie and Kurrawong Mall was packed. Ricardo was bounding about cheerfully, like a monkey. Lucy wasn't in the mood. She tried to walk right past Star Sports. Usually Mum couldn't keep her out of there. Even if she didn't have pocket money, she still loved it. She would look at everything: balls, shoes, boots, even things for sports she didn't play, like hockey, tennis, spear-fishing, abseiling. She knew all the prices. She knew when they went up or down, when new lines came in. She had spent hours in there with Janella fantasising about getting the most expensive boots and balls and trainers and track-suits. And she really wanted a skateboard.

Today, she didn't want to know; but Ricardo was already inside, sucked into a crowd of happy shoppers. Grandma dragged her in and they followed Ricardo's blond head to the punching bags. He was telling Grandma she should buy a huge one. For herself.

Lucy left them to it and drifted up and down the aisles. She saw a crowd gathered around a crate of soccer balls.

Just what she needed. The sign hanging from the ceiling read: 'The revolutionary Ten Star Jumbo. Science meets soccer. Tough as ten elephants. $40.'

Lucy stepped around the crowd, but there was no escape. On the counter were another sign and a pile of leaflets.

TEN STAR JUMBO

Your new Ten Star Jumbo features revolutionary technology
1 The best leather, scientifically treated to
make it as tough as elephant hide
2 Lovingly hand-stitched by trained technicians
in our state-of-the-art workshops

They say elephants never forget
Ten Star Jumbo: you'll never forget.

Yeah, right! That was enough for Lucy. She crumpled the leaflet and threw it at the crate.

'Pick that up, young lady,' said a curt voice.

Lucy blushed, put the leaflet in her pocket and hunched off up the aisle. Luckily the crowd was so busy fighting to get hold of a Ten Star Jumbo, they didn't notice her minus-ten-star exit.

At the end of the aisle, she looked back. The assistant stared pointedly. Lucy turned and kept walking past tennis rackets (stupid game for dorks who couldn't play soccer), fishing rods (who'd want to do that?), abseiling ropes (needed by rocks-for-brains losers), cricket (for kids too dorky to play anything else), punching bags (maybe Ricardo had a point).

Lucy wandered to the back of the shop, near the layby

counter. There was a long queue. A couple of kids had Ten Star Jumbos. Near Lucy was a door marked MANAGER. It opened, revealing a familiar profile.

Lucy ducked behind a rack of surfie gear and slid closer, parting wet suits to get a better look. Yep, Nigel Scar-Skull, talking to a man in a suit. She could only hear a few words.

'No problem . . . one thousand . . . Wednesday . . . won't be sorry . . . I'm telling you . . . ten-star quality.'

Then he smiled that stretchy smile, shook the man's hand and began to walk towards the wetsuit rack. Lucy felt a hand on her shoulder. It was the assistant again, wanting to know if she was interested in buying a wetsuit or just wanted to wipe her nose on one? Because that's what it looked like, and if she wasn't buying a wetsuit, perhaps she would like to leave the shop unless there was something else she *was* interested in buying. Sarcasm plus. Lucy pointed hopefully at the abseiling ropes and ducked out of the aisle.

Over the heads of the crowd, Lucy tracked Nigel Scar-Skull as he left the shop. Near the checkout, she saw him shaking hands enthusiastically with the coach of the team Lucy's side had beaten in the Grand Final. He had a shopping trolley full of Ten Star Jumbos.

Lucy's head was still spinning when she reached the movie theatre. When she was sitting in the dark watching the credits roll up, she suddenly remembered the old lady. She had forgotten to ask Grandma if she had found out anything! On the stairs, the other morning, it had seemed so urgent that they find the old lady, but then they had discovered Telares. Rescuing the kids had overtaken everything.

'Yes, I did find out,' whispered Grandma, 'but shh . . . I'll tell you later.'

Lucy had to sit through the whole movie wishing she had let Ricardo watch his dumb cartoon. Grandma had got sick of them fighting and picked something neither of them really wanted to see. It was the longest movie in history, and the most boring. And Debbie Lucas and Annette Palmer were down the front and she really didn't want to run into them. They'd start asking why hadn't they seen her around lately, even though they didn't even like her and she *really* didn't like them. And Grandma would probably answer them. And that would be bad. Very bad.

Lucy and Ricardo didn't agree on much but they had a deal about this: they weren't going to tell anyone at school about moving house. Not about living in West Kurrawong instead of East Kurrawong. Not about Mum and Dad breaking up. Nothing. Especially not about living in the worst house in Kurrawong.

Lucy felt ashamed about everything. About Mum and Dad. About their daggy house. Ashamed about owning that stupid soccer ball. Ashamed about being ashamed. She sat with hot, lemon-juice tears squeezing out, trying not to sniffle – if she did, Grandma would fuss and everyone in the theatre would know she was crying at a stupid cartoon that wasn't even sad. Especially when Retardo was laughing his head off next to her.

'Did you like it, kids?' said Grandma as they walked, blinking, out into the sun.

'It was great, Grandma, but what did you find out about the old lady?' Lucy said all in a rush.

'It was great, Grandma. What old lady?' said Ricardo and then he remembered and said, 'Yeah, tell us'.

But Grandma wouldn't tell them until they were sitting on the bus.

'Well, you were right, Ricardo, an old lady did live in that house. Still would if she hadn't got sick a few months back. Remember that cold snap? It snowed up in the mountains and your mum got stuck trying to drive home from the hospital. Putrid weather and you kids refused to put jumpers on and . . .'

Lucy knew the signs. Grandma would be off chattering about horrible storms in history and children who died of pleurisy during World War II for the entire bus trip if she didn't get her back on track.

'Who was she, Grandma?'

'Who *is* she, don't you mean, dear? She's not dead, you know, and she's not haunting your house if that's what you're worried about. But she has been very sick. Her name's Nina Hawthorne and she's in one of those old people's hospitals because she broke her leg and then she got pneumonia.'

Then Ricardo made a fatal mistake: he asked one question too many.

'Which old people's hospital?'

Grandma turned suddenly and stabbed them with her eyes and she didn't look like an old lady any more, even though she still had soft pink cheeks and bright blue eyes and fluffy white hair. She looked just like Mum when she was onto something.

'All right, Mr and Miss Curiosity: what's with the questions?'

Oops. Lucy looked at Ricardo so she didn't have to meet Grandma's sharp eyes and put her foot on top of his, ready to crush it if he showed signs of contradicting her. Then she babbled the first thing in her head

'We thought we'd visit her. You know, do a good deed. Visit a lonely old lady. I made a New Year's resolution to do one good deed that I wouldn't normally do, and this is it. Tell her the old house is OK and nice people are living in it . . .' her voice trailed off and she risked a look at Grandma. Her eyes didn't look stabby any more. They were kind of soft and satisfied.

'I knew you had a kind heart, Lucy, but that's lovely. Really lovely! I'll get Beryl to find out where she is and see if she's well enough for visitors. Poor old thing. Dying quietly on her own somewhere. I hope that doesn't happen to me . . .'

Lucy couldn't imagine Grandma doing anything quietly, not even dying. Right now she had launched into one of her incredibly long sentences that Lucy knew wouldn't finish until they got to their bus stop and by that time she would be talking about something completely different.

Lucy didn't mind. It gave her time to plan her next move. When they clambered off the bus Grandma was so out of breath she didn't notice the ginger cat that stepped out of the bushes and wrapped itself purring around the kids' legs . . . and then just disappeared into thin air. One minute purring and twisting, the next – gone. Lucy and Ricardo looked at each other.

'We'll go around the back way,' Lucy said, as Grandma reached for the mermaid door knocker.

'You can do what you like, I'm not walking another step.

Where's that daughter of mine? Oh there you are, Annie. Lucy's had a lovely idea. A lovely idea.'

'Hi, Mum,' yelled the kids, racing up the side path, into the back yard and up the track. Sitting on the mossy steps was the Tiger-cat.

'Grandma did know Mrs Nina, or Mrs Beryl did,' blurted out Ricardo, 'and we're going to see her tomorrow, Mrs Nina I mean, and she's not dead but she's really old and she's in a home for lost old ladies.'

'Sick old ladies, Retardo,' said Lucy, 'and how many times do I have to tell you, the Tiger-cat doesn't talk?'

34

The Old Lady

That afternoon, Lucy and Ricardo stood on the sweeping driveway of St Theresa's Little Flower Nursing Home. Ahead, up sandstone steps, was a grand verandah with massive marble columns. Two ornately carved wooden doors, with brass handle rings as big as breakfast bowls, yawned open. Giant stone tubs brandishing spiky cacti swords stood either side. A startling red tongue of rug poked out.

'It looks like a castle,' said Ricardo.

'Yeah, it's a haunted one,' said Lucy, forgetting her resolution not to tell him big lies.

Anyway, it was haunted – by someone very much alive. A robust matron in a dark blue uniform and red cardigan appeared at the doors demanding, 'What are you young people doing in this vicinity? The park is in that direction. Go!'

She stood with hands on impressive hips, framed in the doorway, not exactly glaring but clearly difficult – no, *impossible* – to get past. She looked as if she could crush them against the door, if they were rash enough to try to sneak past, just by breathing out.

'We've come to visit Mrs Hawthorne . . .' Lucy's voice trailed off.

Blue Uniform raised her eyebrows.

'She's – she's our great-auntie.'

'Mrs Hawthorne? Well, that's unusual. She only gets one visitor.'

Blue Uniform looked the kids over: both were wearing Grandma's Ninja pants, and Ricardo had his skateboard tucked under his arm.

'I didn't think Nina Hawthorne had any other relatives,' she said, oozing suspicion, 'apart from her nephew. You must be related to him too. Why didn't you come with him? It's very unusual to have children arriving here alone to visit *anyone*. She's been very sick, you know'.

'We're from the other side of the family,' Lucy squeaked.

'Speak up! And give me that wheeled contraption, young man. You're not careering around my establishment on that.'

Ricardo advanced obediently up the stairs and handed his precious deck over, which gave Lucy time to think up a good lie. She had to keep going now she'd started.

'Great-Aunt Nina is Grandma's cousin,' she said and stood, mouth open, fresh out of ideas.

Ricardo got the hang of it, though, drawing on some ancient family skeleton Grandma had found out about someone else at bingo and had told Mum while he was slurping Cocoa Puffs. He remembered every word.

'Our grandma was put in a home because she was a poor little illiterate bugger,' he volunteered.

Lucy looked at Blue Uniform, hesitated, then finished in a rush, 'so it's been a big secret and Great-Auntie Nina doesn't tell anyone.'

'Well! That's quite enough. Indeed! I don't need to know any more. What your parents are thinking of, letting you wander all over the country on your own, I don't know. You'd better follow me.'

Blue Uniform swept back inside, marching up the red rug, skateboard tucked firmly under her don't-argue-with-me arm. Ricardo was suitably impressed.

'Is she a guard? Has she got a gun under her cardie? Does she shoot the old people if they try to escape?'

'Shut up!' hissed Lucy, panicked at how far their lies were taking her.

They marched behind Blue Uniform to the end of the hall, where the red rug swung around a corner and they entered a room with a huge desk. Blue Uniform put the skateboard on top of a heavy safe with a combination lock and fixed the kids with a tough look.

'Names and address?'

Lucy felt sick. Blue Uniform's gold pen was poised over a big black book, filled with names and addresses.

'Lucy and Ricardo,' she stammered. '688 Old Mine Road, West Kurrawong.'

Blue Uniform examined her suspiciously a moment longer before thumbing through the book.

'ABCDEFGH . . . here we are . . . Hawthorne: 688 Old Mine Road. Well, I suppose you must be related if you're living in Mrs Hawthorne's house,' she said, smiling for the first time.

It was like the sun coming out in an iron-grey sky. The

matron changed from a stern block of concrete in a blue uniform into . . . well, *a stern block of human being* in a blue uniform. Not so bad.

'Don't look so terrified. Your great-auntie isn't feeling chirpy today, so she'll welcome cheerful faces, but don't disturb the other patients and you're to stay half an hour *only*. If you had come yesterday I wouldn't have let you in at all, but she's much better today.'

She swept around the desk and steamed down the hallway with Ricardo trotting in her substantial wake. Lucy lagged behind, feeling slightly ill. In ten seconds Blue Uniform would know there weren't any great-nieces or nephews and that they were impostors and she would call the Impostor Help Line and she had their address and then Mum would know they'd been telling lies – big ones.

Lucy stopped imagining herself in jail when she noticed that Blue Uniform was waiting for her outside a door with the number 33 on it. She saw a bed with a blue blanket, the same colour as Blue Uniform's uniform, and a foot in a yellow-and-black striped football sock, pointing at the ceiling. It was attached to a leg in a white plaster cast, and the whole lot was held up in the air by a kind of hoist. Lucy heard Blue Uniform's deep voice.

'I've got a surprise for you, Mrs Hawthorne! Come on, children.'

Maybe it was the stripy sunlight streaming through slatted blinds, but when Lucy looked at the face of the old lady with soft, white plaited hair, propped up on the pillows, she *saw the face of a cat*. Then, just like the Tiger-cat's video clips, the cat face and its stripes blurred and

204

resolved into the wrinkles and laugh lines of a familiar old lady's face.

'Aren't you going to say hello to your great-auntie,' boomed Blue Uniform. 'Cat got your tongue?'

Lucy couldn't speak and Ricardo was frozen to the spot.

'Well, they had plenty to say before, Mrs Hawthorne. Don't let Lucy and Ricardo tire you out. I've told them only half an hour.'

Blue Uniform stomped out and Lucy and Ricardo and 'Great-auntie Nina' were left staring at each other as her footsteps reverberated down the corridor into silence. Ricardo turned to run, but Lucy grabbed his arm, and blurted out the first thing in her head.

'The Tiger-cat sent us!'

35
Euphoria

Strange, but the old lady *didn't* reach for the red alarm button next to her bed. With one jab, she could have brought twenty Blue Uniforms rushing back to see if she was having a heart attack. She began to laugh weakly, which brought on a fit of coughing.

'Well! Look what the cat's dragged in: a niece and nephew I didn't know I had,' she said when she could speak again.

Her voice was crinkly – kind of old and husky, but friendly. She put on a pair of glasses with funny winged corners that made her look even more like a cat and peered more closely at her guests.

'Yes,' said the crinkly voice. 'I recognise you now. Euphoria did very well. Now, what are your names?'

'Lucy.'

'A lovely name. You can call me Nina. What about your brother?'

Something unintelligible from under the bed.

'You can get up you know, young man. I'm much less

fierce than Euphoria . . . or Matron. That's better. What was your name?'

'Ricardo – but we don't know anyone called U-furrier.'

'Euphoria, Ricardo, Euphoria. It means absolute happiness. You're a child, so I know you know what I mean. When are you absolutely happy, Ricardo?'

'When he's eating.'

Ricardo opened his mouth to argue, then he saw the jar of jellybeans on the bedside cabinet. Mrs Hawthorne followed his gaze and offered him the open jar, smiling a crinkly ginger smile at Lucy. Her skin was very pale but her eyes were bright, the same warm colour as toffee or ginger-nut cookies. Ricardo took six red jellybeans and put them all in his mouth at once. Lucy didn't try to stop him. She preferred his jaws glued together.

Mrs Hawthorne lay back on the pillows and considered them carefully before speaking.

'Euphoria is my cat. Well, she belongs to herself really, as I am sure you've realised. We have been friends for many years, since long before the Mermaid House was built, in fact. My nephew told me two children had moved in, and Euphoria made sure I knew what you looked like. But now,' fixing Lucy with a penetrating look through those weirdo winged glasses, 'you must tell me everything'.

No way! Something about those smiling ginger eyes made Lucy want to tell Mrs Hawthorne everything, even the really wacky stuff, but she had promised Rahel not to tell anyone about the Telarian kids.

She made a stumbling beginning.

'Well, we met the Tiger-cat, I mean Eupherbia, on the

stairs and she showed me a picture of you and you were crying . . .'

'Mmmm, nnnggg, mbloow . . .' Ricardo tried to speak.

Mrs Hawthorne looked at him with her eyebrows raised and then expectantly at Lucy.

'. . . and I don't know how, but we just kind of knew that you used to live in the Mermaid House, and . . .'

'Mmmm, nnnggg, mbloow, mng!'

'So we asked Grandma and she asked the Octopus Information Exchange and then the Tiger-cat sent a video of you saying 'Little flower, little flower, little flower', and the Octopus ladies told Grandma your name was Nina Hawthorne and you were at the Little Flower Nursing Home and so we knew it was you and we came.'

Lucy was out of breath.

'I'm very glad you did,' said Mrs Hawthorne. 'But tell me, how is Euphoria?'

'She's good.'

'He's good.' Ricardo had finished his mouthful. 'Can I have some more?'

'Yes, dear, but you must tell me – is anything else strange happening in the Mermaid House; anything at all?'

Those eyes again. Before she could stop herself, Lucy was talking about the rug growing a zoo in their bedroom and the horrible dreams she'd been having. Then Ricardo told her how they were dreaming the same things and . . . then they both shut up without either of them saying exactly what they had been dreaming about. They also didn't mention Nigel Scar-Skull or the dragon chest.

There was silence when they'd finished, broken only by

the sound of Ricardo masticating six more jellybeans, green this time.

'Then it's begun.' Her voice sounded very far away.

'What's begun?'

The old lady refused to say anything else, except, with a sharp ginger look, 'Are you sure you're not leaving anything out? This could be very important'.

'No.'

Well, she'd asked about weird things *in* the Mermaid House, not in the back yard, not in a tunnel and definitely not in another country. And they'd promised! Even Ricardo wasn't dobbing, for once. Lucy broke the silence with a question of her own.

'Does Euferbia come to visit you?'

'When they forget to close the window, Euphoria comes. She likes you, you know? She likes you more than my nephew does.'

'We don't know your nephew. We made all that up about being related to get in.'

'I know, dear – I do remember my relatives. Nevertheless, my nephew does know you. Nigel Adams, a real-estate agent. He told me he had rented my house to a mother and two children who could use a lesson in respecting their elders. But Euphoria certainly likes you and now I see those feline instincts were right. She hates Nigel, you know – used to hide whenever he visited before my accident. He's never even seen her.'

'He has now.'

And Lucy told Mrs Hawthorne about the dragon chest and Nigel Scar-Skull wanting it. The effect was instantaneous. The old lady went pale and her hands flew to her face. She looked just as scared as the day the Tiger-cat beamed that first picture.

'You didn't give it to him?'

'Nah. Eufer – the Tiger-cat got rid of him and then we hid it.'

'I can't thank you enough. Now you must do something urgently for me.'

And Mrs Hawthorne undid the black bow of her frilly orange bed-jacket and lifted a long gold chain over her head. Swinging in the sunlight was a filigreed gold key.

36

The Dragon's Treasure

It was ages before Lucy and Ricardo could get to the dragon chest. Grandma wanted to know all about Mrs Hawthorne but what could they tell her? – that she didn't watch TV but she did watch feral cat? In the end Grandma gave up, and they got away and headed for the tunnel.

The key slipped into the ornate lock like an old friend and turned smoothly. They looked at each other solemnly and carefully raised the carved lid. A distinctive perfume wafted up, sweet and strong. In the bottom was a red leather pouch about the size of Dad's wallet. Underneath was a large envelope, about as big as that weird green atlas, yellowed with age. In old-fashioned, faded black writing were the words:

Theodore Hawthorne
January 1942
Private and confidential

Ricardo grabbed the pouch and started to loosen the leather thong around its neck.

'She said not to!'

Ricardo stopped reluctantly. They were under strict instructions from Mrs Hawthorne to open the chest but *not* to look at what was inside. She would explain when they brought everything to her.

'I forgot.'

'Yeah, right,' said Lucy, eyeing the old envelope longingly. She picked it up. It was smooth and dry under her fingers.

Who was Theodore? The old lady's father? Husband? Had she been married before she went crinkly? Lucy tucked the envelope and the pouch into her pack, locked the chest and hung the key around her neck. She had come to a decision.

'Let's go and tell the others.'

Sometimes, changing your mind was the easiest thing. This morning she was never going back to the clearing, now she was too excited *not* to.

Everyone looked glad to see her, when she burst into the clearing. Even Carlos waved and gave a funny half-smile. Lucy didn't hesitate.

'Someone's selling Ten Star Jumbos in the Mall,' she said, pulling the crumpled leaflet from her pocket. Rahel smoothed it, frowning, and read out loud. Pablo put down his tea and Carlos snorted at the bit about leather like elephant hide. When Rahel got to 'trained technicians in our state-of-the-art workshops', they all started talking at once. Ricardo butted in, wanting to know what they were talking about. Lucy still hadn't told him anything about what had happened. All he could work out was that there was a stash of Ten Star Jumbos at the jungle workshop.

His small voice cut through the sunny afternoon.

'We've got a Ten Star Jumbo at home. Dad bought it for us. It's sick.'

'Sick?' queried Pablo.

'Yeah, it's cool!'

'Sick is cool?'

'Yeah, you know.'

'Yeah, sick is cool,' said Toro enthusiatically.

'No,' said Carlos, 'sick is sick'.

Lucy was glad to change the subject. She told them how the Tiger-cat had helped them find Mrs Hawthorne and how she had given them the key to the dragon chest. Lucy pulled out the pouch and envelope.

Carlos got very excited and then freaked out. 'Does this old lady know about us? Will she tell the authorities.'

Silence while the whole camp hung on the answer.

'We didn't tell her about you or the tunnel.'

Collective sigh of relief.

'So open them, then,' said Rahel.

'No, we can't. She said we have to take everything back to her tomorrow.'

Then she told them about Mrs Hawthorne calling the Tiger-cat Euphoria and how it visited her at the nursing home and showed her video clips. No one looked surprised.

'It does that for all of us,' said Carlos.

Trust him to know everything.

'It talks to me,' said Ricardo.

Everyone ignored him, except Toro, who nodded enthusiastically.

Lucy had never considered that the Tiger-cat might send videos to the others, apart from Angel, of course. She felt stupid and a bit jealous at the same time.

Rahel saw her face.

'The Tiger-cat waits until we are alone and then . . . then it does things. It keeps showing me pictures of my parents. They are making rugs in a jail workshop too. And sometimes it shows me my aunt. She is waiting for me.'

Pablo confessed then. 'It also shows me pictures of a dead fish.'

'*A dead fish?*'

'I don't know why.' Pablo looked a bit ashamed that he didn't have a more exciting story.

'What sort of fish?'

'Just a fish. A big pink fish. And then it shows someone's hands with a knife, scraping off the scales and slicing it in to pieces.'

'Any chips? Pineapple fritters?' asked Ricardo.

Toro interrupted: 'I see Ricardo and two Bulls and they are asleep.'

'Who? Me or the Bulls?'

'The Bulls sleep. You have your sword.'

'See,' Ricardo said triumphantly to Lucy, and then he ran around in circles saying, 'I beat them, I beat them,' followed by 'I am the best. I am the best. I am the best'.

'Tell me you made that up,' Lucy asked Toro. He looked offended.

Frowning, Lucy turned to Carlos. 'What does the Tiger-cat show you?' she asked, secretly hoping it would be boring.

'It shows me defeating you 5-0 in a penalty shootout.'

Everyone was silent, watching Lucy's face. In the two seconds it took for her stomach to go *thump*, she saw the look on his face. At the same time everyone burst out laughing.

'Hilarious. What does it really show you?'

He would not say.

Lucy was about to hassle him when she noticed the Tiger-cat lying on her back, with Angel stroking her tummy. The Tiger-cat rolled luxuriously and stretched, then opened its golden eyes wide and held Angel's gaze. The little girl became very still and then, slowly, began to smile. Lucy could hear the Tiger-cat purring intensely.

'Well, I don't know what she shows Angel, but it works,' she said and the others looked over. Watching them, Lucy caught the same expression on each face. First, a sharp, sad look, replaced by a kind of fierce protective tenderness, then a smile. What was it about Angel? It wasn't just that she was cute. There was something about the way she looked at you. As if she was really *wise*. And because she was so little, it was even cuter.

Rahel broke the spell. 'Listen, we must plan for our next raid. Lucy, we have not been able to talk to you since last night. Carlos says you know where the Commander keeps his drugs.'

'Yes. The Tiger-cat made Sarong Lady beam a picture to me last night. I can't explain it, it was weird, but I know they are in a dark bottle, on the table near her window and there's a big tree right outside we can climb up. But we're going to have to get there tonight, before the Commander, or get rid of him somehow, or wait till he's asleep.'

'And I say,' said Rahel, 'that we must ask Bucket Lady for

215

help. We know where she lives. We must take the drugs and solicit her to put them in the Commander's food.'

'Yes and then she will go straight to the Bull Commander and we will all be captured,' said Carlos – and then everyone started shouting at once.

The argument raged on, but in the end it was the Tiger-cat who solved it. She waited for Carlos to stop striding about the clearing and sit down on a rock, then she jumped onto his lap, just as she had done to Lucy this morning, placing a paw on each shoulder and staring into his eyes.

Carlos didn't stop talking straight away and Lucy was delighted to see the Tiger-cat swing back a paw and bop him gently on the cheek.

Everyone laughed, but Carlos was so shocked that he shut up and the next second it was too late – he was caught in the spotlight of that golden gaze. Everyone went quiet. When the Tiger-cat finally relaxed and began washing its ears, Carlos stared into space for a while and then said the fateful words: 'We must ask this Bucket Lady to help us'.

'Well, duh,' said Ricardo.

For once, Lucy agreed with him.

37

Bright Eyes

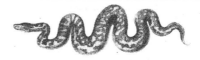

The argument about who should approach Bucket Lady didn't take quite as long as the one about whether they should approach her at all, but it took long enough. Everyone wanted to go. Lucy, who considered herself an expert on old ladies after her encounter with Mrs Hawthorne, said too many kids would freak her out. Ricardo, who considered himself an expert on old ladies after his encounter with Mrs Hawthorne, said all old ladies loved little kids and so he and Toro should go. Everyone except Toro ignored him. Then Carlos and Pablo said they would go, but Rahel said Bucket Lady would think they had come to rob her and raise the alarm.

'It is my view that Lucy and I should undertake this task,' she said firmly. End of argument.

A short time later, Lucy and Rahel stood at the fork of the tunnel.

'Something happens to my eyes in the dark!' Lucy confided. 'Is it happening to you too? Actually, I am not sure if it is my eyes, but . . .'

'It is the same for myself.' said Rahel. 'It's been happening since we escaped, but it is much stronger now. It is confusing. Here and now, in this place, I cannot see the walls, but I *know* exactly their place. And in the jungle, I can see in the dark much better than before.'

'Me too!' said Lucy, excited.

'Perhaps we see with the eyes of the tiger!' suggested Rahel. 'Tigers do not need a head torch like the Bull Commander. I have studied them. They are night hunters. They can see far better than we.'

Lucy pictured a tiger prowling into Dr Baker's clean office in the main street of Kurrawong to have its eyes tested. It would sit up in a chair to read the little letters on the chart on the wall. T for tiger. D for doctor. DOUBLE D FOR DOCTOR FOR DINNER – aaagggghhh. Dr Baker with blood all over his white coat. Gross.

Rahel's calm voice took over.

'Before the Bulls took me, I read all the time about animals. I did many school projects. I especially studied tigers. And Papa took me to the tigerlands when I was little.'

'Where?'

'The tigerlands on the other side of the island. It is against the law to kill a tiger in the tigerlands. There is a legend that Telares belongs to tigers and not people. My grandmama told me when I was little.'

'A legend? Can you remember it?'

'Of course I can. She told me almost every night.'

And Rahel began reciting, as though she remembered the story word for word, her voice keeping rhythm with their feet as they walked in the dark.

'A long, long time ago, Telares had a name that everyone has forgotten but it was a great and powerful island, much bigger than today, with many tigers and elephants and snakes and monkeys and birds and fish, and strange creatures that don't exist any more. The king and queen worshipped the tigers and forbade their people to hunt them. When the king and queen died, their only son, whose nickname was "Young Tiger", was supposed to be king. But his cousin hated him, and one day when they were fishing he pushed Young Tiger overboard and paddled back to shore saying Young Tiger had been swimming and the sharks had taken him.

'The cousin became king, but he hated tigers because they reminded him of what he had done. One day, walking in the garden, the spirit of his aunt, the dead queen, took the body of a tiger and attacked him. The false king almost died and when he was better, he set out to kill all the tigers. He began hunting them secretly. He had to hide the bodies, so he ground their bones into powder and sent secret messages to the rulers of all the other islands, who did not have tigers. He told old kings and queens that his magic powder would make them young again. He said a murderer could not pass through a door with a tiger's head mounted on it. To those kings and queens without an heir, he said sleeping in a bed with a tiger-skin blanket would bring many children.

'The kings and queens of the other islands believed him, and began to ask him for tiger heads and skins. He became very wealthy, but he could not kill tigers quickly enough to keep the other kings and queens happy. And of course he could not ask anyone to help him.

'Then one day a powerful king sent his warriors to demand more tiger bone. They killed the false king. Then they killed many tigers. The people were in despair, and gathered in the sacred jungle on the far side of the island to ask the ancestors for help.

'For three days, the Telarians prayed to the spirits of all tigers, and the spirits of the dead king and queen and the spirit of Young Tiger. And on the fourth day, rain began to fall unceasingly and flood the invaders in their camps. On the fifth day a tremendous storm destroyed the warriors' boats and they were stranded. On the sixth day, the ground shook and Telares broke into two pieces. The warriors saw that they stood on the largest piece and jeered at the Telarians on the smaller island, threatening to build more boats, and return to kill all the tigers. They forgot that the smaller island held the sacred jungle. On the seventh day, a giant wave came from the ocean and drowned the larger island and all the warriors on it. The sacred jungle floated safely away, and its people and tigers were saved.

'And when the sacred jungle floated all the way to the place where the sun is born, Young Tiger appeared in a boat and ruled wisely. And the tigers no longer feared the warriors' spears.'

'Wow! Someone should tell the Bulls,' said Lucy, and suddenly realised they had both stopped walking during the story.

'I know.' Rahel's voice was suddenly hard. 'They are killing tigers too. Before the Bulls came, many people would come on aeroplanes from other countries to see the tigers. Then the Bulls came, and now they shoot them, even in the tigerlands.'

'Shoot them? Because they're scared?'

'Yes, but also Papa told me tiger bone is still worth much money, just as the story says, and they sell the fur too.'

Lucy thought of the Tiger-cat's soft pelt and remembered something.

'The Bull Commander lied to Sarong Lady. He thought he heard a tiger when Carlos trod on a branch and he told her he had shot it and would give her the skin for her bed.'

They contemplated that one silently. Then Lucy remembered what they had been talking about.

'The other night, when we went to the workshop, I could feel the Commander walking on the ground – and I could feel you and Pablo. Is that happening to you?'

'Yes, the same. I could feel you and Carlos. The ground shakes and I can tell what kind of creature is walking. Even I know if Angel is walking towards the pool. But it is best when I lie on the ground.'

Lucy was torn between disappointment that someone had the same talent, and relief that she could share it. 'So if we've got tiger's eyes, what's the shaking thing about?'

'I believe it is the snake!'

'Yuck! I'm not turning into a snake!'

'It's true. Snakes can feel things moving. They sense when you walk towards them.'

'And you read this stuff for fun? I only know science stuff because dad leaves his magazines in the toilet. You should work in a zoo or be a vet or something when you grow up.'

'That is my plan, but first I must go back to school. I have not been to school since the Bulls took me. I have had no books to look at.'

Lucy was about to say, 'Who cares about missing school?', but something in Rahel's voice warned her not to make a joke. She changed the subject.

'All right, I get the snake thing, a bit, but what about how we feel right now, in the tunnel?'

She reached into dense air to touch the wall.

'I really can't see anything. And I don't reckon even a tiger could see down here. There's no light at all. It wouldn't matter how good your eyes were, they need some light, don't they?'

She drew on something else she had read in one of Dad's magazines.

'That's how eyes work, isn't it? The black bit, the pupil, gets bigger as it gets dark so you can suck up more light. But there's no light down here to suck up. But when I try to work out where the wall is,' she kicked it with her toe, 'I know exactly where it is. I try to *feel* where it is and I know! It's as if my thoughts bounce off the wall and I know where it is.'

'Yes. It is the same for me,' said Rahel.

They walked on, deep in thought, feet crunching on the gritty tunnel floor. Then Lucy had it!

'Radar!'

'Radar?'

'Yes, radar! They use it in aeroplanes. They send out invisible waves and the waves bounce off other aeroplanes and a light starts flashing and goes beep beep beep on a computer and it shows where the wave bounced off.

So they know exactly where other planes are and they don't fly into them. We've got brain radar!'

Rahel giggled. 'Beep beep! I will try not to fly into any aeroplanes then.'

Lucy realised it was the first joke she had ever heard Rahel make. It was pretty lame, but they both laughed hysterically and beep-beeped their way down the tunnel with arms outstretched, to avoid other planes, until they heard the familiar purr of the Tiger-cat and bumped into the green curtain. This time it was Rahel who walked straight through, grinning back at Lucy, as the curtain parted before her.

Then a roaring sound erupted behind Lucy and she swung around to see a black geyser burst through the opening, an endless beating of leathery wings, reaching for the darkening sky. The bats were going hunting too. Lucy counted to a hundred and still they kept coming, wings pumping up and away. How many lived in those under-ground passageways and caves? Finally the eruption calmed to a stream, then a trickle. When the last bat had left the tunnel, the Tiger-cat stepped daintily through and the curtain grew into place again.

'I think we have answered our question,' said Rahel.

'What question?'

'The bats. That is why we can find our way in the dark. Do you recall the very first time we came through the tunnel, after you met us on the path?'

'Yeah, Dracula bashed me in the head.'

'This is correct. And since then we have been finding our way without the torch, yes?'

'Oh yeah.'

'And everyone has been able to travel without the torches in the tunnel, yes?'

'Ye-e-es,' said Lucy.

'Bats fly in the dark without bumping into things,' said Rahel.

'Well, they bumped into us! Everyone got a bat in the face.'

'Yes, but you know what I mean.'

Rahel paused. 'I believe you and I are the only ones who can feel like the snake,' she said. 'I have checked with the others, but they do not know what I am talking about when I mention the ground shaking. So I have been thinking. I believe this is because the python touched us that night.'

Suddenly it all made sense to Lucy.

'Of course! And the bats touched all of us. That's why no one needs a torch in the tunnel any more. And the Tiger-cat has given all of us cat's eyes. It still feels like seeing when we walk around at night, as if we've got super eyes. But when we're in the tunnel, it doesn't feel like seeing, it feels like, I dunno, listening, and that's because of the bats. And the Tiger-cat is always touching us. I've started to walk like a cat. And I get this hunterish feeling. Even Ricardo can walk quietly now. He probably still steps in things, though.'

An insistent growl from the Tiger-cat itself warned both girls they were making way too much noise.

They padded on cats' feet down the path, cats' eyes peeled.

38

Bucket Lady Speaks

The Tiger-cat led the way, and Lucy again noticed those distinctive white spots on the back of its ears. Near the jungle jail, the Tiger-cat suddenly darted off the path and turned to face the girls, meowing insistently. They froze. The sound was shockingly loud in the gathering night. The Tiger-cat meowed again and trotted a few more paces off the path, before turning, as if to make sure they were following. Lucy and Rahel looked at each other, and obeyed. The Tiger-cat slipped through the thick under-growth, moving well away from the jungle jail. The girls concentrated on keeping up with those white ear spots. Then the foliage cleared and they were heading downhill, on a narrow track probably made by animals. After a minute Lucy smelt the sea, and then smoke. The Tiger-cat sprang into a tree with a low growl. The girls shrank to the jungle floor. Through the palms of her hands, Lucy felt the vibration of many pairs of feet.

Rahel breathed in her ear, 'I think we have approached the village from another direction. I believe what we are feeling is the villagers and their children walking back from the workshop'.

It made sense. Lucy remembered that army of children who had melted into the shadows the other night. She closed her eyes and concentrated. She felt the vibration with her whole body and a picture began to form in her mind. Yes! Rahel was right. A large group of people was approaching somewhere over to their left.

As if in agreement, the Tiger-cat began trotting along the path which took them around the back of the village and off to the right. Lucy felt her senses stretch out to take in their surroundings. A thought struggled for birth but she couldn't name it. Then she heard it. Running water. Then they were stepping onto a curved bridge over a stream, leading to a round hut. Bucket Lady's house! Quickly they climbed into a tree, near the bridge.

After what seemed like forever, they heard a clinking and rattling. A familiar shape stood silhouetted on the bridge: Bucket Lady. The Tiger-cat leapt out, surprising the girls, who were trying to stay as quiet as possible. The Bucket Lady greeted the Tiger-cat with obvious affection, and then looked up into the tree where the girls hid, saying something urgently in Telarian. Rahel gasped. Bucket Lady said it again and this time Rahel scrambled down from the tree. There was a hurried conversation, and then she turned to Lucy and hissed, 'It's OK, you can come down'.

Inside the hut there was a candle burning on a rough table. Lucy saw the Tiger-cat in the corner, gnawing on the half-eaten carcass of a fish. So she did eat!

Then Bucket Lady began talking softly, as though afraid of being overheard. Lucy understood 'Commander' and perhaps 'tiger'. At one point Bucket Lady got very excited and went outside and brought in yet another, much bigger bucket. From it, she took the most enormous fish Lucy had ever seen. It glowed pink in the lamplight and Lucy was suddenly reminded of Pablo's Tiger-cat video. Rahel began to laugh too. Then Bucket Lady went to the door and looked out. She whispered something that must have meant 'all clear' because Rahel grabbed Lucy's hand and they left, the Tiger-cat streaking ahead.

They didn't stop until they were safe inside the tunnel. Rahel spoke breathlessly, too excited to wait until she had stopped panting.

'She is very pleased with our idea. She says she will help. She will put the medicine in his food herself! She says the fish is the Commander's favourite, but soon his fish soup will have extra seasoning!'

'But we haven't even got the drugs yet. Besides, can we trust her?' worried Lucy. 'Remember, she is working for the Bulls.'

'The Tiger-cat thinks we can trust her,' said Rahel calmly. 'And she told me she has much anger towards the Bulls. They make her work for them. She says the Bulls have torn the heart out of the village. They have taken all the teenagers and the adults to another Bull camp. There are only small children and old people left. On their own, the old people must find food for all the children, and feed the Commander and the militia. Everyone is very scared of the Commander. They do not know what to do. They want their grandchildren to go to school again. She says the Commander closed down the school and put the teacher in jail.'

'Drastic! What about you guys? Does Bucket Lady know your parents are rebels?'

'Yes, the whole village knows. She said that some of them hate us too.'

'Why! You haven't done anything to them.'

'Yes, but they blame the rebels for making the Bulls angry. They say if the rebels stopped fighting, the Bulls would stop making the children work.'

'Is that true?'

'I do not think so. They make much money out of us.'

'But if your parents had not joined the rebels, you might still be at home.'

Lucy sensed Rahel's anger, even before she had finished speaking.

'My mama and papa joined the rebels after many innocent people were taken away. After Carlos' mama and papa were killed, they knew things had gone too far. I am proud of them.'

'Look, I didn't mean it was your parents' fault or any-thing . . . I just meant . . .'

'Of course it was not their fault,' Rahel said coldly.

Then they had reached the pit and there didn't seem much point saying anything else.

'Bye,' said Lucy, but Rahel veered off towards the camp without replying. Then T-Tongue charged up the path, almost exploding with excitement to see Lucy. That was the best thing about T-Tongue: nothing she could ever say or do would ever offend him. Had she blown it for good with Rahel? It was bad enough having Carlos so touchy. But as she walked towards the glowing kitchen she could have sworn she heard a faint 'beep beep' waft on the warm evening air.

That night she was so tired she almost fell asleep in Grandma's meatballs. The only reason she didn't was that Grandma started going on about how she had seen something horrible on the news – something about the jails in the desert, where the boat people were kept. Lucy lifted her head. Something about people's lips being sewn together.

'Gross!' said Ricardo. 'How do they eat?'

Grandma said the boat people were doing it to them-selves.

'Why?' Lucy was flabbergasted.

'Well, I only heard what their lawyer had to say,' Grandma answered. 'He said they think no one listens to them, so they may as well sew up their lips. Some of them are only teenagers, not much older than yourself, Lucy.'

Lucy put down her knife and fork, met Ricardo's eyes across the table, and felt her mind glow white-hot like a Christmas tree again. There was no way the kids from Telares were going to end up in one of those jails in the desert. Not after what they'd been through. Ricardo's eyes grew big and there was no need for words. Slowly he nodded.

The Telarians must never be captured.

39
Rug Games

Lucy, sleeping in after the night's adventure, was shocked awake by a screaming Ricardo.

'It's alive!'

He dived onto her bed.

'The snake. It's got skin!' and scrambled under the blankets.

'Sshh! Grandma will hear!'

'She's at the chooks. That thing's got skin!'

'Sure, and the tiger's growing fur,' replied Lucy, yawning. She swung out of bed, placing both feet on the tiger – and yelled as loudly as Ricardo. Her toes had sunk deliciously, deeply, into burnt-orange fur, punctuated in charcoal and white. Wonderingly, Lucy traced the outline of the tiger with her toe. Rich, soft fur was inviting her to curl up in a ball and dream tigerish dreams.

Lucy pushed a pile of clothes off the monkey. Its golden fur was much brighter and softer than before. She cleared more clothes and faced the python squarely. Its gold diamonds glowed and pulsed before her eyes if she stared at it for a long time, but when she blinked the effect was gone. From certain angles, if she turned to face it quickly enough, it even seemed to move. The scales looked smooth. She stretched out her toe and her skin met the cool discipline of snake skin. Gross!

Lucy jumped back and landed on the elephant's jewelled trunk, leathery, rough and smooth. She ran the tip of her finger over the red jewel in the centre of its forehead. It was lustrous, and ungiving as glass.

What about the bat? Its wings looked like skeleton hands with leather stretched over them, but its back . . . Lucy touched fur, soft as the fox stole at the bottom of Grandma's wardrobe.

The rug wasn't just growing itself new again. It was growing itself *alive*.

Ricardo broke into her thoughts. 'We've got to give the stuff to the old lady.'

Ten minutes later they were boarding the bus. As they climbed the stairs Grandma handed up sandwiches and reminded them to go to the library first because she needed a book. They sat up the back and Lucy filled in Ricardo about last night. He kept repeating her words.

'Bucket Lady had a big fish?'

'Yep.'

Then they were jumping off at the Little Flower Nursing Home. They ran as fast as they could, arriving out of breath at the great wooden doors and stone steps. No Blue Uniform. They looked at each other.

Just do it. Silent personal jinx.

They walked quietly in and followed their noses around winding corridors to the old lady's room, number 33.

Right number, wrong room. The funny sling for her leg was gone and the sunlight melted on an empty, perfectly made bed. No jellybeans.

'We'll have to ask Blue Uniform.'

'No way!'

'We have to! C'mon! She's still got your skateboard, remember. You left it in her safe.'

Ricardo went pale and started tiptoeing up the hall. Blue Uniform had that effect. They'd almost reached the corner leading to her office when Lucy heard a sound that sent her dodging for cover.

'. . . aware it's short notice but there was no other option, I'm afraid. It's a rather delicate financial matter.' Nigel Scar-Skull!

They heard Blue Uniform's booming voice.

'Regardless, I must express my absolute displeasure at how this business was conducted. Most irregular. Mrs Hawthorne was making sound progress here. With a bit of family support, she would have been ready to *go home* in a few weeks. If she really had to go elsewhere, surely it could have waited a few days. As a professional in this field for forty years, I feel obliged to warn you she simply may not receive the care she requires in that establishment. In all my days, I have never seen a transfer handled so abruptly, and I must say, I hope I never do again. Mrs Hawthorne was in no condition for the sort of stress she faced this morning. Most upset, she was, Mr Adams, and I hope you have learned something from the experience. Now, if you'll excuse me . . .'

Wow! Lucy felt the advance of heavy, angry strides and tried to sink into the wall of the corridor. Something jabbed her back. A door handle. She grabbed Ricardo's hand and they slipped into a dark space, just as the footsteps rounded the corner. Lucy held the door open a crack and watched Nigel Scar-Skull retreat towards the front door. His entire skull and the back of his neck were as red as one of Grandma's prize tomatoes.

'I don't think Nigel Scar-Skull likes Blue Uniform very much,' whispered Ricardo.

'I don't think Blue Uniform likes Nigel Scar-Skull very much,' whispered Lucy.

Then she felt something *she* didn't like very much. More heavy footsteps. She shrank into the shadows. It didn't help. The door was wrenched open, revealing an ample shape.

'You will come to understand: there is nothing, repeat nothing, that takes place in this establishment, that escapes my attention, least of all the patter of little feet. I've had just about all I care to put up with this morning.'

A red-cardiganed forearm snapped on the light to reveal five brooms, four mops, three huge vacuum cleaners and two kids.

'But I must say I am very glad to see you! Come this way, please.'

Lucy and Ricardo couldn't quite believe that Blue Uniform was smiling at them. A minute later they were in her office, Ricardo was clutching his skateboard again and Lucy held an envelope bearing, in flowery script the words:

Ricardo and *Lucía*.

'Mrs Hawthorne asked me to keep that letter safe and give it to you when you came,' boomed Blue Uniform. 'She did not have time to finish it, but she asked me to tell you to open the other things.' Blue Uniform sniffed disapprovingly. 'She did not explain *what other things* because she said you would understand. She said to look after Angel and the others. Do you know anyone called Angel?'

'No.'

'Yes.'

'Maybe.'

As they followed the red rug outside, Lucy's head was spinning. How long had the old lady known about Angel and the others? How did she know Lucy was short for *Lucía?* It sounded like Loo-see-a, that's how they said it in Portugal, and it was her real name but only Dad called her that. And how did Blue Uniform hear their footsteps from so far away when they were tiptoeing on thick carpet?

Ricardo must have been thinking along similar lines.

'I bet she doesn't know U-furrier jumped in the old lady's window,' he said hopefully.

Loo-see-a wasn't so sure.

40

The Pattern

Grandma was delighted when Lucy handed over the book she had got from the library: *So You Think You're a TV Quiz Master? 1000 Brain Teasers for Fun and Profit.* She sent them off for the rest of the afternoon, telling them not to worry about cleaning up their room. She'd been going psycho about it until she saw the book.

Now Lucy and Ricardo sat with the other kids around the campfire, with the leather pouch and two envelopes propped up like forensic evidence on the flat kitchen rock.

'Mrs Hawthorne knew my name was Lucía,' said Lucy, 'but only Dad calls me that, ever!'

'The Tiger-cat,' said Pablo simply.

'The Tiger-cat's never seen Dad!'

'The Tiger-cat is playing games with your mind,' said Carlos, sounding pleased.

'It hunts your thoughts like mice,' smiled Rahel. She seemed to have got over whatever had been bugging her last night.

At that moment, the striped thought-hunter strolled in,

relaxed and confident. It jumped up on the kitchen rock, next to the exhibits and looked expectantly at the kids.

'Open them!'

Lucy tore open the small envelope, took out a thin sheet covered in loopy handwriting, and read aloud:

My dear Ricardo and Lucía,

By the time you read this I will be a long way from Kurrawong. I was very much looking forward to our next discussion but circumstances outside my control have intervened. I have so much to tell you. I cannot risk this information falling into the wrong hands, so will not go into detail. Euphoria has kept me informed. You have been very brave and you must be even braver. Forever Telares! The contents of my pig may be of some use to you. Now you must open the chest and

The sentence was incomplete, as though Mrs Hawthorne had been interrupted. Lucy flipped the note over but found nothing but a blank page. They must open the chest and what? And what was that about a pig?

'This old lady, she is one of us,' announced Carlos triumphantly. 'I told you we should get all these old ladies to help us.'

Everyone sat opened-mouthed at that.

'You didn't even want Bucket Lady to help until the Tiger-cat slapped you! You were discrurnimating against her,' said Ricardo, ever the diplomat.

'*Discriminating*,' said Lucy, but Carlos was off again.

'I tell you, she is one of us! *Forever Telares!* It is the rebel slogan. How does she know this? Where is she now!'

Lucy was downcast. Why hadn't they asked Blue Uniform where she'd gone? How dumb was that?

She remembered the red leather pouch. In it was a small silver casket with a hinged lid, decorated with tiny stones in the shape of a tiger, orange, white and black. Its eyes burned: two tiny jewels, the same vibrant, rich red as the jewel on the rug elephant. Something rattled inside. Lucy swung open the casket to reveal another key, the same shape and size as the dragon-chest key.

'It must be the key to the Commander's chest!' exclaimed Carlos. 'He made the militia search the whole jail for it, but they could not find it.'

Suddenly Ricardo began jumping up and down. 'The pig,' he shouted, and bolted out of the clearing, with T-Tongue in passionate pursuit.

Everyone looked at each other and shook their heads, but they were all too preoccupied with the tiger casket to wonder what Ricardo was up to. They passed it around, admiring the jewelled tiger.

Finally, Lucy opened the Theodore Hawthorne envelope. A heavy, folded sheet of paper fell open, revealing ruby red, forest green and brilliant gold. Everyone gasped. Golden eyes gazed up at Lucy. It was the tiger rug, painted like Lucy had never seen it, with glorious animals and birds in every corner and cranny and tiny turquoise butterflies twisting between them. There were too many new animals for Lucy to count, but the tiger still held pride of place. The painting was just how the tiger rug must have looked when it was new; just how the Bull Commander wanted the one in the jungle jail to be.

'It is the pattern!' breathed Rahel, awed.

'The Bull Commander, he would kill us to get his hands on this,' Pablo said in a hushed tone.

'Give it to me,' demanded Carlos.

But Angel trotted up to Lucy and wordlessly, held out her little hand. Surprised and curious, Lucy gave it to her. Quick as a flash, Angel darted over to her favourite tree and sat down with the map on her lap.

'Angel, bring it back!' Lucy laughed. But the little girl looked up, shook her head and went back to examining the map and its menagerie.

Then Ricardo burst back into the clearing carrying the pink piggy bank he had found on their first day at the mermaid house. *The contents of my pig may be of some use to you.* Of course! Ricardo was already removing a cork in its tummy and coins clattered onto the kitchen rock. Cool! Two, four, six – $20 in $2 coins. T-Tongue sniffed them excitedly. There were many strange silver coins. Carlos twisted one in the light. It bore the image of a crouched tiger on one side, and on the other a man's head.

'Telarian silver sovereigns!' he crowed. 'Enough to buy food for a month for all of us! We will need them if we are going to get Angel back to her grandparents in Telares City.'

Lucy had forgotten all about that mission. Everyone got serious then, thinking about what had to be done tonight. To Ricardo and Toro's disgust, they were voted out of the action *again*. Lucy had to go because she knew where the drugs were. Carlos and Pablo would create a diversion, giving Lucy time to climb the tree. She would give the drugs to Rahel, who would take them to Bucket Lady. And tomorrow night, after the Commander and the militiamen had eaten, the real action would begin. It was a good plan, and it *definitely* didn't need Ricardo's special touch.

41

The Dad Show

At the end of the day, Lucy and Ricardo trotted down the path into the welcoming light of the kitchen.

'Lucía! Ricardo!'

They were swamped in the hugest hug from Dad.

T-Tongue went berserk.

Dad had got back from China this morning and was going to stay the night because Mum had been called to Sydney again on another emergency.

Of course they had pizza and Coke for dinner. Then they made Dad play indoor soccer up and down the hall (even though he was really tired), until the ball bounced too close to one of the dragon vases and they all froze and Dad said *oops*, and made them stop.

He'd bought them a new soccer training video, so they stayed up late watching it and then did a bit more training in the hall before he tucked them into their sleeping bags. Lucy could tell Dad would be asleep before her. Jet lag had made him greyer and more ghostly than ever. But he was happy to see *them*.

It seemed like only a few minutes later that Lucy woke up with the Tiger-cat's fishy breath on her face and a soft paw patting her cheek. She got up quietly, dressed and headed for the back door. She checked her watch. Midnight. That made it 3 a.m. Telares time.

She followed the Tiger-cat and T-Tongue up the path. The waning moon briefly lit up the faces of the three Telarian children gathered at the stairs. Wordlessly, they swung down into the pit and entered the tunnel. For a few seconds the enormity of what she was about to do swept over Lucy and she stopped walking, frozen to the spot. But the brush of fur on her legs and the rumbling purr of the Tiger-cat brought that hunterish feeling rushing back. She trotted down the tunnel after the others, senses stretching into blackness.

As they stepped into the Telarian night, the Tiger-cat made a strange growling meow, trotted a few steps, and turned back as if to make sure they were following.

'We'd better do what she says,' Lucy said.

There was just enough moonlight to illuminate the Tiger-cat's white ear spots. The creature led them purpose-fully along a network of narrow animal paths, winding ever deeper into the jungle. Soon they stood hidden in the trees, gazing at what could only be the round walls of Sarong Lady's hut. A candle burned in a high window, framed by the branches of the tree Lucy had 'seen' the night before.

Carlos and Pablo melted away, working their way around towards the other side of the village. The Tiger-cat padded to the tree and leapt into its branches, disap-pearing. Rahel touched Lucy on the shoulder as if to say

'Good luck', and she felt that hunterish feeling flood her veins. She signalled to T-Tongue, who dropped to the ground. Lucy prowled silently forward and leapt gracefully into the tree. She climbed higher and higher, following the Tiger-cat. The tree was huge. Among its great spreading branches she was in a sailing ship, riding through the stars. The sight of the Telarian moon low in the sky sobered her up. It would be sunrise here soon if she didn't hurry up.

Then she was straddling a thick branch which grew right up to the window, peering through a fringe of leaves, right at Sarong Lady's back. The Telarian woman stood away from the window, holding a candle up to see something hung on the far wall of the hut. Lucy saw that distinctive lonely seagull shape: a map of Telares. Why was Sarong Lady up in the middle of the night, looking at a map?

Then Lucy noticed a man lying on a mat on the floor, under a curtain of mosquito net. Her heart almost stopped beating. Even asleep, the Bull Commander was scary, that vicious scar distorting his face in a gruesome leer. If he were awake, he would be looking straight at her.

Next to the mat was a familiar shape: a carved wooden box. The other dragon chest! But that was not what Lucy had come for. Over near the map, on a low table against the wall, was a tall dark bottle with a medicine cup next to it. That must be the sleeping drug. But how on earth was she going to get it with Sarong Lady wide awake, standing right next to it?

The Tiger-cat brushed against her skin and Lucy felt that white-hot feeling grow in her body. She closed her eyes and let it happen. It began as a warm glow in her fingers and toes, and then the fever swept over her and she was pulsing with that same white-hot intensity again. She opened her eyes and found herself staring at Sarong Lady's back. She heard a low purr, and at the same time Sarong Lady turned around and faced the window. Lucy could not move, she could only sit in the tree feeling as though she must be glowing in the dark. Then Sarong Lady picked up the medicine bottle and the measuring cup and walked slowly, purposefully towards her. She placed the medicine on the table by the window, only centimetres from Lucy's face, turned and walked casually back to the map.

Lucy's electric pulse slowed. Had the Tiger-cat made Sarong Lady do that? Should she take the bottle now, or wait? What if the Commander woke up? She broke out in a cold sweat at the thought.

Then an ear-splitting howl made the hair on the back of her neck stand up. It rose higher and higher until she got goosebumps. She had never heard anything like it.

There was a scream from out near the fire. As another howl rose to the moon, Sarong Lady ran outside. Lucy heard the urgent rustle of the mosquito net and the Bull Commander jumped to his feet and thumped out the door, calling out a harsh command. As he pounded down the stairs, Lucy reached for the bottle.

Then she was climbing stealthily down the tree. Many voices shouted in the clearing. The Tiger-cat appeared below and T-Tongue, who had shown enormous restraint in all the commotion, stepped shivering from the shadows and licked Lucy's hand. Rahel moved from behind a tree and gestured, 'Time to get out of here'.

They melted into the jungle. It was none too soon. A gunshot from the direction of the village wrenched an involuntary cry from both girls and a whimper from T-Tongue. They froze. Another shot cracked the night open, and the shouts in the clearing grew louder. The Tiger-cat gave an urgent low growl and the girls sprinted after her on the narrowest of trails.

In a few minutes Lucy smelt fresh water again and then they were racing across the wooden bridge over the creek to Bucket Lady's hut. The Tiger-cat jumped through the open window and Bucket Lady opened the door, beckoning, 'Come in, come in'.

Lucy didn't have to understand Telarian to know the old lady was telling them to hurry. Lucy just had time to give her the bottle of medicine before more shouts came from somewhere close to the hut. Bucket Lady tore a curtain aside at the back of the hut, revealing an open window. Lucy threw T-Tongue out as the shouts grew closer. Rahel and Lucy jumped together, landing outside just as heavy boots thumped over the wooden bridge. They darted into the jungle to the sound of heavy fists hammering on Bucket Lady's door.

In their fear and panic, it was all the girls could do to keep track of the Tiger-cat's white ear spots. It led them on a track so overgrown and dense that Lucy had to crouch low to the ground. Her heart was pounding but the sounds of shouting and running feet gradually slipped away.

They were exhausted by the time they reached the pit. The girls sat on the pile of rubble and waited for the others. It seemed an eternity before Carlos and Pablo emerged, grinning.

'That,' said Carlos, 'was very much fun'.

'No,' said Lucy and Rahel together, 'it wasn't!'

'But we sent them crazy!' said a delighted Pablo. 'We pretended to be ghosts and the villagers panicked. The Commander called the militia, but they were scared too. We led them everywhere but they did not even know what they were chasing.'

'Yes, Lucy,' said Carlos with an unexpected smile, 'your Ponytail Zombie was too scared even to hunt. We saw him hiding from the Commander behind a bush'.

'Finally the militia caught something,' said Pablo. 'It was some animal, I think, but it was not us!' The boys burst out laughing.

By the time Lucy stumbled into her room, she was so tired she didn't even bother getting into her sleeping bag. She was so tired she didn't notice Ricardo wasn't in his bed.

42

Oh, Brother!

Lucy awoke to the smell of smoke. She looked across at Ricardo's bed but saw only his empty sleeping bag. His sword was gone from his bedside table, which meant he had gone to the base without her. Dad poked his head in the door.

'Good morning, Lucía! You and T-Tongue slept in late. Can you smell the smoke? There's a bushfire down south. Deliberately lit, the radio said. They've declared a total fire ban.'

Total fire ban! The campsite. If Pablo or one of the others started a bushfire . . . Lucy didn't even want to think about that.

'Um, Dad, I don't really want breakfast yet. I'm just going for a walk.'

'That's fine, Lucía. Have a look for Ricardo while you're up there, would you? He went out before I got up and I'd rather you two stuck together today. We might have to get out of here fast if things turn bad.'

Lucy ran all the way to the clearing, to find Pablo boiling the billy.

'Put it out! There's a total fire ban!'

'A what?'

'A total fire ban. You're not allowed to light any fires. There's already a bushfire burning down south. If they see smoke up here, they'll send the fire brigade up!'

That did the trick. Pablo doused the flames with the contents of the kettle, sending a cloud of steam up. Rahel filled a pot at the pond and dumped the contents on the fire, and then Carlos kicked soil over the embers.

The little group stared mournfully at the remains of their campfire. Toro looked the saddest of the lot. Lucy noticed Ricardo was not with him.

'Where's Ricardo?'

Toro looked puzzled.

'He has not come today. He was supposed to go swimming with me when the sun came up.'

Lucy's stomach lurched.

'Are you sure? You're not just hiding him from me?'

'No. He did not come.'

Angel trotted up and grabbed her hand. As she did, Lucy felt that Christmas-tree fever again. Angel's hand felt hot and dry like paper, then Lucy was pulsing with electricity just like with the Tiger-cat. She met Angel's dark eyes. They were glowing like polished stones. Lucy wrenched her hand free and turned urgently to the other kids.

'He's in Telares. I know it, I mean, she knows it,' she said, gesturing at Angel. Everyone looked at her blankly.

'You've got to believe me! Ricardo wasn't in his bed

this morning and he's not with you. He's missing. And Angel thinks he's in Telares. She just told me . . . Well, not quite . . . Never mind! I can't explain. Just trust me. He must have followed us last night!' Lucy didn't want to think too hard about the implications of that.

'You are pale,' said Carlos, and there was no trace of scorn in his voice.

Everyone had gone very quiet, thinking about Ricardo down that tunnel, alone, with the Commander and the militia on the alert after last night's disturbance.

'If he did follow us, why didn't he come back?' Lucy said to no one in particular.

She didn't like any of the possible answers.

Lucy had already swung into the pit before the others caught up.

'Wait, we are coming with you,' said Carlos.

They swung down the rope and into the tunnel. Lucy ran, senses stretching to find her way as never before. In no time they were at the green curtain, and Lucy trotted into the first Telarian day she had seen since this whole adventure began. She looked at her watch and made the calculation. Just after lunch Telarian time.

'Lucy, we must have a plan,' said Rahel, sounding like an echo of Lucy on earlier trips.

'I've got a plan. Bring Ricardo home.'

She spoke too loudly.

'Hush. Remember where we are! And we do not know where Ricardo is. We must be careful and clever. He may simply have hurt himself and be hiding in the jungle hoping we will come to get him. First we must search.'

Lucy looked desperately about for the Tiger-cat. She would know where Ricardo was, for sure! Why wasn't she here when Lucy really needed her?

It would have been more sensible and quicker for everyone to split up, but no one wanted to. Close to the jungle jail, they crawled on their bellies until they had a clear view of the firepit and the padlocked gate, with the rickety, rotting mermaid house behind it. What they saw didn't make anyone feel any better. Three militia patrolled the fenceline, and for once they didn't look drunk.

As one, the kids wriggled backwards and melted into the jungle. It was a long time before they felt safe to talk.

'At least they are just militia and not Bulls,' said Pablo.

'But soon the Bull reinforcements come,' said Carlos.

'That's it!' said Lucy. 'If Ricardo is in there, we must get Ricardo *now*. He can't stay here any longer, if that's where he is.'

Rahel spoke soothingly: 'We do not yet know where he is or what has happened to him. Let us check the workshop.'

Carlos led the way, taking the back route. Once again the kids lay on their bellies and looked at the building. Another three militia were on patrol. The Bull Commander was taking no chances. Again the kids wriggled backwards and regrouped, gathering in dense jungle under a tree.

Suddenly, the girls lay on the ground, palms spread on the dirt.

'What do you think?' breathed Lucy into Rahel's ear.

Rahel shook her head and concentrated.

What Lucy could feel was like a small earthquake.

'It's a truck,' she whispered.

'Yes,' Rahel said. 'The reinforcements, or they may be bringing more children from the city. Or taking some away.'

Lucy felt her face set into the expression she had seen so often on Rahel's face. Determination, pure and simple. No one was taking her little brother to Telares City.

'We still do not know if he has even been captured,' Rahel said, seeing her face. 'Let us check the village.'

They climbed under the tree close to the village and watched the scene below. A string of villagers was straggling in from the jungle, each dragging a heavy log to add to the woodpile. There was no sign of Sarong Lady, the Bull Commander or Ricardo.

'We must ask Bucket Lady,' whispered Rahel.

In single file, they threaded through the jungle. Luckily, T-Tongue seemed to remember the way. He trotted confidently ahead, ears pricked. Soon they were huddled under cover near the little bridge.

There was no sign of life in Bucket Lady's hut. Then Lucy got a distinct whiff of fish and felt the clump, clump of approaching feet. 'Get down!' she gestured at the boys. Rahel was already on the ground. Lucy dared to lift her head and saw Bucket Lady and her distinctive buckets, with large fish tails poking out.

Just as Bucket Lady stepped up to her front door, the Tiger-cat appeared, rubbing about her legs, purring so loudly the kids could hear it from near the bridge. The effect on Bucket Lady was instantaneous. She dropped her buckets, plodded wearily but quickly back to where the kids were hiding and said something urgent in Telarian.

Rahel jumped up immediately but Carlos, Pablo and Lucy needed a little more encouragement.

'We must,' said Rahel urgently.

Bucket Lady muttered something else and Carlos and Pablo leapt up and, looking over their shoulders, scuttled over the bridge and through the front door after Rahel, with Lucy and T-Tongue bringing up the rear. Bucket Lady grabbed her buckets of fish and closed the door firmly.

Once again Lucy could not understand a word anyone was saying and had to scrutinise their faces for clues. She learned a lot she didn't want to. When Rahel mentioned Ricardo's name, Bucket Lady looked grim and shook her head. She put her finger to her neck, as though slitting her own throat.

'What did she say? Is he *dead? Tell me!*'

'No, no,' said Rahel, 'but he has been captured. The Commander is very angry. The militia searched the whole village last night and found a strange white-faced little boy hiding nearby, but she does not know where he is being held. A truck has come from Telares City and will take him there tomorrow. The Bull Commander found his medicine missing and blames the little boy.'

A strange buzzing filled Lucy's head and her limbs didn't feel as though they were attached to her body any more, but her stomach still belonged to her, tight in a vice of regret. Why had she kept coming down here? She had led Ricardo into danger. The skin on her face felt cold and heavy like old leather, and she wanted to speak, say something, anything, but she had no words.

Rahel went on. 'Bucket Lady, actually her name is Soella, she says she does not understand why the Commander is getting so upset about a little boy. But ever since we escaped he has not been the same. She says he has got crueller and if anything goes wrong in the workshop or with the tiger rug he flies into a rage. The militia is searching every hut in case there are more children. There is a search party coming this way soon. Remember Ponytail, Lucy, how he complained of the "girl ghost"? The Commander thinks there are other white-faced children helping the others escape. That truck we felt, it is bound to be more Bull soldiers.'

Rahel explained to the others and there was silence as everyone thought about the implications.

'Soella says tonight she will put the medicine in the soup.' Rahel tried to sound confident. 'She thinks that there will be enough to go around, even if there are extra soldiers. She says she knows that the Commander only gives the children a few drops and they sleep. It is very strong.'

'Look, I do not like to say it, but there is nothing we can do in daylight,' said Carlos, showing unusual restraint. 'We must wait for our moment tonight. We will find your little brother and rescue him and the other children, once and for all.'

'Yes, we must wait,' said Rahel.

'But we don't even know where he is,' said Lucy.

'Soella said she will try to find out where they have taken him,' said Pablo, seeing Lucy's stricken face.

Lucy looked about for the Tiger-cat, but she had disappeared again. Suddenly she remembered the image the Tiger-cat had sent to Toro, about Ricardo and his sword and two sleeping Bulls. She forced her leather lips to move so she could remind the others.

'Yes,' said Pablo, pointing at the largest of the fish in Soella's buckets, a beautiful pink and silver specimen. 'And that is the fish I saw through the Tiger-cat. Soon it will be sliced and filleted and the Bulls will sleep.' He looked positively bloodthirsty.

It gave Lucy some hope.

Then both Rahel and Lucy felt it at the same time: the shuddering of many approaching feet. The shock galvanised Lucy into action. Rahel spoke rapidly to Soella in Telarian and she quickly hid the medicine in the bucket of fish and shooed everyone out the back window.

The kids melted into the undergrowth, T-Tongue in the lead. There was no sign of the Tiger-cat, but T-Tongue led them through the jungle to the tunnel and got lots of praise when they got inside.

Lucy trudged through the darkness like a zombie. This was worse, far worse, than she had ever contemplated. She felt hollow. *This was real!* She was confronted with the fact that somewhere inside her she had still been clinging to the idea that no harm would come to her or Ricardo. She had seen the Telarian kids in danger, seen what they had gone through, but *she* had felt protected because, in some dark corner of her mind, she didn't really *believe* what was happening. Didn't really believe the evidence of her own eyes and supercharged senses because recent events were *impossible.*

What really *was* impossible was going home and explaining to Dad first, then Mum and Grandma, that Ricardo was currently overseas, a prisoner of the Bull army. And how had he got there? Through a magic tunnel, of course.

'Bulls? Magic tunnels?' Mum would say. 'You're telling us you took your little brother into that hole I told you not to play in and he's lost somewhere under the mountain, and you think he may have been arrested by foreign soldiers?'

Then the ambulance would come and take Lucy away.

Dad would never believe her story either. But the biggest problem was that Lucy *hadn't believed her own story*. Because everything that had been happening had *seemed* like an action video or some super-charged dream, she had believed she could do *anything* and still wake up in her own bed in the morning. She hadn't thought about the implications. She had been scared, of course, in the beginning; intimidated, as Rahel would say. But lately, Lucy had felt indestructible – crazy enough to lead her own little brother into the clutches of the Commander. She should have known he would follow her if they kept leaving him out.

Lucy had made the same mistake as Dad. When Mum told him he was turning into a ghost, he didn't believe her. Scientists don't believe in ghosts. But Lucy knew what Mum meant. He *had* turned into a ghost in their house. His body was there in the lounge room, but his mind wasn't. It was off in the stars. And he didn't believe Mum until it was too late. He had believed what he had wanted to believe. Then one day his indestructible family got sucked into a black hole while he gazed at the stars.

Ricardo had believed what he wanted to believe, too. He really had believed his sword would protect him. And it hadn't. He'd believed he could fend off armed guards with a plastic sword. Lucy hadn't believed what was staring her in the face and she had led her little brother into danger.

254

The conversation with herself was endless. It went round and round but always, at its core, was how much she wanted to see Ricardo. *Now! With his stupid sword.* Lucy had never felt anything like it in her entire twelve years. In a rush, she was sorry for all the times she had ever been mean to Ricardo, especially since they had moved out of home.

You knew you were taking it out on him, but you did it anyway, she told herself bitterly.

Then she reached the end of the tunnel and saw the Tiger-cat stretched out in a shaft of light as though there was nothing in the world to worry about.

Well, thought Lucy grimly, *you'd better be right.*

But, once again, the Tiger-cat wasn't telling her anything.

43

When All Else Fails

The acrid stench of smoke, much, much stronger than before, greeted them as they clambered out of the pit. The sky had a strange glow and the hot wind had swung around, gusting from the south, where the bushfire was. Great. That was all Lucy needed. But the knowledge broke through the grey skin of shock she was walking around in, and blood flowed in her veins again.

'Listen, do you guys know about bushfires?'

Everyone shook their heads. The trouble was, Lucy did know about bushfires. She had lived in Kurrawong all her life, and every summer the smell of a bushfire was in the air. Once she had seen a whole swathe of the escarpment up in flames. She didn't want to see it again.

'You're going to have to get up to the camp and get everything out of sight under the waterfall,' she said urgently. 'Dad's going to come looking for Ricardo, so you won't have much time. Make it look as though only Ricardo and I have been playing up there. If you can, get everyone back down into the tunnel. At least we know that's safe.

The Tiger-cat won't let anyone else in.'

Lucy hoped that last bit was true. She was worried about the fire.

'If you run out of time, just get under the waterfall,' she warned. 'You'll be safe under there, even if a fire comes through, probably safer than our house. I'm going home now to stall Dad. I'll tell him that Ricardo is having such a good time up here that he won't come home. But when Dad can't find him, he'll call the police. You've got to be out of sight. Please try to get back to the tunnel.'

She waved goodbye and plunged off the stairs and down the hill, ready to tell the biggest lie of her life. She had no choice. No one would believe the truth. They'd lock her up and then she wouldn't be around to help Ricardo. And in her bones, she knew she was the only one who could.

'Hi, Dad,' she called from the back door. But he wasn't alone. Mum and Grandma were there, looking worried.

'Lucy! Where have you been?' said Mum. 'They sent me home because they're afraid the fire will cut the highway. I've been worried sick about you!'

'I was trying to get Retardo to come down off the mountain. But he's having such a good time that he won't listen to me about the bushfires.'

Dad was hunched over the radio, listening to the news.

'The wind's swung. It's not too strong right now, but they're worried it will pick up and drive the fire this way. They're trying to stop it at Rocky Pass. They think they have a good chance.'

'I don't care, I still want Ricardo off that mountain,' Mum said. 'You should have made him, Lucy. He does what you want if you really try. You know that. I'm disappointed in you.'

'It's not my fault,' she began out of sheer habit and then gave up.

Grandma was more sensible.

'Let's just go up and get him, shall we?' suggested Grandma. 'Where did you say he was, Lucy?'

'Mum knows where he is – at the waterfall.'

'All the way up there! For goodness sake, anything could happen. I'll go. Lucy, you go and start packing a bag in case we have to evacuate. Not much, just the essentials. Clothes, toothbrush, things you don't want to lose.'

What about the tiger rug? Somehow Lucy didn't think they'd let her roll that up and take it away.

She walked through the dragon vases standing guard at her door and stared at the wreckage on the floor. Morosely she began to tidy up. Somehow it didn't matter any more if the grown-ups found out about the tiger rug. Maybe they would believe her about Ricardo if they could see what had happened to it. Mum and Grandma knew how old and crappy it was when they first found it. Maybe they wouldn't think she was crazy after all. Suddenly enlivened, Lucy began clearing Lego and magazines and clothes as quickly as she could. Soon the whole menagerie was spread at her feet. The tiger in all its soft, rich fur, the monkey with its glamorous ruff, the python that still sent a tremble through her bones, the bat which was no longer a smudge but a distinct creature of delicate leather and fur, and the elephant, with that red jewel glowing like blood.

With a start Lucy realised there was something new, way

over there, near the tail of the tiger. It looked like letters. Hang on, it *was* letters. Lucy sprang over the python and fell to her knees in luscious tiger fur to decipher the new addition. There, woven in golden thread, were the words: *I hav been a Retardo agin. From Ricardo.*

Lucy's whoop of joy brought Dad and Grandma charging up the hall.

'Look,' she said triumphantly, pointing at the carpet scrawl, 'Ricardo's sent a message. We have to go and get him!'

She had abandoned all caution. This was evidence even Dad couldn't ignore.

Dad and Grandma looked from the carpet to Lucy's excited face, then at each other.

'Now, calm down, Lucía,' said Dad, soothingly, his face greyer than usual. 'If we can't find him we'll call the police and the fire brigade. They'll get him off the mountain.'

'But he's not on the mountain! He's gone down a time tunnel and the Bull Commander captured him and he's a prisoner in the jungle jail and he's just woven a message to me in the carpet, look!'

She traced the letters in the carpet and recited Ricardo's words.

'I think,' said Grandma in her sternest voice, 'on the day when your little brother might be in serious danger you could stop calling him that dreadful name.'

'I didn't say it, he did,' Lucy objected. Then she saw the looks on their faces.

'How much sleep did she get last night?' Grandma asked Dad accusingly, then lowered her voice. 'I think she may have a fever.'

Turning back to Lucy, Grandma spoke in a bright, cheerful voice. 'Pop back into bed, petal, and we'll bring you a couple of aspirin. All this excitement has been too much for everyone. You'll see, your mother will be back soon with Ricardo and we'll all just listen to the radio and jump in the car if we have to. We get these scares every year, but I really don't think we have anything to worry about. Now, you get some rest.'

Before Lucy knew what was happening, Dad was tucking her into bed, walking all over the animals as though they just weren't there. It was only then she realised, with a sinking heart, that for him they weren't. She was on her own. And it was going to take more than lying around in a sleeping bag to rescue Ricardo.

Grandma bustled back in with two aspirin and insisted that Lucy take them. Dad sat on her bed and read her a story. Lucy felt her arms and legs go heavy and her eyes start to close. Just as she drifted off to sleep she mumbled, 'Mustn't go to sleep,' followed a minute later by, 'They weren't aspirin, were they?' Then she was drifting in strange dreams of elephants and tigers, monkeys and bats, snakes and the Ponytail Zombie and the Bull Commander, smiling, smiling, smiling . . .

44

Let's Go Hunting

When Lucy finally woke, it was afternoon. That meant it was sunset, Telarian time. Time to get down that tunnel. But when she stepped out of her bed, her legs felt rubbery and her head was foggy. The house was terribly quiet. She walked down the hall and peered out the front door. Two police cars were parked out the front. Buzzing filled her head again. An insistent purr brought her back to earth. The Tiger-cat rubbed against her legs, gazing up at her. Lucy fell into that golden gaze and saw . . .

Ricardo, sitting with his back against a wooden wall, his plastic sword clutched in his right hand. Two Bull soldiers asleep on either side of him.

Lucy shivered back into her body. Her legs felt strong again and her head was clear. She looked directly at the Tiger-cat. 'OK,' she said. 'Let's go hunting.'

Lucy ran into the back yard. No sign of anyone. They must all be searching the waterfall. She darted up the path, T-Tongue and the Tiger-cat streaking ahead. Just as she got to the pit, she felt a familiar vibration. One, two, three, four people striding down the track above the pit. Without a moment to lose, she swung in and was relieved to see the tail of the Tiger-cat disappearing into the darkness. She ran to catch up and for the first time, the tunnel entrance closed behind her. The Tiger-cat was taking no chances. It was pitch-black instantly, but Lucy trotted confidently forward.

She reached the miners' room quickly and found Rahel waiting at the door.

'I felt you coming,' Rahel said. 'We hid everything under the waterfall and came down here, but we almost were caught. Someone came to the clearing and we had to hide. I felt someone walking and took everyone under the waterfall just in time.'

'It was Mum,' said Lucy. 'They think I'm crazy. They gave me sleeping pills and called the police to look for Ricardo.' Her words spilt out in a torrent. 'And the Tiger-cat sent me that same vision she sent to Toro – Ricardo awake with his sword and two Bulls asleep. So the extra Bulls did arrive. But get this! Ricardo sent a message – he wove it into the carpet. That means he is in the other mermaid house. So let's just go and get him.'

Lucy paused for breath. Through the open door, she saw Carlos with Angel on his knee, and Pablo and Toro at the candle-lit table. It seemed like forever since she had sat around the table, feeding a bunch of strange children Cocoa Puffs.

The others jumped to their feet, eager for action.

'If Soella has done her work, then the guards will be asleep,' said Carlos, excited.

Rahel spoke in Telarian to Toro and he sat down with Angel on the lounge.

'We don't want any more little brothers lost,' Rahel explained to Lucy.

Lucy was the last to leave the candle-lit room.

'Goodbye, Angel,' she said gently.

It seemed important. She didn't know what her connection to the little girl was, but she knew it was nothing she had ever experienced before. And Angel's mother had told her to look after her, just as Lucy's mum had told her to look after Ricardo.

'See you, Toro. Thanks for looking after Angel!'

'It's OK. Bring back Ricardo.' His little face looked pinched and serious in the candlelight.

Lucy caught up to the others just as they entered the Telarian night.

The scene that greeted them as they lay looking down on the jungle jail couldn't have been better: six guards, three Bulls and three militia, slumbering around the blazing firepit, their meals half-eaten. There was no sign of the Commander.

'He has gone back to Sarong Lady,' Lucy whispered to the others.

Carlos took the keys from Rahel and crept to his feet. He ducked from tree to tree and made a dash for the gate. It was excruciating watching him try each key on the lock and fail.

'The Commander must have changed the locks!' Lucy hissed.

Carlos must have worked it out too. He looked desperately up to where the others lay hidden and shook his head. Then he padded carefully over to a sleeping Bull. The hair on the back of Lucy's neck stood up. He chose one, carefully patting his pockets. Nothing. Then Carlos began undoing the buttons of his shirt, one by one. Lucy clearly saw the bunch of keys on a chain around his neck. Just then the Bull yawned and rolled over, flinging his arms wide open, whacking Carlos on the leg. Carlos jumped, and almost fell on another guard. Lucy held her breath until the guard began snoring again. Soella's fish soup was something to be reckoned with. It was a delicate operation to get the chain over the guard's head, but Carlos juggled ever so gently, cradling the snoring head first in one hand, and then the other. Gradually he worked the chain free!

Lucy reached the gate as Carlos unlocked it, then they were padding up the stairs towards the peeling door with its mermaid knocker. Suddenly, Lucy was overcome with the memory of the first time she had seen her own mermaid house, Ricardo finding the right key, the door swinging open to release musty air. It felt like a year ago.

Then the door to the jungle jail swung open to show two more drugged Bull soldiers lying on the threadbare mermaid carpet. The kids tiptoed past. Carlos went straight to unlock the ballroom where, until, a few days ago, he had been held prisoner. Lucy was dimly aware of a host of bodies lying on the floor, before Pablo stepped past her, whispering urgently in Telarian.

It was time to get her little brother out of here. Lucy padded up the hall and pushed open the door. A lamp burned in the corner. There, as before, was a litter of children chained to the tiger rug. Dark eyes wide open and frightened, the children stared in silent shock at Carlos, Lucy and Rahel. At the far end of the loom, Ricardo jumped to his feet, plastic sword outstretched. Silent shock was not in his repertoire.

'What took you so long?' he demanded, uncaring of the two Bull soldiers stretched out asleep at his feet, next to the remains of their fish soup. 'The food's disgusting here. Fish soup! No way was I eating that!'

'Shhh,' said Rahel urgently.

Carlos tried key after key on the chain around the children's necks, but none worked. Lucy wanted to scream in frustration. They were running out of time. And she had a bad feeling about the Commander. What if he came back?

Pablo appeared at the door, with frightened shadowy faces peering over his shoulder.

'We must hurry!'

'But we don't have the right keys!'

Then Lucy felt that familiar shaking: someone was coming. Rahel dashed for the front door, listened and then dived down the stairs. In a few seconds she was back.

'Close, but not so close. One person, I think, but we still have some time. Pablo, you take the children in the other room to the tunnel now, and wait. We'll see if the guards have the keys for these chains.'

Pablo vanished and Lucy and Carlos checked the pockets of the sleeping guards. Nothing. They undid the guards' shirts. Nothing.

'We'll have to smash the frame,' said Carlos.

'It will make so much noise!'

'We have no choice.'

That vibration was getting closer. Lucy looked frantically at the chain on Ricardo's neck. It was only a tiny padlock and tiny chain. Surely if she just twisted . . .

'That hurts!' said Ricardo, way too loudly.

That's when Lucy felt the vibration intensify. Feet, running. A few seconds later she heard the front door of the house creak open and footsteps pound up the hallway. Carlos and Rahel shrank behind the door and Lucy was left with one hand on her little brother's chain. Ricardo raised his plastic sword in defiance as the Ponytail Zombie lurched into the room, a ghastly smile on his face. But when his bloodshot eyes swept over Lucy he took two steps back, an involuntary hand going to his throat. He made a choking sound.

Incredibly, he turned to run, but Carlos and Rahel leaped from behind the door and pushed him. Already off balance, he stumbled and fell, hitting his head with a sharp crack on the door frame. He groaned once and was quiet.

Rahel bent over him.

'He's still breathing.'

'Check him for the keys,' hissed Carlos.

Rahel searched.

'He does not have any.'

'What are we going to do?' Lucy was distraught.

'I'm going to check the other guards,' said Carlos. Rahel darted outside after him but was back in seconds.

'Someone else is coming. We must hurry!'

Lucy stared at the lock on Ricardo's neck as though concentration alone would be enough to break the lock. It wasn't, and those feet were getting closer. With a last desperate look at Ricardo, Lucy breathed: 'We have to hide. Don't tell them anything'.

Lucy ran down the hall after Rahel. As she reached the

verandah she registered the smell of cigarette smoke. Too late, she knew something was wrong. Like a slow-motion movie, she watched Rahel trip over an outstretched leg and tumble down the stairs. Then a brown-shirted figure turned and tackled Lucy, throwing her after her friend.

Lying breathless in the dust, Lucy felt heavy footsteps, and she rolled over instinctively to see what was coming. A bright torch flashed on, and the Commander loomed over her.

He took a leisurely drag on his cigarette before speaking to Rahel, but not in English. Lucy risked a glance at Rahel. Whatever he'd said had made her white with fury. She clenched her fists and tried to scramble up but the Commander crunched his heavy boot down on her wrist. Rahel cried out in anger and pain.

'Leave her alone!' Lucy screamed and jumped up. She wasn't quick enough. The Commander's gun was trained on her before she could take a step. He stared at her curiously. In the light from the blazing firepit, his scar shone silver.

'Ahh, another visitor,' he said in English. 'My idiot militia speak of a girl ghost, but I do not believe in ghosts. I believe in foreigners who visit without being asked and cause trouble. This is what you were looking for, no?'

He opened his shirt and Lucy saw a chain with a set of tiny keys around his neck.

'If you want the other little visitor, then you will have to talk to me first. I will look forward to that tomorrow in Telares City.'

As he stepped towards her, something seemed to catch his eye. He looked sharply at Lucy, then lunged and ripped the key to the dragon chest from around her neck.

'So, you came to steal a key and you have had one stolen instead,' he gloated.

He didn't gloat for long. A furious, growling mini-tornado leapt from the undergrowth and wiped the smile from the Commander's face. T-Tongue sank his teeth into a uniformed ankle. The Commander kicked him off, but T-Tongue came back for more. Inspired and suddenly free, Rahel launched herself, just like the Tiger-cat in one of its furies, at the Commander's head. She clung to him, scratching and clawing. He dropped the torch, threw her violently to the ground and with T-Tongue clinging valiantly to his calf, drew back a boot to kick her.

That's when Lucy felt a rumble begin in her feet – no, not in her feet, in the very earth itself. She felt thunder boil up in every cell, making her very bones tremble. A storm gathered in her chest in a mighty coil. In the instant of silence just before she unleashed a roar of pure fury, Lucy saw that the Commander had stopped in mid-kick, his foot still swung back. He was staring appalled at Lucy, as though mesmerised with fear. Her eyes bored into his. He was transfixed, unable to move, held captive by some force Lucy couldn't see, let alone control. Then a mighty roar erupted from her throat and he jerked into action again, aiming his gun.

Too late – the storm was upon him. But the fury that descended on the Commander came from an unexpected direction.

The tiger struck so fast, Lucy was aware only of blinding speed and power, and then the Commander was face-down in the dirt, screaming in fear and pain, his back a bleeding mess of fabric and flesh. Golden eyes held Lucy's for a long second, before the beast gathered itself in a sinuous crouch and leapt with muscular grace into the darkness. The Commander's fists clenched and unclenched as he tried to rise, then he lay still.

And Lucy could *taste* the tiger's fury.

In the blistering silence, a clear voice spoke from the shadows.

'That is one tiger who will not be a blanket for your bed!'

Sarong Lady stepped from the shadows, an ancient curved sword in her hand. She held its lethal tip to the Commander's neck.

'I promise you, if the man-eater had not attacked first, you would have been bleeding from my claws. Never would I let you hurt my own niece!'

'Larissa?' Rahel breathed.

'Greetings, Rahel. I told you I would help you.'

Lucy had her own family to think about. She ran to the Commander. The tiger's claws had torn the chain from around his neck. She grabbed the tiny keys from the dust and ran back inside the mermaid house, T-Tongue faithfully at her heels.

Ricardo sat with his head bowed. When he looked up she could see he had been crying. He must have thought she would not come back. T-Tongue launched himself at him, taking full advantage of Ricardo's prisoner status.

'What happened?' he asked, as Lucy unlocked his collar. 'I heard something roar!'

'The tiger clawed the Commander and Sarong Lady is Rahel's auntie.'

'Huh?'

'Really, she's Rahel's auntie. She must be a rebel. And you're going to love this – she's got a sword! Help me get these kids free.'

They unlocked the children's chains and the little Telarians stood shivering, as though afraid to move.

'We have to chain these guys up,' said Lucy, pointing at the sleeping guards. It looked as though they would sleep for days, but Lucy didn't want to take any chances. Then she remembered the Ponytail Zombie. He was gone!

'Hurry. We have to get out of here!' she urged Ricardo. 'The Ponytail Zombie is somewhere around here! And the drugs didn't seem to work on him.'

They slipped the neck chains around the ankles of the guards and beckoned to the Telarian children to follow, but they just huddled closer together.

'They're too scared. They don't know us. We need Rahel,' Lucy said.

Lucy and Ricardo ran outside. Sarong Lady still held her sword to the Commander's neck.

'Cool sword!' said Ricardo, 'I've got one too,' he said helpfully, brandishing his own.

But Sarong Lady was not listening. At a distinctive bird-call she laughed and whistled in return. In that instant, she took her attention and her sword off the bleeding soldier on the ground. It was the break the Commander needed. He stumbled to his feet, catching Sarong Lady by surprise, and pushed her violently to the ground. Then he staggered with surprising speed into the jungle in the direction of the village, a hand clutched to his blood-soaked shoulder.

Shadows jumped from the trees, some brandishing the same old-fashioned swords as Sarong Lady, some carrying simple axes. They chased the injured Commander, but Sarong Lady jumped to her feet and called them back with a sharp Telarian order.

'He will not get far,' she said reassuringly, seeing Lucy's concern.

'Not without these,' said Carlos, appearing from nowhere. He swung a cluster of spark plugs triumphantly in the air, freshly liberated from the Commander's truck.

Everyone grinned admiringly.

'And without this,' said Sarong Lady, picking up a mobile phone from the ground, 'he is lost. I believe there may be some interesting numbers in here. Let's see . . .' She pressed a series of buttons with an expert hand.

'Just as I suspected. The Bull General will not enjoy his next phone call.'

Carlos looked delighted.

On a sudden hunch, Lucy stepped forward.

'Is there anything under A, A for Adams?'

Sarong Lady looked at her curiously and checked.

'Abero, Acullio, yes, Adams, Nigel Adams.'

'Nigel Scar-Skull!' Lucy and Ricardo repeated together.

'But this is an international number,' Sarong Lady exclaimed.

'Well, it's a long story,' started Lucy, but Sarong Lady had turned abruptly to Rahel.

'Where is Toro?' she asked, frowning.

'He's close and he is safe,' said Carlos. 'It will not take long to get him.'

'There are many more children inside,' said Lucy. 'They are very frightened.'

'By tonight everyone will be safe in the rebel base,'

promised Sarong Lady. 'We have planned this for many months. That is why I was sent to the village. The Commander never suspected.'

'But you were so close and I didn't know,' Rahel protested. 'I would have felt so much better if I had known you were there.'

'No one could know. Someone would have betrayed us otherwise. But someone was helping anyway. Soella, the old woman. It was she who drugged the soldiers, yes?'

'Yes. We must take her with us!'

'And here is my other helper,' said Larissa, as a familiar figure stumbled down the stairs.

'The Ponytail Zombie?' said Lucy, Rahel, Carlos and Ricardo together.

The Ponytail Zombie saw Sarong Lady and his face lit up. Then he saw Lucy, took a step sideways, swayed, and fell down the stairs.

'Yes, Bernardo has been helping the rebels for months, giving us information. That was how I knew what camp you were held in.'

'But he is drunk all the time!' Lucy couldn't believe Ponytail Zombie was working with rebels.

'He may be drunk, but he is loyal,' said Larissa. 'And when he is not drunk, he is very useful. He tells me everything the Bulls do not want me to know.'

'Oh,' said Lucy.

The Ponytail Zombie sat up and stared at Lucy again, his hands creeping to his throat nervously.

'But lately he has been worse,' said Larissa. 'He keeps speaking to me of a girl ghost who turned into a snake and strangled him. Perhaps he *should* stop drinking.'

45

Goodbye

Soella the Bucket Lady had done a really good job. When Larissa and the rebels dragged all the militiamen into the jungle jail and locked them in, not one of them woke up.

Then things happened so fast, Lucy felt as though she were in a dream. Larissa gathered all the Telarian prisoners together and her shadowy rebels led them into the jungle.

'We must leave immediately,' she told Lucy. 'We have a truck hidden not far away. You must come with us. You will not be safe here. It will be crawling with Bull soldiers soon enough. You have helped my family and Telares. Now it is our turn to look after you.'

'No thank you,' said Lucy. 'We'd better be getting home. Mum and Dad don't really know where we are.'

Larissa looked puzzled. 'But where is your home? There is nothing around here but tiny villages and they are all under the boot of the Bull. I do not understand.' She looked suspiciously from Lucy to Ricardo.

Rahel jumped in.

'I will explain later, Larissa. Lucy and Ricardo will be

OK. They will get home safely. Now we must fetch Toro and the others.'

Then Lucy was running through the jungle with Carlos, Rahel and Ricardo. The Tiger-cat was waiting for them at the turnoff to the tunnel and once they were inside she would not stop purring.

Pablo and Toro could not believe the news.

'Sarong Lady is Larissa?' breathed Pablo wonderingly. 'I thought she was a traitor!'

Rahel shot him a dangerous look but he did not notice.

'And the Ponytail Zombie, he is with the rebels?' he continued, incredulously.

'Yes, he told them where we were. That is how Larissa found us.'

But then they had to hurry. It was hard for Rahel to convince all the new kids that it was safe to go back, but she managed eventually. The procession swayed like a blind centipede down the tunnel and into the Telarian night.

With Lucy carrying Angel, they gathered in a huddle at the jungle jail.

Carlos started to speak but started coughing instead and couldn't stop for ages. He was getting worse.

'We will take you to a doctor,' said Larissa as though it would be the easiest thing in the world.

Carlos grinned at her gratefully.

Then Lucy realised what was happening.

'I'm not ever going to see you again,' she said to Rahel, Carlos, Pablo and Toro. 'And Angel, I was supposed to keep her safe and take her back to her family in Telares City.'

Larissa shook her head sadly.

'That will not be possible for a very long time. The Bulls have brought reinforcements into Telares City and no one is going in or out. Angel is safer with us in the mountains. We have a well-equipped base, with a school and doctors. One day, we will all return to Telares City.'

And that was that. Lucy didn't know what to say. They just all stood about awkwardly and scuffed their feet in the dirt.

Then Ricardo made the supreme sacrifice. He walked up to Toro and looked him squarely in the eye.

'You're going to need this,' he declared, and drew his sword from his scabbard with a ceremonial flourish. Toro's eyes grew as big as saucers and he took it wordlessly.

Everyone burst out laughing, but suddenly Lucy felt like crying.

She gave Angel a big hug and passed her to Rahel.

'Please, look after her for me – and for her mum.'

'I will,' said Rahel seriously. 'I must thank you for your service to Telares.'

'No probs,' said Lucy, embarrassed. 'Thanks for helping me get my little brother back.'

'No probs,' said a chorus of Telarian voices.

'This time it was Carlos who had to say it: 'Personal jinx!'

The last Telarian sound Lucy heard was their laughter. The last thing she saw when she turned back to wave was Angel. Her dark eyes were locked on Lucy's and she raised a tiny hand and waved back.

46
Charcoal

When Lucy and Ricardo emerged from the pit, it was just on sunset. T-Tongue sniffed the air carefully and sneezed. Ricardo was too busy chattering about Larissa's sword to notice the smoke in the air, and even when he clambered onto the stairs he didn't see that the slopes above were black and charred. But Lucy did. It had come close, very close, to the pit. Who knows what had happened to the campground. And what about the *house*?

Lucy flew down the path, desperate to know if the mermaid house was still standing and everyone was safe. A shout went up and a man and a woman in orange overalls and hard hats burst from the trees nearby.

'Hey! We've found them! Here they are.'

The next instant Ricardo and Lucy were locked in Mum and Dad and Grandma's arms. A jumble of words came out, and all the grown-ups were crying.

'Where have you been? We thought you were dead. The bushfire came through the top and we thought you must have been burnt.'

'What bushfire?' said Ricardo.

Then the emergency services team were checking them for injuries and giving them hot tea. The local TV station arrived to interview them and Mum said 'No way!', and the kids begged, and she said 'OK'.

An hour later Lucy was watching herself on the news, and the next thing she knew, she was a hero. She had walked bravely into the teeth of the biggest bushfire in the area for years to save her little brother. The reporter used words like 'just when all hope was lost' and 'miraculous rescue' and 'mystery surrounds just how the children survived their ordeal but they are in too much shock tonight to give details'.

For two kids in shock, Lucy and Ricardo ate rather a lot of pizza that night.

Then there was the difficult moment when Mum, Dad and Grandma wanted to know exactly what had happened.

So Lucy told them about a tunnel that opened up in the earth just when she thought the fire was upon them, and how they had gone down it and waited for the fire to pass. When they had climbed out and looked for the tunnel again, it was gone.

The adults exchanged significant glances and Grandma asked her if she wanted another aspirin. Then Dad started going on about the complex geological formations in this part of the coast until Mum told him to shut up. But she was smiling when she said it. Lucy liked that.

When they finally went to bed, Lucy lay for a long time looking at the tiger rug in her newly cleaned bedroom.

Her gaze fell on the monkey and the elephant.

'We haven't met them yet,' she said to Ricardo, pointing.

'We will,' he said with absolute certainty.

'How do you know?'

He opened his mouth but Lucy said it for him: 'I know, the Tiger-cat told you.'

'Yeah,' said Ricardo. 'He always tells me things.'

And for once, Lucy didn't have the heart to argue.

Epilogue

In the still of that smoky summer night, no one noticed a handsome ginger cat wriggle through the kitchen window. The cat showed no interest in the remains of a peperoni pizza on the table, but padded purposefully across the hall, between two dragon vases, into the bedroom of a sleeping twelve-year-old girl with long dark hair. The cat leapt lightly onto the bed and gazed intently at the girl. She didn't stir, nor did the puppy on the end of her bed.

But Lucy's dream changed.

A crinkly smile and golden eyes.
Mrs Hawthorne!
'You have done well, Lućia, very well.
Now, your task is to keep my pattern safe for me.
It matters more than you can know.
I cannot risk visiting you yet, but soon, Lućia, very soon,
I will.
It has begun . . .'

Lucy slept on, dreaming deeply,

Angel is smiling right into her eyes.

She can hear the Tiger-cat purring loudly, and somehow she knows that Angel is speaking to her.

Angel speaking!!!

'Angel wants to go home. Lucy take Angel home! Lucy will take Angel home!'

And in her dreams, Lucy knew it wasn't over yet.